I0777488

Not Just a Homemaker

The Extraordinary Life of

Sheila MacGregor

Not Just a Homemaker

The Extraordinary Life of Sheila MacGregor

A Novel

Paulette Brooks

~ Top Drawer Publishing ~
Noblesville, IN

NOT JUST A HOMEMAKER: THE EXTRAORDINARY LIFE OF
SHEILA MACGREGOR

Copyright © 2024 by Paulette Brooks

ISBN 979-8-9912873-0-2 (pbk.)
ISBN 979-8-9912873-1-9 (e-book)
First edition: September 2024

Front cover photo courtesy of Sheila Connett
Back cover photo: P. Brooks
Cover design: Phil Brooks
Ink sketch illustrations by David Coffey

To Sheila and Millie, whose friendship and resiliency
are an inspiration

For my mother, Margaret
Gone too soon to tell me her own stories
This book is for you

Prologue

"You shall walk where only the wind has walked
before and enter the living shelter of the forest."

- Nancy Newhall

2014

When I set foot on the weathered front porch, I did not know that a dead woman would save my life.

The little white farmhouse where Sheila lived beckons to me at first sight. Although I have been living with my former college roommate and her young family, quarters were tight in their two-bedroom bungalow; I am relieved to move my things over to this woodland shelter.

On my first afternoon, I am literally walking in the steps of a woman I have never met, but I can perceive her spirit in the primordial forest that she loved so much. In a year's time, this property is to become a nature preserve, just as Sheila requested in her final years. Why was this place so special to her? The little that I have learned of her is that the Scottish-born woman was a hardy soul who walked the perimeter of this parcel of Indiana farmland every morning. She lived here all alone for twenty years, but her faithful dogs kept her company as she breathed in this air, centering her soul in the tranquility of birdsong.

A thirty-five-year-old librarian, I am also grateful to be on my own and begin anew in this town. The lawyer handling her estate, and who arranged the rental, told me Sheila was a foreigner who made her way quietly in social circles. Curious to know more, I imagine myself as a detective who has stumbled upon a mystery. To me, Sheila is an enigma shrouded in the mists of the past. I hope to uncover more about her life's story so I can more fully understand the woman whose presence I can sense. It's as if we are both admiring the view from the top of the hill. Pausing at the entrance to Sheila's home, I silently ask for permission to live here and invite her back in.

2002

Gordon sits in his office at the Indianapolis Star newspaper, pondering his retirement. He writes for the society page, noting the passing of the city's greatest and most accomplished people. However, a name occasionally crosses his desk that stirs neither notoriety nor significance. Sheila Beals was unknown to him until today.

He finds in an online database that her spouse, Mr. Lyndon Beals, who worked at the newspaper his whole life, merited two obituaries. One listed all his achievements in life and another included glowing reflections of his character. The seasoned journalist remembers meeting Sheila's remarkable husband as a teenaged apprentice, when the veteran took the time to encourage Gordon in his career. It's the least he can do to find similar information on his widow, so he scans the dusty old paper files for a reference to Sheila. Ah, a simple note in Lyndon's file about his wife: homemaker. The term strikes him as old-fashioned, but Gordon is under deadline.

He begins: *Sheila MacGregor Beals, 93, Noblesville, died Dec 6. Widow of Lyndon Beals. Memorial contributions: MacGregor Park, Westfield … She was a homemaker.*

Chapter 1 - Meg
(September)

"When I was growing up, I dreamed about becoming a cowgirl, a detective, a spy, a great actress, or a ballerina. Not a dentist, like my father, or a homemaker, like my mother - and certainly not a writer, although I always loved to read."

-Judy Blume

The sparrows burst out of the bush outside the window that affords me a peaceful view of nature, startled by the sound of my fist thumping down on the desktop. The birds settle back into the foliage, but Badger, my faithful guard dog, has awoken from his slumber and comes running.

"Unbelievable. How can anyone think of encapsulating the essence of a ninety-three-year-old with the phrase **she was a homemaker**? It may reflect her 'official' occupation, but in my mind, that summary is an outrageous injustice. So typical for an obit written in the 1950s, but she died in 2002. There must have been more to her life than performing household duties. Sheila deserves more."

My best friend, Charlotte, always says that I get worked up over the slightest issue. When we were rooming together at UW Madison, she'd find me fuming over some miscarriage of justice, or getting ready to pack my bag in order to help earthquake survivors. Practical as ever, she would calm me down and make sure that I finished my library degree before saving the world. She would often remind me that as a librarian, I could help others to discover opportunities to be engaged with those in need and teach them to sort through

3

misinformation. The time will come, she'd say, when you can take on the problems of the downtrodden.

Here I am venting again in my cozy home office space, tucked off to the side of the main farmhouse entrance. Badger, my brindled Catahoula Poodle mix, looks up at me with his attentive and soulful eyes. If he were human, he'd be asking what was so important to have disturbed his naptime. Thankfully, my canine companion is always there to listen and to never question my passion.

"Let's take a walk and I will explain." Stepping out onto the porch, I take a deep breath of the crisp fall air. "I know we had a rough patch with Trent." A shudder goes through me just saying my ex-husband's name out loud, but it feels good to acknowledge how that chapter of my life is behind me. "Things are so much calmer now with a new home, a guard dog at my side - yes, that's you - and hopefully a new job."

I pause and hold my index finger up in the air. "However, Sheila's sparse obituary with that terse tally of her legacy has touched a nerve. Is it the assumption that women of a certain age must have spent all their time doing household tasks with no time for employment or other serious pursuits like art or literature? Am I sensitive about the anonymity that befell my mother, who indeed lived most of her life being perceived as just a housewife?" My fingers comb back locks of my sandy-colored hair as I consider why I am so worked up with these thoughts and emotions.

"Or could it be that I don't know how to characterize what I have accomplished with my life thus far?"

Badger moves closer to me. His silky fur is the tactile comfort I need to calm down, and I bend over to rub behind his ears. "Maybe this project of correcting the meager record of Sheila's life is the beginning of making a difference for women who deserve to have their stories told." He wags his tail in agreement.

We set off on an exploratory walk, following a well-worn path out into the verdant forest. This woodland route will be open to the public in a year's time as part of a newly established nature preserve. It's late September and I admire the old-growth trees that are stretching their branches overhead to create a glorious canopy. Their leaves, with hues of green, yellow, and orange, are a vivid contrast to the clear blue sky. A noise in the distance interrupts my reverie.

Badger and I round the corner, catching sight of men on a work crew up ahead. They are placing posts along the trail with phrases such as "Streams at MacGregor," "The Dismal Swamp," and "Sheila's Trail."

Intrigued, I call out as I get closer, but they can't hear me over the din of machinery. I try again, louder this time.

"Hi! I'm renting the farmhouse."

They look up and one short middle-aged man clad in denim and sturdy work boots steps forward. He yells out over his shoulder, "Cut the posthole digger!"

When quiet ensues, I repeat my introduction.

The fellow who appears to be the crew chief approaches with his hand out to shake mine. "Welcome to the soon-to-be MacGregor Park. The name is Bruce, and the parks department told me that a single gal would rent the farmhouse. I'm glad to see you have a dog to keep you company, since you're staying here on your own."

"Yes, he is indeed an excellent guard dog. I'm Meg and I don't mind the solitude. Can you tell me what these markers will be when you finish up here?"

Bruce explains how he is overseeing the creation of the official trails and that the stakes show the places where they will install the informational signage.

"If you're interested, I can arrange for you to see the signs ahead of time. Consider it a consolation prize for putting up with all the noise we're making."

"Thank you," I say. "That would be great. Just let me know where and when to show up."

"I'll leave a note on your front door with the clerk's name and phone number once I let her know you're coming. You can work out a time to meet her at the township building."

I smile and continue with Badger at my side. I can't wait to learn more about Sheila. Perhaps the ordinary homemaker may have led an extraordinary life after all.

After I contact Linda, one of the park employees, she is kind enough to invite me to their office, which occupies a section of a newly renovated historic county building. They are working on the mockups of the trail signage, which will feature interesting facts about the history and geology of the farmland. My interest grows as I get a peek at one sign titled "Sheila's Trail." I am delighted to see a black and white snapshot of Sheila. The image of a slender young woman in a strapless top tucked into a midi skirt made of Buffalo check material, cut on the bias, fascinates me. Perhaps the day has turned warm, as she has removed her matching jacket and is clutching it to her chest. She is standing in a field wistfully gazing off into the distance, her face turned away from the camera. The background of the picture is blurry, giving the photograph a dream-like quality. Was this Sheila seeing her new Indiana home for the first time?

I read the caption which states: *"Sheila MacGregor Beals was brought here from Scotland by her husband Lyndon after WWII. They met in England during the war as she served as a driver for officers."* Caught up in the romantic notion implied by those few lines about a war bride brought to Indiana by her smitten fiancé, I think this is the seed of an idea for a short story.

"Would it be okay to copy this information?" I am already reaching for my backpack. "I have a notebook where I am recording facts about the woman who donated this land. If it's okay, I'd also love to take a photo of Sheila with my phone."

Linda nods. "As long as you don't publish what you see here before the park's opening."

My mind is racing ahead, and I jot down a few questions that are forming: When they met, was Lyndon in London on Army business or elsewhere in England? Was Sheila a part of the British war effort known as the Mechanised Transport Corps? I have the image of the fictional character of Sam in the popular *Foyle's War* TV series. I know the volunteer organization included women who offered their own vehicles to help with war work. When did she arrive in Indiana? I plan to follow up on those points of inquiry and search online for Sheila's immigration paperwork.

Despite a desire to stay and linger over more of the signs, I close up my notebook and thank Linda profusely, promising to keep in touch. I have to prepare for a meeting with the person who I hope will be my new boss.

***

Seated in front of the library director's desk, I nervously pull my sleeve down over my wrist tattoo of the word "more" and think how this job could be just that: a chance to be a more independent woman with a fresh start in a new state. I am dressed conservatively in black pants, a white blouse, and a dusty rose brocade jacket. Jan, with jet black hair cut into a bob, is in her late fifties and has an office filled with neatly stacked reference books and her favorite mystery novels. Wearing an elegant forest green sweater, herringbone pants, and a gold locket, she looks over her glasses at me and smiles.

"We are happy to offer you the part-time position of adult reference librarian here at our library. I only have one question."

Releasing the breath I was holding, I sigh with relief.

"Fantastic."

I pause. "What is the question?"

"The Library Board and I were impressed by your qualifications and references. However, you list another name on your C.V. Is there something we should know before you begin your employment?"

"I'm divorced, so I've gone back to using my maiden name and my preference is to use my middle name as my mother did. I'd request that you keep that information private."

She concurs with a nod. "Yes, of course. Then, I am pleased to have you join our team. Here is your paperwork to fill out for Human Resources and a schedule for September. Welcome to Westfield Public Library."

We rise, and she takes me out to meet the staff. The burden of seeking employment gone, I move forward with relief to meet my new coworkers, who seem eager to learn all about me. I answer their friendly questions as briefly as I can. Careful to drop hints of moving around the Midwest, I promise to cheer for the Indianapolis Colts football team; after a pause, I warn them that when they play the Minnesota Vikings, my true loyalties will surface. No mention of my beloved Green Bay Packers. Teasingly, I finish with a fact that is sure to take their minds off the details of my personal life. I plan to bring in freshly baked muffins weekly. If there is one thing that library staff members love, it is treats.

My goal is also to learn everyone's favorite reading genres, their allegiances to sports teams, and the names of their partners and children. Just when I think I've met everyone and have committed their faces to memory, a rumpled looking, forty-something man comes bursting through the back door. He has a messenger bag slung haphazardly over his shoulder and an apologetic look on his face.

"George, what have I said about being tardy?" Jan chides.

He looks sheepish, then catches sight of me. Grinning, George comes over to shake my hand.

"Ms. Livingstone, I presume."

Surprised that he already knows my name, I return his banter.

"Why Mr. Stanley, you found me. It's Meg to my friends."

"My name is George, and I only wish that I was a relation of that intrepid newspaper reporter who tracked down the famous David Livingstone."

"When I was growing up in Toronto, my Scottish grandfather proudly stated that the acclaimed African explorer was his relative."

"So, you're a Canuck, eh?"

I like this guy already. "Yes, and proud of it," I reply, satisfied that I can establish myself as a Canadian. I will keep my more recent past in Wisconsin private.

***

After a week of orientation, I am enjoying my new routine at the information desk. Happy to identify some of the library's regular patrons, I greet them by name; that goes a long way in being accepted as the new librarian in this tight-knit town. Jan shares her love of British detective novels but surprises me with the fact that she follows Formula One racing with a passion. George entertains me with his favorite things about Canada, like Tim Horton's donuts and All Dressed potato chips. My muffins have been a big hit, although one of the staff has informed me that, for him, rhubarb is an acquired taste. I ask George more about his preferences in baked goods.

Library duties keep my mind engaged, but my MacGregor Park project simmers like a pot left on the stove, bubbling away at the back of my mind. I have a tendency to get caught up in my research, so it helps me to chat once a week with Charlotte over coffee. She is glad to hear about my new job and intriguing research, but recognizes the glint in my eye from our college days together. I would get so absorbed in a class assignment, I'd hardly remember that I had roommates. My best friend does such a good job of keeping me grounded, especially after all that has transpired in the last year. She reminds me about work/life balance and I promise to keep in touch and not get consumed with my investigation.

When I get home, I fix a quick supper and feed Badger. My brain is full of potential avenues to pursue, and I sit down at my laptop to sketch out a scene about how Sheila and Lyndon may have met in London during the war. Evening shadows creep down the wall and Badger can wait no longer, reminding me with a howl that we have not done our walk. It's getting late, but off we go to explore the property together. He seems to know his way around the meandering tracks already, skillfully sniffing out real wildlife while I explore mental rabbit holes.

I plan to stay late after my library shift tomorrow to log into genealogy websites to track down immigration paperwork and information about Sheila's family. My research into her story and why she wanted to create the park is in full swing. I have folders ready to be filled with information about her time in London, the history of this farmland, and the Beals family starting with Lyndon, her husband. The notebook that I carry in my pocket is brimming as the questions pile up: What was Sheila doing in England when she met Lyndon? What kind of dog did she have to keep her company here on the farm? Are there any older people in the area who might have known Sheila personally?

Checking my watch, I remember needing to find a warmer sweater for work in the morning. I realize I haven't completed my seasonal wardrobe shift in my closets. There are two bedrooms at the top of the stairs, and I need to move summer outfits across the narrow hallway to the spare room. Feeling a little disheartened seeing the disarray of unpacked suitcases and boxes, I realize I haven't yet organized all my belongings. I bring my sweaters over and throw them down on my bed, laughing at how my tangle of woolens resembles the state of my research notes. When I back into an old dresser, I turn to see a piece of yellowed paper flutter to the floor. The air shifts and I sense Sheila beside me. Badger, who has followed me up, whines as if he too notices a change in the atmosphere. Excitedly, I snatch up what appears to be a student claim ticket for the Herron School of Art in Indianapolis. So, maybe Sheila was an art student there when she first arrived in the States? First thing tomorrow morning, I'll make an appointment with the school officials to discover where this ticket may lead. Is it possible that they kept the contents of student storage bins for over fifty years? It will be worth the effort if I uncover something substantial like a senior portfolio. A frisson of anticipation ripples down my spine.

***

Next Monday, I follow the GPS directions to the old, two-story brick buildings, which stand proud and stalwart in the heart of downtown Indianapolis. One of the two edifices housed the Art Museum before it moved to the lovely grounds at Newfields in 1970. Plans are now in the works to move the

Art School to a beautiful new home at Eskenazi Hall, which is part of the IUPUI campus in midtown Indy. Then, the newly formed Herron High School will make use of this historic campus at 16th and Pennsylvania Streets. That's good news for me because the staff has been going through the archives to lessen the amount of paperwork they will need to transport to the new location. It's a miracle, but I've been told that Sheila's portfolio remains intact and unclaimed. An administrator has verified my librarian credentials and agreed to an appointment.

A member of the faculty meets me in the lobby. She has dust on her pants, no doubt from moving old files, and looks exhausted.

"Thank you, professor, for agreeing to meet with me," I say as I hand her the yellowed piece of paper.

"Where did you find this?" she inquires, turning the claim ticket over in her hand.

"I'm renting Sheila MacGregor's farmhouse and found it in her old bedroom. It's my understanding that she was a student here. I'm doing research on her life in Indiana."

Handing her my business card from Westfield Public Library, I continue, "I've learned that she did not have any family in the U.S., but I assure you I will work hard to preserve her art."

The professor seems relieved that the collection of ink sketches will find a loving home. They can keep only the essentials from the school archive.

I practically dance my way back to the car, ecstatic about uncovering clues to Sheila's life and interests. Treasure in hand, I head home and turn into the farm driveway. I text Charlotte right away to tell her about this new breakthrough and we arrange for a time when she can come over and see the art in person. After a quick walk and a meal, I'm ready for an evening of discovery.

Only the country kitchen table has enough space to spread out the artwork, so I bring over a gooseneck lamp to add illumination. I reverently carry the portfolio over and position it on the wood surface. I feel as if Sheila is looking over my shoulder as I unbuckle the dusty clasp of the old leather portfolio. Carefully, I open it flat, trying hard not to damage any of the papers inside. I don the white cotton gloves the professor recommended I purchase, thankful that I found an art store on my way home.

The first sheet reveals the theme of the portfolio: *My Life in Ink Sketches.* The very first drawing is of a kind-looking minister in his collar, standing in a quiet churchyard with moss-covered gravestones behind him. There is a serene look on the man's face, as if he bears the weight of being shepherd over both the living and the dead, yet is equal to the task. Another page shows an alcove with a sculpted stone knight lying on a rectangular slab with his arms folded on his chest, a little stone dog keeping watch at his feet. On the back of the page, someone carefully printed the word "Fordyce."

Chapter 2 - Sheila

"Life can only be understood backwards, but it must be lived forwards."

- Søren Kierkegaard

Fordyce, Scotland 1913

The warm-hearted man coughs into the sleeve of his clerical garb. He chucks the chin of his four-year-old daughter and tucks an escaping auburn curl underneath her tartan homespun scarf.

"Who is ready to be the assistant to Reverend MacGregor this morning?"

"Ach, aye, Da," Sheila replies, a look of intense concentration on her small face.

He laughs and the two carefully set off along the cobbled village streets, which are frosted over in the October air.

"After we visit the McLeods, shall we head over to the churchyard and find our secret friend?"

His young daughter nods in response, her grey eyes wide and bright with anticipation.

After concluding his pastoral call, they push open the ancient cemetery gate and weave between the lichen-covered gravestones, heading to their favorite place. In an intricately decorated enclosure lies the stone effigy of a recumbent Elizabethan knight in his armor with a canine companion resting at his feet. The little girl looks inquiringly at her father.

"Aye, go ahead," he directs her with a gentle nudge.

She steps forward, bows to the nobleman and then, on tiptoe, carefully strokes the head of the little stone dog with his frilly collar. Captured in time, he has remained faithfully at the feet of his master, even in death. Her fingers trace the stone ruff around his neck, feeling the coarse surface under her fingertips. Her touch is as delicate as if the statue's fur is soft.

"Good wee dog," she whispers.

She returns to her father and they leave, venturing home to the manse hand in hand.

When the family has gathered, the minister clears his throat, and all eyes turn in anticipation. Sheila knows what is coming, so she ducks her head. The generous parent often gives from his own pocket or table to support the needy families of his flock.

"No dinner tonight, but we will have tea and toast," he announces, and little moans escape around the table.

Sheila winces as her mother responds with a sigh of exasperation. "Really John, must we sacrifice yet again?"

He replies to his wife, Anne, "The Lord tells us to care for widows and orphans."

His words fall on deaf ears. The new baby has exhausted her, and she excuses herself to retire for the evening. Coddled as a child, Anne's parents never once denied her requests for sweets or anything her heart desired. The maid takes away their white pudding supper and delivers it to the poor unfortunates waiting at the back door. Sheila's stomach rumbles, but she is glad to share her food with the hungry McLeod children.

In the following months, the reverend's health falters, and he cannot perform his ministerial duties. One day, Sheila and her older sister Mona are in the hallway and notice their father's bedroom door is open. Despite the admonition of not bothering their da, they edge forward. There lies the man who is the center of their world, and they hear him hacking. When his coughing fit subsides, he whispers, "Dance my fairies and see what happens."

Delighted with his unexpected request, they swirl in place. The house has been colder and more somber than usual; it is December and the cold North Sea winds have found their way inside. They will not celebrate Christmas this year, but Sheila is unaware of space and time. She is, at this moment, dancing joyfully for her father. Then a miracle happens as coins clink on the stone floor at their feet. She and her sister squeal in surprise and eagerly bend to pick up this treasure.

"Pennies from heaven," the patriarch says softly. His face brightens with the image of his innocent children. Wearily, he closes his eyes.

***

Grateful members of the parish attended the wake and funeral of Rev. John Charles MacGregor, who ministered to his flock with compassion. Only two days have passed since the burial and the air inside the bare vicarage is bone cold. Sheila clings to the warmth of Mona and their younger brother, Iain, as they sit next to the stove in a corner of the drafty kitchen. Sorrow hangs like a shroud and there is a great fear abroad; consumption, common in the village, has been ravaging both the young and the old.

The appearance of their formidable grandmother transfixes them. Dressed in black with her grey streaked hair pulled back into a tight bun, she barks out orders to men who are hefting enormous trunks onto a cart outside. Their grandparents have arranged transportation; they have known all along their daughter shouldn't have fallen in love with a humble vicar who mingled with the sickly lower classes.

"Why is Grandmother here?" Sheila whispers to her sister.

"She is taking us to her house." Mona draws in her brother and sister with a fierce hug.

"Where is da? Is he coming with us?"

Her sister wipes tears from her eyes. "No, he's sleeping with the knight and his wee doggie."

They hear wailing that comes from the bedroom where their oldest sibling, Anne, seeks to comfort both her distraught mother and baby sister, Biddy.

A gruff voice announces, "The carriage is here. Children, where are you? Come here immediately."

Mona stands and pulls her little trembling brother up to his feet. Sheila follows suit and the three children obey their grandmother.

Sheila is unaware of the future that stretches ahead for herself and her siblings; she only feels an emptiness in a place that was once filled by her gentle father. Now on the cusp of 1914, how could they imagine the beginning of the "War to End All Wars" in Europe? Sheila and her family members must prepare for survival in their own war that will bring separation and misery.

Aberdeen, Scotland 1919

When Sheila reaches age ten, her grandfather, the last responsible adult in her brief life, departs this earth. Her grandmother passed away two years ago, her mother succumbed this year to tuberculosis, and her uncles either died in the war or are overseas. With no male relatives in Scotland, the attorneys are now in charge of the MacGregor children.

A teary Sheila is sitting on the bed clutching a book, watching Mona pack a school uniform and a few treasured belongings into a suitcase. They both have their "pennies from heaven" which their father had given to them. The tokens are reminders of a loving parent now gone but not forgotten.

"Why can't we stay together? How will I ever survive without you?" she asks of her older sister. She is still stunned by the news that the siblings are to be separated and assigned to different guardians. Little Biddy and Iain, both young and golden-haired, are on their way to live with a middle-aged couple in the city. Sheila goes alone to live with a widow from the church where her grandparents attended. The oldest sister, Anne, is already at boarding school, and Mona is to join her. Their frail Aunt Margaret still lives in the family home and will take in the older girls on term holidays with the help of Jean, the family cook.

"One foot in front of the other, like always," Mona replies in her best no-nonsense voice, just like her teacher uses. "We will still see each other when I am home on holidays." A thought occurs to her, and she continues. "Remember when I was walking in the garden and my dress caught fire because of a stray spark from the burning trash pile?"

Sheila nods and shivers at the memory.

"My burns were so bad that Grandmother asked if I wanted to go to the hospital or stay home. She thought I would not last the night, so she put me up in the guest room all by myself. I was so scared, but you snuck in and stayed by my side. You and my boxer dog, Rufus."

Sheila smiles at the thought of her daring subterfuge. Even though she was only eight years old, Sheila had stood up to their fierce grandmother, who discovered the pair the next morning. Ready to banish Sheila and Rufus from the sick room, the old woman finally gave way to their stubborn refusal to leave. Expecting her granddaughter would not live long, she let Mona's sister and the faithful pup remain by her side for all that next week. Sheila remembers whispering continuously, "Mona, I'm here. Please don't go away and leave me." Knowing Mona's fondness for the fawn-colored boxer, she would add, "Look, Rufus has also come to stay with you." To emphasize this, the dog's wet nose would nudge Mona's hand and she would stroke his silky ears with her fingers.

There had been little affection shown by their distant mother and stern grandparents once they were certain Mona would survive. However, the ferocious and demanding love of a tenacious sister and a loyal dog kept her going.

"All that terrible year when I couldn't get out of bed and the pain was unbearable, you were there urging me to not give up." Mona continues in a serious tone, "So now I am telling you, stiff upper lip, my girl."

Sheila repeats her sister's admonition in her mind the next day. The weather in Aberdeen is dank and dreary to match her mood, as the attorney escorts Sheila to her new home. Mrs. Campbell, a stout and severe-looking widow, motions the shivering girl into a cold and dimly lit parlor.

"Well, I am a member of the church where your grandparents attended. God rest their souls. You should know that I am giving you refuge out of the goodness of my heart.

The Lord commands me to do my Christian duty to take care of orphans."

Sheila holds tight to her carpetbag as her new guardian continues. "Be thankful. Listen well. It is my belief that children should be seen and not heard."

The child nods, but the old lady has more to say.

"Another thing, you will walk to the primary school every day and then straight home. No playing with any of the urchins who live nearby. They are below our station, so they will not be your friends."

Quietly, Sheila follows the rustling grey skirt up the narrow stairs. Her new bedroom has a sloped ceiling and bare wooden floorboards. She sets her bag on a small metal frame bed and notices a Bible placed on the nightstand. The chest of drawers sits in the corner and an oil lamp rests on a faded doily. A small window lets a little tepid light into the dingy room, but at least she can read during the day as time allows.

"This is your room. Keep it tidy. Come down for teatime after you have put away your belongings."

Alone, Sheila slumps to the bed, her lip quivering and her grey eyes filling with tears. The young girl imagines Mona there beside her and straightens her back. In just two years, she can join her sisters at boarding school. Regardless of her experiences of misery and deprivation, Sheila is determined to picture a brighter future.

Village of Kemnay, Scotland 1930

"Dear sister, are you sure that you are going to be safe traveling to South Africa to visit our Aunt Helena and Uncle Jack?" Mona is bustling about their shared room, checking drawers and shelves for anything of Sheila's she might have missed packing. They have been living together in a boarding house called The Grove, in the village of Kemnay. Their oldest sibling, Anne, has graduated from a nursing school in Glasgow. Her career choice was a natural progression after all her practice in caring for ailing family members.

"I will be more than fine in the warmer weather of the Transvaal, so you can stop fussing." Sheila retorts, her eyes flashing, "Now that I have finally come of age, I intend to be away from Scotland for a spell. Our older cousins will be protective escorts, and you will be busy with your teacher's training. Besides, your handsome gentleman caller, Malcolm, will distract you while I'm away."

Mona blushes and is about to protest, but her sister continues. "One glorious year with you, attending classes at Gray's School of Art in Aberdeen and seeing paintings of beautiful places, convinced me of the need to travel as soon as I came into my inheritance. After all those horrible years, it's time to spread my wings further before they get pinioned with marriage and responsibilities."

Mona sighs and surreptitiously tucks a little envelope into Sheila's trunk for her to discover later. In it is a cherished photo of their father and a letter which has sentiments she wants her sister to hold close while she is away. Checking the luggage tag, she calls for the hired hand to transport it to the railway station.

"You know we will miss you. I am worried that you might not come back, just when the family is almost together again. Young Iain is itching to enlist in the Royal Air Force as soon as he is old enough. Biddy is an overindulged child and no doubt wants to continue to be pampered, but boarding school should knock those notions out of her pretty little head."

Sheila smiles and gathers the last of her art supplies, including sketchbooks, willow charcoal sticks, and colored pencils. She arranges them carefully in her carpetbag. She aspires to be a fashion designer and will have plenty of time to add to her portfolio on the ocean voyage. Her mind is always whirling with new designs.

"I will write lengthy letters and regale you with my African adventures. Never fear, I will come back, but for now, it is time to explore." With a last hug, she is out the door and into the fog of Kemnay's cobblestone streets to meet up with her cousins to board their train. Today, Sheila begins a new stage of her life.

Chapter 3 - Meg (October)

"An early morning walk is a blessing for the whole day."

– Henry David Thoreau

I've formed a habit of walking each morning before work on what I consider Sheila's trail, thankful to find solace from self doubt. In nature, I feel peaceful and confident in this new direction my life has taken. The autumnal foliage is cascading, creating a magical carpet of gold before me. The lovely birdsong and susurration of the trees calms my soul and puts me in a good frame of mind for the rest of the day.

Tucked up in my little farmhouse, I have a sense of security with Badger, my companion and protector. He was a rescue dog from my local Wisconsin Humane Society, where I volunteered. I knew, looking into his caramel-brown eyes the first time we met, that I needed him as much as he needed me. This dog, with a tender disposition, has a coat of many hues that also reveals the scars of mistreatment. As two battered souls in search of a little tender loving care and attention, it was a simple decision to adopt him.

Sometimes the farmhouse feels a little secluded here in the Indiana countryside, so I'm grateful to have met my neighbor Carol, who raises horses on the adjacent farm. I want to express my appreciation for the warm welcome she has given me, so I have baked pumpkin muffins infused with cinnamon and nutmeg spices to deliver today, on Canadian Thanksgiving. I've called ahead to confirm that she has a break from her equine chores and is expecting me. Rather than walk on the busy road, I hike up the hill and through the woods that divide the properties, appreciating the crunch of leaves under my feet.

When we settle in at her beautiful oak kitchen table, I warm my hands around a mug of freshly brewed coffee. She is in her late fifties, with calloused hands that are proof of a hardworking farm woman. She wears a flannel shirt and blue jeans and will be back mucking out the stables when we are done with our visit. There is warmth and curiosity in her green eyes as we trade stories.

"I'm new to the area and just started working at Westfield Library. This part of Indiana is so beautiful. How long have you owned this farm?"

Carol gets up from the table, retrieving an old photo from the wall. A black-and-white portrait features two adults and two young children, all on horseback in front of this house.

"This was taken in the 1950s when my brother and I were first learning to ride. That's our parents, who were so proud that their kids were following in their footsteps. Working with horses has always been a family business, and we have owned the farm and stables for years. I have relatives who settled here just after the Civil War. This amazing forest is something I would miss the most if I had to move, but I plan to stay put for some time. I heard you are renting Sheila's place. Are you settling in okay?"

"Oh, yes. The old farmhouse is cozy, and I have my dog, Badger, to keep me company. I've been doing some research into the past owners of the property. By chance, did your mother know Sheila MacGregor Beals well?"

"My mother and father were both friends with Sheila and Lyndon. As a teenager, I heard the story of their wartime meeting in London and Lyndon's invitation for Sheila to come to Indiana as his bride. I was part of the initial committee formed to establish the park," Carol says proudly.

"Living in her home, I'm interested in learning more about Sheila's life on the farm. I'm also looking for information on her family members so I can search for her family tree. I hope this doesn't sound like too personal a question, but would it be possible to arrange for me to talk with your mom sometime?"

"Well, it would have to be on one of her good days, as her memory is not the best, but I can certainly ask Mom if she ever talked with Sheila about her relatives in Scotland. I'm afraid I was too young to have gotten to know her well, but I loved listening to her Scottish accent. I remember a memorable presentation she gave for the Hinklettes Home Demonstration Club, where she talked about tartans and how to wear them properly. My friends and I all wanted our own kilt to wear. She certainly was a kind lady and encouraged me to ride my horse on the trails through her forest." She smiles at that memory.

I nod and add, "My maternal grandparents also emigrated from Scotland, so that gives me a special connection to Sheila."

"A cousin of mine has dabbled in compiling our family's history in this area." Carol laughs wryly, "If I ever have the time, maybe you could show me how to look up my relatives at the library?"

"Yes, I'd be happy to teach you how to get started, but fair warning, genealogy is an addictive hobby."

I share some of the promising results from the genealogical research into my parents' family, like how my grandpa might actually share relatives with the famous explorer David Livingstone.

"It's discouraging to find some gaps in my mother's story. I was only twenty years old when she died. My father and I disagreed over the simple obituary he had published in our local newspaper. He provided the dates and places of birth and death along with funeral information and then agreed to add a line that she was a housewife. When I read it in the paper just before we buried her, I was heartbroken to think no changes to her obit were possible. There was nothing about her kindness, her fabulous baking skills, or her talent for listening and putting people at ease. It fills me with regret that in our grief we didn't leave a better record of her life."

"You poor dear, to lose your mother so young," Carol murmurs.

"If I could write a letter to my teenage self, it would be to sit down with my mother and ask her to tell me stories about growing up in Toronto. My parents were married for twelve years before they had their first child. That is a dozen silent years. Was my mother working during that time? I really knew little about her hopes and dreams. Come to think of it, I heard her say once that she really hoped to travel to Scotland one day."

My neighbor puts down her mug and says, "Good advice for me. When her mind is clear, I should video my mother talking about her life raising horses. I'll let you know if she remembers anything about Sheila."

She takes the last bite of her muffin. "By the way, thank you for these delicious treats."

"You're welcome. Sorry that I must get back home now, but perhaps we can meet up again soon."

As I walk back along the path leading to my farmhouse, I jot a reminder in my notebook to follow up with Carol's mother. I add my neighbor's recollection that Sheila and Lyndon met in London. Printouts and post-it notes with potential lines of inquiry cover my desk, so I label some file folders and organize my paperwork. I also create a spreadsheet for both Sheila and her husband, Lyndon. It would be great if I knew the names of their parents and siblings so I could find more information about both of them through digital files such as census records and ship manifests. This is all great preparation for the class I am going to teach at the library next week - How to Track Down Your Family Online.

That evening, I jump onto a popular genealogy website and find a 1947 immigration form for Sheila MacGregor, who has her destination as Indianapolis. I feel like a prospector striking gold. This might be the breakthrough I need. Badger hears me giving a whoop of joy and comes running to join me at this exciting moment. He gets a treat and I pour myself a glass of Malbec to celebrate. On the entry document, she lists her birthplace as Fordyce, Scotland, and her birth year matches with the obituary I found for Sheila. Smiling, I remember seeing the word Fordyce written on the back of the graveyard sketch in her portfolio.

I am thrilled when I discover a family tree on another website with Sheila's parents and siblings all living in that same village in 1903. Her parents are John and Anne, with five children in total. I have work in the morning, so I reluctantly shut down my laptop. Tomorrow, I'll pan for more gold, using all these additional details to see what more I can uncover.

When I first retrieved Sheila's art portfolio, I looked at every section of sketches, which seems to be organized chronologically. Now, I want to scrutinize the art, a few pieces at a time, to see what clues they hold. As I find more references to where Sheila was living from old records, I add to the timeline of her life and adventures. So far, I've confirmed that she was born in 1909 and lived in a little Scottish village named Fordyce. Her father was a Presbyterian vicar at a church which had an old graveyard next door to the manse. I even found a photo of the stone knight and his dog, posted on a Scottish travel blog, that matches Sheila's sketch.

***

On the weekend, Charlotte and her daughters come for a sleepover. We feast on pizza and fizzy drinks. After many rounds of Uno with Maya and Tara, we notice the yawns and help them into their pajamas. With the girls tucked into bed, it's time to share my research progress with my best friend.

"Remember how I told you about my visit to the Parks Department's office and my sneak peek at the future park sign titled *Sheila's Trail?* Well, here is the image they used."

I bring out my phone and show her the photo of Sheila. It is wonderful to have an actual image to reference as we open her art portfolio. We linger over a section of drawings: one of a train engine with N. R. stenciled on the side and another of a colonial-looking house with a gentleman and his dog in a tropical setting. The last drawing is of a dapper young man holding a book up to his chest. On the back of the handsome gentleman's portrait are the words: *Gilbert -Blantyre*

I muse aloud, "So Gilbert is the man in the sketch, but where have I seen Blantyre referenced before?"

Charlotte watches over her wineglass as I sort through my files and folders in search of the name. I pull out two different copies of a ship's manifest to compare with what turns out to be the name of an African city. Charlotte points out that both documents have a passenger listing for Sheila MacGregor, her occupation listed as a Children's Nurse. She is bound for Africa in 1933 and three years later returns to England. As listed in the former manifest, she appears to be sailing to Blantyre in the British Colony of Nyasaland with a civil service doctor, his wife, and their young child. A few lines down on that same list of passengers, we find the name of a single man, also a civil servant, named Gilbert Rennie. Charlotte and I crow over this connection. Perhaps it was in a small English ex-pat community where Sheila and Gilbert met?

"I've never heard of Nyasaland." Charlotte has her finger on the word.

"Let me look it up." I perform a Google search and discover that the African colony of Nyasaland is now the country of Malawi, with a major city named Blantyre.

"It seems strange to have a Scottish sounding city in Africa. Ah, here's the answer. In honor of the famous Dr. David Livingstone's work and explorations in the area, British colonial officials renamed the settlement after his birthplace in Scotland."

"Livingstone? Any relation of yours?" Charlotte teases.

"Perhaps. My grandpa always said he was a third cousin twice removed from the great man."

After all my solitary hours of research, it's fun to have Charlotte here to share in the uncovering of such splendid details; we both turn in for the night, pleased with ourselves.

Sleep is slow to come as I ponder these new discoveries, feeling a kinship with Sheila over a potential geographical connection in Africa. Imagine, Sheila lived for a time in Blantyre, where David Livingstone worked. Is my grandfather's claim of being related to the African missionary and explorer accurate? More interestingly, what happened in Africa between Sheila and this young man named Gilbert?

Chapter 4 - Sheila

"… I shall try to hold myself in readiness to go anywhere, provided it be forward."

- David Livingstone

London, England 1933

Sheila stiffens her resolve and crosses the busy London road, entering The Royal Societies Club with its luxurious furnishings and hushed atmosphere. She removes her brimmed hat with the faded flower band and nervously smooths her brown suit jacket and skirt. Taking a deep breath, she approaches the concierge.

"Excuse me sir, I have an appointment with Dr. & Mrs. Irwin."

He looks up at her brown hair pulled back into a tight bun and down to her sensible Oxford brogues with one eyebrow raised, but says nothing. He leads her through an elegantly appointed room with burnished wood trim and plush furniture, to a middle-aged couple sitting by the fireplace. She takes a seat in the chair that is positioned in front of them and then primly places her hat and small clutch in her lap.

Dr. Irwin sports a mustache and has the air of the upper middle class. He glances at a portfolio that is open on a side table. He seems weary, as if preparations for his journey have taken too much of his time thus far.

"Miss MacGregor, I presume."

"Yes, sir." Sheila nods.

He asks about her experience with children and Sheila gives him an outline of the time spent caring for her young charges in Scotland. Although she is in her mid-twenties, she already has glowing letters of recommendation from former employers, a sign that she aims to succeed wherever she focuses her attention.

Mrs. Irwin leans forward slightly and her pale-yellow dress rustles. She pulls a flowered shawl over her slight shoulders and inquires, "Have you been to Africa before?"

Sheila replies, "Yes, when I was twenty, I took a trip to South Africa with my older cousins. My uncle and his wife owned a ranch in the Transvaal, and I stayed with them for a bit." She does not add that although the exotic animals were a wonder to behold and the country was beautiful with its breathtaking views of verdant hills, the established customs of racial segregation were intolerable. She could not abide the unjust rules of viewing some people as less than human and departed after only two months.

Dr. Irwin catches his wife's eye, and she demurely glances down. He takes back the interview. "I am a physician with the Colonial Civil Service and my post will be at Blantyre Hospital in Nyasaland."

"In the town named after the birthplace of David Livingstone. I have heard the mission has a reputation for its excellent medical care of the natives," murmurs Sheila. She knows from her reading that most of the staff of the hospital in Blantyre are indigenous men and women, contrary to practices she encountered in South Africa.

"Why yes, are you familiar with this particular town?"

"I read a biography of David Livingstone and his explorations in the area. My father was a Scottish minister, and I believe in his youth he had aspirations of going to Africa someday as a missionary. Alas …" Sheila trails off when she sees that Dr. Irwin is losing interest.

"Yes, yes, reading is good."

The doctor taps a stack of folders next to him.

"Well, Miss MacGregor, your references speak highly of you. You are healthy, yes? Will you be able to tolerate the heat? Are you ready to leave immediately?"

Sheila answers in the affirmative to all his questions.

He ends with, "We will contact you as before when we have made our choice."

"I will await your decision." Then Sheila hesitates and adds, "Pardon me, sir. If you choose me, I would make a request that I be able to meet your child first before I officially begin." If Sheila is to assume responsibility for the care and welfare of the child, she wants their daughter to feel that her nurse will not be harsh. She will be strict and fair in her discipline as a nanny should be, but she will also show kindness to her young charge. Unconventional as it is, this ritual shows who she is, and if that makes her new employers uncomfortable, then Sheila is content with the outcome.

Taken aback, Dr. Irwin harrumphs, "Most unusual. We will make those irregular arrangements if we decide to hire you."

A few days later, they summon her back to the Club where the four-year-old Grace shyly meets with her new nanny. After a hushed consultation, the unconventional young woman and the little girl seem to conclude: Yes, this new situation will suit them nicely. Sheila helps the child in packing her clothes and a favorite toy in order to be ready to embark on the *Dundurn Castle* bound for Nyasaland.

***

The ocean liner is more like a floating hotel for the first-class passengers; not so for those in second and third-class. Sheila is grateful that she shares tight quarters with only one other person, Laura, a children's nurse from Plymouth. The children in their care sleep in the cabin next door. During the day, all the young ones and their nurses gather on the second deck to keep each other company, out of sight of the mothers and fathers.

Sheila welcomes the chance to get to know her charge and is grateful that Grace, with her curly brown hair and sweet smile, has a mild temperament. Miss Laura is constantly trying to wrangle the rambunctious brother and sister who keep making up new games to evade their nanny. Sheila is relieved that Grace is young and sits contentedly on her lap, listening to the drone of conversations around her, while Sheila reads a book.

The domestic staff are free to take the air in the evening, so long as they do not stray too far from the children's cabins. Thinking of her upcoming three-year stay in the middle of the African continent, Sheila wants to take advantage of the cooler weather while she can.

"Do you mind if I stretch my legs and walk around the deck?" Sheila asks, already throwing a plaid shawl over her plain black dress.

"I'll keep a listen for the children, but I think they are finally asleep." Laura looks fatigued, and Sheila expects to hear her roommate snoring softly when she gets back.

Sheila checks on the cabin next door and, hearing only steady breathing, sets off for a stroll on the promenade deck in the soft moonlight. She is used to hiking in the countryside, so she grows restless if she does not at least walk the perimeter of the ship every day. Relishing the smell of the ocean, Sheila recalls her earliest childhood memories from living close to the North Sea.

Tonight, Sheila sees a young man on the deck. He is also part of the Civil Service contingent going to Blantyre, just starting out in his career and brimming with confidence. When she overheard him speaking with Dr. Irwin, she caught the hint of a Scottish accent. He notices her tartan and quietly hails her with a greeting.

"Halò ciamar a tha thu."

Sheila replies, "Tha gu math, tapadh leibh."

Looking around, they switch from their Gaelic *Hello, how are you?* and *Fine, thank you,* to English.

"So nice to hear someone speak who is from the Old Country. I am Gilbert Rennie, at your service." He doffs his Harris Tweed trilby and puts it back over his neatly trimmed red hair.

"Pleased to meet you, sir. My name is Sheila MacGregor, bound for Blantyre."

As the wind picks up, he grabs his hat, and she laughs. "Is this your first ocean passage? You will want to hang on tight to that trilby in these gales."

He grins, "Aye, my maiden voyage." They fall into step and a comfortable conversation begins about all things Scottish. In the coming nights, when they meet again, Sheila shares her experiences in South Africa, as well as what to expect in terms of climate and the conditions of poverty in Nyasaland. She has been to the British Library and read previous Civil Service reports on the area. She impresses him with her initiative to learn about Central Africa in advance.

"So, you like to read?" he questions her in his soft brogue.

"Books are my friends. Are they not your companions as well?" she teases. Sheila has often seen him reading in a deck chair.

For the rest of the voyage, she takes advantage of the freedom to chat with Gilbert about literature and gratefully borrows some books he has already finished. It is a delight to share in the admiration of authors such as Dickens and Hardy. She ventures to encourage him to try her favorite novels by the Bronte sisters and Jane Austen. Even if Mr. Rennie finds in her a mind equal to his own, she is below him in station; they both know that fraternizing in Blantyre will be inappropriate.

They dock at Beira, a bustling port in Mozambique that is the gateway to the colonies in Central Africa. Grace tugs at Sheila's skirts, a frightened look on her small face. "Where are we?"

"We have arrived in Africa. We must take a carriage and then get on the train that has a big letter N and R painted on the side," she explains, hoping to make it sound like a grand adventure.

At the railway station, Dr. Irwin herds the family to their compartment. Sheila gently waves a fan over Grace to cool her down during the overnight excursion. She whispers to the sleeping child, "All will be well when we arrive in Blantyre and get settled in your new home."

Beyond exhausted herself, she looks out the grimy window as the light fades. Sheila has composed a letter to Mona, her sister, about her voyage and will post that when they get to Nyasaland. After the weariness of travel has passed, in her next missive, she plans to note her first impressions of Africa.

September 1933

Dear Mona,

Landed safely in Beira and caught the train on to Nyasaland. After an exhausting twenty-four hours of travel, we and all our luggage arrived in Blantyre. Poor little Grace was weary of confinement, as we all were. The weather is hot and sleeping under the mosquito netting at night has taken some adjusting for us both.

A few weeks have sorted us out and now life in Blantyre is becoming a routine of meals and nature study and strolls about the garden.

You will be pleased to hear about the guard dog, whom the last resident of this house left behind. He is a frisky Jack Russell terrier who follows us about, warning of potential dangers that lurk in the yard with barks and growls. Grace and I have renamed him Jack. We both love when he settles down in the evenings, content to sit between us and listen to nighttime stories. I'll send you a sketch of our new dear doggie with this letter.

I've also made friends in the kitchen. Mrs. Irwin insists the cooks provide the usual British fare, but they cook deliciously spicy local dishes for the household staff. I occasionally try these out. My tales of haggis elicit gasps and giggles, while they offer a roasted fish called Chambo with a spicy gravy or serve me Nsima, their traditional maize porridge.

Dr. Irwin invites the other civil servants and their wives over for weekend dinners. Mrs. Irwin hosts weekly gatherings of English matrons who come for tea and cake while exchanging news from home. Sometimes, the nannies meet up to compare notes or share the latest gossip.

A highlight for me is when Mrs. Irwin walks to town and allows Grace and me to accompany her. My favorite stop is The Times Bookshop on Victoria Avenue, which has a large palm tree out in front. Inside, one can

One bright spot in the usual cycle of weekly activities is
attending church. The whole family dresses in their finest and
walks toward the magnificent Presbyterian Church. Scottish
missionary Rev. David Clement Scott designed the building
and Sheila marvels at how he directed the construction, despite
not having any training as an architect. They built the exterior
walls using bricks formed from the local red soil. This choice
of building material signified that St. Michael and All Angels
Church was to be the first parish where Africans of any race,
who inhabited Nyasaland, were welcome to worship there.

On her first Easter in Blantyre, Sheila and her charge
choose a place in the back pew. She is ready to swoop up Grace
if she makes a peep during this special holiday service;
however, the child sits quietly, fascinated by the colors of the
stained-glass windows. The organ music brings back memories
for Sheila, and tears form in the corner of her eyes. Now, in a
moment of wistfulness, Sheila imagines the presiding Rev.
Thomas Maseya to be the Rev. John MacGregor there at the
lectern. Her father's plan to go as a missionary to Africa
changed because of the beautiful socialite who would become

his wife; her mother protested that she was ill suited for a tropical climate, or anywhere else that was so far from her own family. Would it have pleased him to know that his daughter is here now, listening to a sermon on God's love for all people?

She is grateful to be employed, as the Great Slump in Scotland had taken many jobs away. No one had extra cash to pay an artist and Sheila had no desire to be a teacher like her sister Mona. While she has some money tucked away from her inheritance, Sheila knows that if she is to satisfy her curiosity about the wider world, she needs this job to provide the means and method of travel.

Her employers have brought her back to what Europeans refer to as the Dark Continent, and she is happy to do what exploring is open to her from her base in Blantyre. She finds she learns a great deal just from the acquaintances she makes amongst the expatriate community. To her surprise, she has the unexpected pleasure of meeting one of the few women doctors in the Central African colonies.

While the Irwins are entertaining one night, Sheila brings little Grace to say goodnight to her parents. She is a charming child and is making the rounds with her father to curtsey and greet the guests. It is heartening for Sheila to observe that he seems to cherish his daughter. As she stands against the wall, waiting to take the sleepy child back to her bedroom, the woman next to her leans over and comments, "How well this little one looks. Well done in attending to her health and welfare."

"Ach, well, I make sure that she gets plenty of fresh air and activity," Sheila smiles politely.

Nodding, the woman extends her hand and introduces herself. "I am Nurse Muir, pleased to make your acquaintance. They call me a nurse here, so as not to confuse the hospital staff, but I trained at the London School of Medicine for Women. When I return to England, I shall receive my license as a practicing physician."

"I am very pleased to meet you. My name is Sheila MacGregor. My sister, Anne, has just graduated from Nursing School in Glasgow. Although I have no formal training, I try my best to take care of Grace. There is an interesting book I have been reading, *The Universal Home Doctor*, to see if I can learn more about infectious diseases."

"My, I admire your desire to become more informed. If you have questions, I would be more than happy to meet with you when you have time off from your duties."

A thought comes to her as Nurse Muir chats about cases of smallpox and dysentery at the Blantyre Hospital and shortages of medicines. Sheila has long been curious about Dr. Irwin's work in overseeing community health; she has tried to listen in on conversations concerning medical concerns when voices carried down the hallway to her back bedroom. Sheila's official job title is Children's Nurse, yet her own meager medical training had been a course in childhood ailments and treatment of injuries. She would love to learn more about the diseases in this country and what she can do to protect her charge.

She advances an idea. "Would it be possible for the wee bairn and I to come to the hospital one day to see her father?"

"With his permission, yes, I can arrange a time. I'm sure some patients would love to have a young visitor, but not on the isolation ward. In the meantime, keep up the regimen you have established for your charge."

It's time to take Grace to her room, and as they leave Sheila's new acquaintance whispers to her, "I will be sure to let Dr. Irwin know that this outing was my idea."

True to her word, Nurse Muir arranges an appointment within the week for Mrs. Irwin, Grace, and Sheila to visit Dr. Irwin at his office. As a clerk ushers them in, the doctor tidies away a small mountain of paperwork into a neat stack on the corner of his desk. When an attendant rushes in a few minutes later with an urgent request for the physician, Nurse Muir comes along and takes them to visit the women's ward. Mrs. Irwin covers her mouth with a handkerchief, but Nurse Muir strides confidently along the row of beds, greeting each patient. An African nurse is dispensing pills and smiles as they pass by. The floors are spotlessly clean, and the open windows bring a slight breeze into the room. The attention to hygiene and patient care makes a positive impression on Sheila.

"We must be on our way," Mrs. Irwin insists, hurrying Grace outside after the minimum time required by politeness. "Come along, Nanny."

"Thank you for your tour, Nurse Muir. I am sorry we must leave in such haste," Sheila apologizes.

"I am glad you saw some of our work here. It is not a place all people feel comfortable in." She nods toward the door of the ward Mrs. Irwin passed through with a sympathetic smile. "Please don't keep your employer waiting. I would like to continue discussing preventive methods for avoiding childhood diseases." Nurse Muir winks at the prospect of a continued conversation.

December 1933

Dearest Mona,

I hope you are well, sister. Thank you for your letter that arrived yesterday. As I suspected, you have grown fond of Malcolm, and I couldn't be happier for you both.

Do tell of his prospects. You mentioned he might be in line for a job in Elgin at the Woolen Mills there. How far is that from Kemnay? Oh, don't they say that the heart grows fonder with distance?

Did I tell you the previous occupants of this big old house had an ample library? I have asked for permission to peruse the volumes, and Dr. Irwin allows me to borrow anything that strikes my fancy. Picture books, of which there are a few, fascinate Grace, and most nights I read her to sleep.

I am sad to report that conversations with Mr. R. are restricted to a simple hello at church on Sundays. He often comes to the house when Dr. and Mrs. Irwin entertain, but alas, I am usually occupied with Grace and her bedtime rituals.

However, there have been some occasions when I have been near the foyer when he has come in. One night, we were alone briefly, and he caught my eye. Imagine my surprise when he placed a book on a side table, alongside a portmanteau he had brought in. He tapped the book gently and left to join the others at the table. I recognized it as a volume I had lent him on the ship. When all the guests were being served in the dining room, I carefully gathered up the novel and took it back to my room. I quickly found a book that I had purchased at the bookshop and wrote a hasty note about how I hoped he might enjoy this novel as much as I had. Quietly, I went back and slipped the novel and note into his briefcase. Oh, Mona, how I felt like a spy!

It has become a game now. Inside each book, we exchange our carefully worded comments about our impressions of an author, or setting, or plot. It is impossible to meet in public, so these missives will have to do. I know my place, but these little interchanges lift my spirits.

How exciting that our sister Anne has found a nursing placement in Glasgow! Are Biddy and Iain behaving at boarding school? I also want to hear more about Malcolm. Will he be able to celebrate the holidays with you? Happy Christmas to all there in Kemnay!

Missing you,
Sheila

Blantyre, Nyasaland September 1934

It is Sheila's half day off, and she is sitting in a tea shop on Victoria Avenue, smiling as she reads a long-awaited letter from Mona. When she looks up, she sees Nurse Muir entering and walking toward her.

"Good news from home?"

"My sister was married last month!" Sheila reveals, grinning. "I'm so happy for Mona, and only regret that I could not attend her wedding in person. At least our youngest sister, Biddy, was there."

"Let's have tea and cake to celebrate the joyous occasion." Seeing Sheila hesitating at the suggestion, she adds firmly, "I insist."

Their tea arrives with delicate little petit fours on a pretty porcelain plate. They raise their teacups to toast Mona and Malcolm.

Relieved that Nurse Muir doesn't stand on ceremony, Sheila is glad of the opportunity to engage in a conversation with this intelligent woman. She asks her about the treatment of spider or snake bites and what medical procedures to take if anything untoward happened to Grace. Sheila knows that there are two hospital buildings in town, one for the British and one for the locals, and knows that her new friend works in them both.

"I am impressed by your interest in my work here in Blantyre. Please call me Mabel when it is just the two of us. I wonder if I might give you a draft of a paper I am writing on the mission, regarding the health and welfare of the natives in the region. You seem very well read and I need someone to check for grammar mistakes in my article before I submit it to the Free Church of Scotland Missionary Society."

"It would be an honor to help you in this way, Nurse Mu … ach, I mean Mabel. I may not help you with the medical terms, but I would be glad to put another set of eyes on the document."

"Thank you. I am sure you will do well. I suspect you have a keen eye for detail."

Teatime over, they proceed down the main street and Sheila quietly asks, "I wonder if I might ask for a favor. I have been exchanging books with a gentleman friend. As we are not equal in our social standing, it is difficult to make our literary transactions in the presence of his peers."

Mabel laughs out loud, then slips her arm through Sheila's and draws her closer as they walk together. They are an odd couple, the tall doctor and the petite nanny. "I would be delighted to assist you and Mr. Rennie in this delicate situation."

"But how do you know his name?" A worried look comes over her face.

"We are a small expatriate community here, and I have seen the brief glances you have exchanged. Such utter rubbish that people are not free to associate with whomever they wish. It will be a pleasure to help you both." Mabel gives her arm a squeeze.

February 1935

Dear Mona,

How are you? I think of you in the cold of winter and trust that you have enough coal to warm your flat there in your new home with Malcolm.

As I imagine the Scottish winter winds blowing about you, I hesitate to mention that the heat is upon us here. Yet this climate yields such a unique landscape. In discovering new vegetation, I have taken delight in the lushness of nature all year round. What a place to be a gardener! The hot spells mean drought, but when the rains come, it seems like the Biblical flood. Still, these plants are so resilient in the heat and spring back to life with a little moisture. The profuse flora also provides homes for creatures that I encourage Grace to observe, albeit from a safe distance. I have located a field guidebook and when we notice an interesting insect, it's straight to the "bug book" and we look it up. Is Grace going to be a naturalist someday? I wonder.

Jack the terrier is our constant companion, and I am relieved to have him by our side. When he growls, it gives us time to back away if he senses danger. Good old Jack!

Spiders can be a grave hazard, but nothing like the snakes in the area. I have asked my new friend, Nurse Muir, for advice on how to handle a poisonous bite just in case. Don't start worrying! It seems there is always a manservant around to wield his machete or use his rifle to dispense with a threat. I have learned to be cautious, especially at certain times. Here in Africa - the adage is to never venture out at night when one can glimpse eyes glowing in the dark!

Enjoy some of my sketches of the flowers. Must dash!

Fondly,
Sheila

One morning, Sheila must take matters into her own hands: as she is watching Grace play in the yard, a deadly puff adder takes them by surprise. Jack alerts Sheila with his low growl and she looks around for the gardener but doesn't see him. Thinking quickly, she picks up a rifle leaning against the house and aims at the snake before it gets within striking distance. The thunderous sound of the shot brings everyone in the house running, and they all gather to examine the dead reptile. Sheila scoops up the sobbing Grace, bringing her inside to the parlor as a hysterical Mrs. Irwin follows, reaching for her daughter. Later that evening, the dinner guests discuss the incident, then summon her to tell the story.

Sheila stands uncomfortably before the group. "I saw the snake and knew Grace was in danger. The gardener was elsewhere and there was no time to call for someone else, so I took a shot at the adder myself."

"You didn't put that you could handle firearms on your references." Dr. Irwin guffaws, and Sheila blushes.

"My grandfather was in the 6th Battalion Donside Highlanders and was an excellent marksman. He showed all his grandchildren how to handle a rifle when we were young," she states matter-of-factly. "Also, I had some experience shooting with my uncle in South Africa."

Grace's parents speak of their gratitude. Sheila looks at the gathering of civil servants, a little abashed at the fuss that people are making, and then notices the smile on Mr. Rennie's face. He is shaking his head in surprise, while grinning broadly at the discovery of yet another side to the deferential nanny. She hopes they will engage in a private conversation later, perhaps on the ocean voyage home; she wants to confirm there is more to their friendship than just the books they exchange.

April 1936

Dear Mona,

How are you holding up? I am heartbroken to learn that Anne is in the TB ward at Tor-na-dee Hospital. I have written but have received no letters back from our dear sister. How I long to visit her upon my homecoming in May. Do you remember going to visit Mother in the sanatorium and being asked to recite poetry for her? We were so young and there was Anne as a teenager making her rounds to greet all the patients and inquire after their health. It seems the TB curse has brought down another member of the MacGregor clan and it gives me great pains to think she is suffering. Do give her my love if you are allowed to visit.

It's hard to believe that three years have passed since I first sailed to Nyasaland, and now it is time for me to return to England. I would dearly love to visit you and Malcolm in Scotland, but I am not sure when that might be. There are many stories to tell of my time here. I have been faithful in my sketching, so will show you the likenesses of the people I have met.

Yes, I have a sketch of Mr. R. and yes, I hope to correspond with him. We have become quite fond of each other. I would even venture as to say that he is my gentleman friend. However, I have been guarding my heart, for while he is bound for London, he is unsure about where the Civil Service will post him next.

Who knows what the next few years will bring us all? Dr. Irwin was talking this morning about Germany moving troops back into Rhineland in violation of the Treaty of Versailles. Please let there be peace upon my return, not rumours of war.

It's peaceful there in your village of Elgin, is it not? I'm dreaming of sitting in your parlor listening to stories of your little schoolhouse and of Malcolm's fishing exploits.

Lovingly,
Sheila

Chapter 5 - Meg (November)

"I awoke this morning with devout thanksgiving for my friends, the old and the new."

- Ralph Waldo Emerson

November is the month of thanksgiving, so I've created a gratitude list to revisit throughout the month. I am thankful for …

- A Thanksgiving dinner invite from my old college roommate in Indiana
- My new job and coworkers
- Badger, my buddy
- My cozy new home
- New freedom to begin a writing project
- The progress I am making with Sheila's research, including her obit, immigration paperwork, and the MacGregor family tree
- New places to explore: Monument Circle in Indy, Potter's Bridge trail in Noblesville, The Indianapolis Museum of Art

We have arranged most of the Thanksgiving Day feast on the dining room table, and I circle around to find my name, Aunt Meg, on a cute place card in the shape of a turkey. There are only five places set, so it doesn't take long.

"Well, look at that - I'm sitting between Maya and Tara, my two favorite kiddos. I wonder where they got the name cards …"

Hearing giggles, Charlotte's young daughters pop up beside me. With no nieces of my own, I am delighted to be an honorary aunt to these two.

"We made them by tracing our hands on brown paper, then cutting out the shape of a turkey. Then we cut out feathers in different colors and pasted them on. The thumb is the head of the turkey." They are both showing their technique with their hands held up in the air.

"Oh, yes, I see." I admire their artwork with a smile.

Charlotte enters the dining room, bearing her world-famous sweet potato casserole with a pecan crumble topping. I inhale the spicy aroma of my favorite part of this holiday dinner. Don't get me wrong, I love turkey, mashed potatoes, and stuffing, but this festive dish is the best.

"Ooh, that looks delicious. Do I smell cinnamon? I know I had the recipe at one time, but can you write it out for me again?"

Her husband, Raffi, lanky compared to her petite frame, follows her in with a Tandoori turkey to appreciative comments. He sports an apron that has *"That's what I do, I cook and I know things"* printed on it. He points out that this year he has also made his mother's Indian sweet-and-sour tomato chutney instead of cranberry sauce. We sit down, holding hands and bowing our heads as Tara says grace. Her child-like sincerity shines through as she thanks God for the yummy food and for all the people gathered around the table.

"Amen" echoes around the room, and we dig in.

With the dishes cleared, Charlotte and I sip coffee and enjoy our pieces of pumpkin pie. We are relaxing on her sofa that had been my bed before I moved into the farmhouse.

"Thanks again for putting up with me and Badger when we arrived in Indiana. You cannot imagine how grateful I was for a place to land."

"No problem. The girls miss having you around. We're just glad to see you safe after all that trouble with Trent. How are things at the farmhouse?"

I cringe at the mention of my ex-husband's name. "Blissfully quiet and uneventful. Badger and I take invigorating walks every day. It's a shame that the rental period is only for a year, but they have scheduled MacGregor Park to open next September. I'm soaking up the peace and solitude of my woodland setting, plus the bonus of living alone is that I have plenty of free time to research when I get home from work."

"How's your Sheila project coming along? Any more discoveries?"

"I've now talked to two sources: a parks department clerk and my neighbor, Carol. They both reference how Lyndon and Sheila met in London during WWII. This has been my inspiration to write a charming wartime tale. Imagine the romance of a war bride brought to Indiana by her smitten fiancé. I've delved into stories of women who volunteered for the Mechanised Transport Corps in England. It was not an official branch of military service, so I can't look up to see if Sheila's name was on any registration lists. Still, I can fill in the blanks and imagine how Sheila drove Lyndon around London, and they fell in love."

"Please let me read what you have written so far. You know, I've heard authors say how they started writing a short story and it just organically grew into a novel." My friend nudges me, reminding me how I have declared more than once that I would like to write a book one day. She is such a voracious reader and is always asking me for book recommendations.

"Don't get me started, or I may recount every detail of my research so far. If you knew how many hours of facts I could unleash on you …"

My friend pretends to hold her hands up in surrender. "Oooh! Maybe not tonight. We will have to plan a time to have dinner together soon. Then you can tell me all about the lives of Sheila and Lyndon."

"Over wine. Agreed."

I return home with leftovers and a warm heart filled with thanksgiving.

The library is closed the next day, and I launch into creating a timeline for Lyndon, searching especially for details of his military service in war-torn London. Online, I find a black-and-white photo of him in his army uniform. Lyndon's picture goes up on my research bulletin board next to the one of Sheila that I captured on my phone and printed out. He has a receding hairline, broad forehead, and a half smile, but it's the penetrating look on his face that holds my attention.

His draft card registration form notes he was 6-foot, 1-inch tall, with brown hair and blue eyes. In 1943, his mother died, and her obituary had the following note: *Lyndon Beals, who is in the United States Army, stationed at Camp Breckinridge, Kentucky.* From his own obituary, I make a list of all the different organizations with which he was involved. He worked for the *Indianapolis News* for his entire career; the newspaper editors also published a personal piece about his life and charming personality traits. I'm thankful for this wealth of details that reflects his interests and passions. I also gain a sense of the man who convinced Sheila to move to Indiana to be his wife.

***

Over the next couple of weeks, I delve into Lyndon's family history, which goes back to pioneer times in the county. This helps me understand how, since the Civil War, various members of the Beals family owned the land where the farmhouse rests today. I reach out to the staff at the Indiana Room, which is part of the Hamilton East Public Library in Noblesville; they are very helpful in suggesting sources for Hamilton County archives. Westfield Library has its own history room as well, and sometimes I take my notebook and settle in at a table for a couple of hours after my reference desk shift. Exploring the details of area plat maps is fascinating. I learn that Lyndon's maternal grandfather had a farm close by that was in their family for one hundred years.

Tonight, I will review my recorded thoughts and the remaining questions. Taking another look at Sheila's immigration form, I realize that I have not figured out the identity of a person listed on her entry paperwork. She designates Imelda Ostrom as "FR" in the margins of the document. I conclude it stands for "friend" rather than a relative. That Sheila lists this name and address as her destination upon arrival in America opens a whole new avenue of exploration. Hurrah for research databases where I can search old Indianapolis City Directories from the 1940s. When I plug in the address from the immigration form, I discover Henry F. and Imelda Ostrom listed as owners of the property. It designates Sheila MacGregor as their renter in the 1949 and 1951 directories. Another cry of delight, another treat for my assistant Badger, another celebratory glass of wine. I create a new folder for the Ostrom family and add an item on my research "To Do" list: investigate Imelda's family history and her connection with Sheila. Did they know each other in England? Was this Imelda also a British war bride like Sheila?

The next section of sketches from Sheila's art portfolio seems to reflect her experience of living in England during World War II. There is one of a forlorn looking young girl with her doll, a battered rucksack beside her on some stairs, and one that seems to be a crowded London Underground platform. That lines up with the evidence I found of a 1939 address for Sheila living in London at the beginning of World War II near the Earl's Court tube station. Was this a scene of people sheltering during the Blitz? I desperately want to learn about the stories behind the sketch of the dog on a pile of rubble with *Jordy the Blitz Dog* written on the back. If only Sheila were here to tell me about her war experiences.

Chapter 6 - Sheila

"Carry on! Carry on!
Fight the good fight and true;
Believe in your mission, greet life with a cheer;
There's big work to do, and that's why you are here."
- *Robert W. Service*

London, England 1940

September 1940

Dear Mona,

What has our world become? It's been a year since we have declared war on Germany, and it seems all we hold dear is at risk.

No news from Mr. R. and I am wondering if he has received my letters. The post office must be in disarray, and I fear he does not have my correct address through all my moves, nor I his. So many men have enlisted, and he could be one of their numbers. Has our brother Iain said anything to you that would suggest he is also considering that path?

I am relieved that Biddy has moved to Oxford to join her new husband and is relatively out of harm's way with the recent bombings in London. Were you as surprised when she <u>finally</u> let us know about her marriage to Jim? I'm still flabbergasted that Biddy kept it a secret for two years that she wed a medical student! I felt sad when I was in Africa and missed your nuptials, and sadder still, knowing that no one in our family attended Biddy's clandestine wedding. I'm sure she also wrote to you about how she *didn't want a fuss then, and now they are just getting on with things. Our little sister has always had a mind of her own.*

Speaking of determination, I cannot help but admire a young girl whom I recently met. Greta is from Vienna and arrived in London a year ago as part of the Refugee Children's Movement. Have you heard about this organization which has helped to rescue almost 10,000 Jewish children from the Nazi threat? She captured my heart the first time I saw her at the shelter - such a waif, with her black hair in braids, clutching a doll with one hand and her rucksack with the other. I could relate to the pain of separation from her family at such a young age.

I have been volunteering at a Salvation Army hostel here in London. They provide shelter for some of these poor unfortunates, and I do my bit by pestering my friends to donate some of their ration cards to help feed them. This morning, I had to say goodbye to dear little Greta and the other children I have gotten to know. They are being evacuated today to farms in Shropshire. I hope she finds refuge with a kind foster family.

It feels just now like life is loss after loss, and I am feeling quite alone in this great city. What else is there to do but carry on? Please write and cheer me up with news from Elgin. Saying prayers for your safety, dear sister.

Much love,
Sheila

London, England 1941

Sheila stops at the motivational war poster that hangs at the factory entrance and reads,
"*Your Courage, Your Cheerfulness, Your Resolution Will Bring Us Victory.*"

She inhales deeply, pulls back her shoulders, and takes her place in line next to her new friend and roommate, Imelda, who insists that everyone call her Millie. Her life has changed once again. She spent two years in Surrey in domestic service after getting back from Africa. Then her sister Biddy helped her find a position at the Selfridges Department Store in

London. She has listened on the wireless to the speeches of Prime Minister Winston Churchill in which he reminded the people of their island nation to do their bit. So, she is starting her first day at the munitions factory on the outskirts of the city. Sheila chafes at the feel of the stiff new coveralls against her skin, but they are required for the job. It is a far cry from what she wore when working as a beauty specialist at the swanky cosmetics counter. "Needs must" is her motto as she resolutely ties her reddish brown hair back with a bandana. With so few men available, women are stepping forward to work the tedious hours in factories of all sorts.

Fitting together the pieces of the weapons, she turns her mind to stories of brave soldiers across the Channel to take her mind off the fumes and dust. On particularly long days, she mentally recites the poetry of Robbie Burns. Sheila will also think about her brother Iain, once a banker and now a Leading Aircraftsman with the Royal Air Force Volunteer Reserve. As his older sister, she is grateful that for now he is still in England but worries about what may happen once they send him to the Far East. Sheila puts her shoulder to the wheel with the determination of a woman who now is choosing to carry on with the work set before her, knowing that every bit of effort is necessary.

At the end of her shift, weary from her labor, Sheila settles in at her second-story Kensington flat she shares with three friends, eager to rest. She has just fallen asleep when she awakens to the sound of air raid sirens.

"Blast, I was hoping for a decent night's sleep," she groans. For safety, Sheila dons her utility garment with its CC41 insignia. Her blond and perky roommate Millie sleepily shucks on trousers and a jumper. Heading out the door, she checks on Sheila, who is applying her go-to lipstick. Spending the night underground in the Earl's Court Tube station with strangers, she just wouldn't feel comfortable not looking her best.

"The bombs will be falling soon, and you are worried about makeup? Get a move on, my dear Sheila, or the only person who will appreciate your looks will be the undertaker."

Smacking her lips, Sheila grimaces and grabs her tartan for warmth. She draws courage from the memory of her Scottish ancestors and knows the shawl can serve as a pillow as well. The two young women, shelter tickets in hand, join the queue to the Underground station that serves as a bunker for their London neighborhood. It is going to be another long night.

***

The street is lit by the pale dawn light when they sound the all-clear siren. Millie and Sheila stagger out of the air raid shelter, trying to stretch out the kinks from their cramped muscles. The air is heavy with acrid smoke, and the street coated with the filthy grime of smashed bricks as the friends stumble to find a clear path back to their flat. They have seen bomb damage before, but none has come this close to home until now. Millie shudders in the chilly morning, wishing for her bed.

Before they even turn the corner to their block, they hear screaming. A distraught, dust-covered old woman is straining against an air raid warden who is preventing her from going back into her basement flat. The volunteers had just pulled her out from the rubble of her home.

"Madam, it's not safe!" he insists.

"He's all I've got … my dog, my dog!" the woman wails, collapsing to the ground in tears. She continues to repeat the phrase.

Sheila anxiously approaches. "What's the problem here?"

"This poor lady's dog is stuck in the basement. He did not follow her out," one rescue worker says, shaking her head. "We can hear him whimpering but can't get down there. The space is just too narrow …" she trails off.

Sheila cannot bear to hear the dog in pain or observe the grief of this old lady who now lays in a heap on the sidewalk.

"What is the pup's name?" Sheila gently asks the owner.

"Jordy. His name is Jordy, and he is all I've got since my husband died," she sobs.

Sheila tightens the belt on her siren suit and, turning to the block warden, orders him.

"Lower me down with your ropes. I'm small enough to squeeze in."

"I will grab him, and you can pull me up," Sheila says over her shoulder, as she picks her way through the rubble, following the sound of the dog's pitiful barking.

The warden puts his hands in the air in surrender. The other workers watch anxiously but prepare to help her. Even in her bulky suit with the shawl around her neck, Sheila will do what she can to save this little shaggy creature who is cowering underneath a table that somehow remained intact. He is afraid and only, with a great deal of coaxing in a soothing voice and the offering of half a biscuit, is Sheila able to grab and cradle him against her chest. They are both filthy when they emerge, but before Sheila places the little dog in his owner's arms, he licks some of the dirt from her face in gratitude.

"Ah, there, you are my pet. Look who is waiting for you, wee doggie," Sheila tells him.

She pats Jordy as he wiggles in the old woman's embrace. The look of relief on the wizened face and the joy of the terrier mutt are all the thanks Sheila needs. Scanning the rubble and sighing with exhaustion after the night of destruction, she shakes out her now dusty tartan and wipes her brow with a clean corner of the shawl. Perhaps the roommates should think about leaving London.

July 1941

Dear Mona,

Greetings from a beleaguered Londoner. I was grateful to get your letter, as the mail service has been spotty. Work in the factory continues, but my friend Millie has finally convinced me to apply for a posting with the Women's Land Army. Our applications will go in together and we hope that Millie's Aunt Cecilia will put in a good word with her friend Lady Holcroft, who oversees the Land Girls in a place near the Welsh border. Wouldn't that be something if they assigned us to the same farm? Fingers crossed.

I hope that I might have a quick visit with Biddy soon. Did you know that Jim - or should I call him Doctor Jim? - is working day and night for the Royal Army Medical Corps in Oxford? She is going a little stir-crazy with their first baby on the way and no family or close friends around. They will ship him overseas after the baby comes, and then Biddy and the babe will live with Jim's parents in Beaconsfield. I wonder if she plans to visit with you as well?

I trust that all is well in Elgin. Malcolm must be busy as the new manager at Johnson Woolen Mills. You mentioned he is conducting drills with the Home Guard. I feel that your small section of Scotland's coast is more secure with Malcolm on duty.

Give all those dogs who dwell under your roof an affectionate pat on the head for me. You can also pass along a peck on the cheek for Malcolm.

Fondly,
Sheila

"Come on, Sheila." Millie shouts up the stairwell, "I want to get our applications in the post today."

Sheila leans over her paperwork again and thinks hard about how to answer the question which asks for "short particulars of any training or experience in agriculture." Neither her current position as a worker in a munitions factory nor in her prior position as a department store beauty specialist are at all farm related. She sighs and notes on the line that she is an excellent markswoman from her time in Africa. Oh, and she is a first-rate nanny. Sheila looks the form over one last time, then trundles down the stairs to join Millie. She slips her form into the envelope Millie is holding out and gives her friend a smile in anticipation of a positive outcome. Hopefully, Millie's Aunt Cece will come through with her connections.

***

The need for Land Girls is urgent, as the time for harvest is just around the corner. Within the month, Sheila and Millie arrive at their designated farm outside of Shrewsbury. This new rural assignment will prove to be a life-changing period in both their lives.

Chapter 7 - Meg
(December)

There is a light dusting of snow on the forest trail, so I place my feet carefully and navigate my way up and down the forest hills. It's like a setting for a fairy tale, and I'm content in my current state of seclusion. Despite living alone, I am feeling settled and happy here in my new state.

Work provides plenty of contact with people, both friendly coworkers and library patrons alike. Jan watches over us and the library with the skill and compassion born from years of experience as the director, and George keeps us entertained with engaging gossip from the literary world.

I'm delighted with my weekly exchanges with a fellow science fiction reader, one of the regular patrons. Simon is a handsome, middle-aged EMT who works at the fire department station close to our library. Like clockwork, once a week after his shift, he swings by the reference desk to give me a review of the latest novel he read and enjoyed. We swap favorite classic authors like Isaac Asimov and Ray Bradbury, then compare notes on the newest books.

Many people dread being on their own during the holidays. As an only child, Christmas has always been a time of melancholy since my parents died. I'm grateful that I have Charlotte's girls to spoil with gifts; we did the present exchange early as their family is traveling out of town this year to be with relatives. On the bright side, I am thrilled to have three days to do research: Christmas Eve, Christmas, and what I refer to as Boxing Day, which is what Canadians and Brits call the day after Christmas.

With the library closed and nowhere to be, I vow to make use of this time to myself. My plan is to dig deep into the online newspaper archives to find more information about Sheila.

I've made a big pot of turkey soup and stockpiled some of my favorite red velvet treats from a place in Noblesville called Rebellion Doughnuts. I grin at the thought of rebelling by wearing my red and white candy cane fleece pajamas all day. There is no one here to tell me I need to always look presentable.

Trent would insist that I dress up for every work function so that I could make the best impression on his business associates. My husband also insisted that I never leave the house without wearing something stylish. No schlepping around town in leggings and sweatshirt for the wife of an important accounting executive. Overly conscious of his reputation, he wanted me to project his success in my wardrobe, regardless of my comfort. I rub my sleeves and feel the soft material under my fingers, relishing the freedom to choose my weekend attire.

Setting up my laptop, I start my research marathon by reviewing what information I have found so far. As a reward for a set number of hours of finding connections between Sheila and Imelda, I've queued up *While You Were Sleeping,* one of my mom's favorite holiday flicks. I always get a little teary when Sandra Bullock's character points to which of the two brothers is the man of her dreams. After the movie and popcorn and content with a day well spent, I slip into bed and dream of finding my own happy ending here in Indiana.

Bright and early the next morning, Badger is wearing a special Christmas gift while I am bundled up with the new pink scarf and mittens. These are presents that Tara and Maya picked out for us, so I take a selfie and send Charlotte and the girls a pic of Badger with his plush reindeer antlers headband

and me in the snowy woods. Back at the farmhouse, he forgives me the indignity of having to pretend to be one of Santa's helpers and gnaws happily at a rawhide chew. I pour myself a mug of coffee and settle in for another fact-finding session while holiday music plays in the background.

Every bit of information is a gift today as I immerse myself in searching the library databases that give me access to digitized birth, wedding, and death notices. I verify multiple connections between Sheila and her friend Imelda. A marriage announcement lists her as Sheila's matron of honor. I also find an obituary for Imelda; I now have a full list of her family members.

Another piece of good news is the engagement announcement for one of Imelda's daughters, noting an address in Indianapolis. Here's a potential primary source who may still be alive and have personal stories about what Sheila was like. To my knowledge, Lyndon and Sheila did not have any children of their own. Is this woman the closest to family, as I will find in the United States? The death certificate for Sheila has this same daughter recorded as the informant, listing her relationship with the deceased as a goddaughter. Badger wonders if we have won a big prize as I jump up and down in celebration. He joins in by barking excitedly and spinning in circles around my feet.

Once I calm down, I dive into checking to see if the goddaughter and her siblings might still live in the area. It's amazing how much personal information you can find on the Internet. I make a mental note to check on my own digital footprint. With a bit of Facebook sleuthing, I find contact information and compose an email using the message line: *"Librarian researching Sheila MacGregor Beals - would love to talk to her goddaughter."* With fingers crossed, I send my request into cyberspace.

I still have one full day to myself, and I want to ride my research adrenaline rush in search of more people who may have known Sheila. There are a lot of details to slot into my timelines that I have created for both Imelda and Sheila. A further scan of the Indianapolis newspapers results in a major find. It is a newspaper society page article about Sheila's niece, who visited Indianapolis in the 1960s. My guess is that she is the daughter of the youngest MacGregor sister, Biddy. This young woman was on her way to a very successful career with the British Broadcasting Corporation in England. Evidently, she became a distinguished radio host and presenter in England who interviewed celebrities and wrote a tell-all account of her life. I tracked down and ordered a used copy of her book, also emailing her agent to ask if she would be available to answer some questions about her aunt in America. Boxing Day is ending, so I sigh with satisfaction and tidy up my files. That will have to do for tonight.

***

A few days later, I discover one of my favorite things, a book-shaped package in my post office box, and eagerly unwrap my copy of the memoir I ordered. It turns out to be a treasure trove of MacGregor family information. After just one evening of reading, multiple post-it notes poke out from the pages. I now know the complete names of Sheila's siblings and their spouses. It also answers a lingering question about a doctor whom Sheila listed as her brother-in-law on one of her U.S. entry forms. His name was Dr. James MacGregor, and I presumed incorrectly that it was a typo and that he was Sheila's brother. It turns out her younger sister, Margaret, married someone with the same last name as her own. I also found it sweet that her husband used her childhood nickname, Biddy, throughout their marriage.

New Year's Eve finds me at home, enjoying a Reuben sandwich and my favorite German-style Dunkel lager from the local Westfield restaurant called Field Brewing. I am mulling over the information in my research folders; there is one each for Sheila, Lyndon, and now Imelda. If I could, I would thank the local newspapers for providing a wealth of family information in their archives. These old weekly publications shared features with our modern social media, recording social events and naming people and places.

59

My most exciting find this evening is a critical reference in the niece's memoir when she and her mother visit Sheila, who is working as a Land Girl on Holcroft Farm, near Shrewsbury in England. It turns out that Sheila's overseer, Lady Holcroft, was part of the British aristocracy. Her formal photo on the National Portrait Gallery website doesn't evoke the description of an eccentric woman who preferred to be known as Aunt Topsy instead of her more formal title.

It is time to research the Women's Land Army (aka the Land Girls) to see if Sheila shows up in the records. My questions about this part of Sheila's life are mounting. I can verify a London address for Sheila in 1938-39, so why did she give up living in the city to move out to the countryside? What was her experience on the farm like with Aunt Topsy in charge? I can verify that Sheila and Imelda were close friends in Indiana, but can I find evidence that Imelda and Sheila were acquaintances in England?

My phone lights up with a "Happy New Year!" text from Charlotte as the seconds tick to midnight. I respond with fireworks emojis while raising a glass of bubbly to the new year and the unearthing of proof that Sheila has led a full and noteworthy life.

On the first day of January, I find new material online about Land Girls in Shropshire County. There is even a mention of Mrs. Holcroft, who they have listed as a local representative for the Women's Land Army in the Church Pulverbatch district. Her address is simply "Wrentnall," which seemed to be a historic home called Wrentnall House. I suppose that Aunt Topsy may have billeted the land girls working at Holcroft Farm in her home.

Now some of the ink sketches I discovered in Sheila's portfolio make sense. There are depictions of farm life with a uniformed Land Girl offering part of her lunch to an English Spaniel and a woman milking a cow. Knowing the location of the farm where Sheila was working has led me to information about a British military station near Shrewsbury. It was called RAF Atcham, and Britain transferred the base to the United States Army Air Forces in 1942. Could that be the location of the sketch with men in uniform dancing with women in summer dresses, and an American Flag in the background? Now I need to find out if Lyndon's military assignment was to that base in order to confirm the story of how they met. What I've found so far about his war experiences is minimal, and there have been no references to his time in England. I might have to submit a request to the U. S. National Archives to uncover his military service records.

Glancing down at my phone, I see it is almost midnight. There is my morning shift at work tomorrow, so I place all my paperwork into their respective folders before rising from my desk. Looking out the window, I see a clear sky, with stars twinkling between bare branches and a luminous full moon. A quick walk will clear my head, which is still buzzing with all the new material I have uncovered. Badger is excited and charges ahead along the path that runs the perimeter of the silent meadow. Breathing in the cold, clear air, my body is still. This is a sacred moment for me as I stand where Sheila once did, with all her hopes and dreams. I whisper to her, "I resolve to prove that you were far more than an ordinary housewife. Happy New Year."

Chapter 8 - Sheila

"The land army fights in the fields. It is in the fields
of Britain that the most critical battle of the present
war may well be fought and won."

- Lady Denman, Honorable Director of the Women's Land Army

Shrewsbury, England 1941

After a brief training period, Sheila and Millie arrive on the
doorstep of Holcroft Farm. The sleepy village of Church
Pulverbatch is home to titled nobility who own a manor house
with an attached working farm. Lord and Lady Holcroft are
billeting some of the Land Girls in their Edwardian home, with
bunk beds installed in some of the many guest bedrooms. Lady
Holcroft has taken leadership of the Women's Land Army for
the district of Shrewsbury. Millie and Sheila settle in and marvel
at the size of their room that comfortably houses six girls, yet
still gives them plenty of room to move around.

Preparing to report for duty, Sheila lays out her cotton
corduroy breeches, fawn-colored cotton shirt, and bottle green
jumper on a chair next to her bed. She runs her fingers along a
green tie with diagonal yellow stripes bearing the letters
"WLA" on it. A brown felt hat and yellow socks with brown
shoes complete her uniform. She also has cotton dungarees,
which might be preferable in this warm weather, and gum
boots to wear in the barn and farmyard.

Sheila looks up as the mistress of the manor enters the
bedroom. She has a regal bearing and fine manners, but the
twinkle in her eye belies her air of propriety.

"Lady Holcroft, we are just unpacking. My name is Sheila MacGregor, and thank you ma'am for the lovely room," Sheila babbles, glancing uncomfortably over at Millie, who is reclining on her bunk.

"Oh tosh, call me Aunt Topsy. I can't abide formality when we will all be at the same breakfast table. Are you settling in?"

"Yes, ma… I mean Aunt Topsy."

Millie is now on her feet. "We so appreciate being able to stay in the house. The bunk beds remind me of boarding school, but your home is much nicer."

"Hmm, who are you and where did you attend school, young lady?"

"My name is Imelda Mountford, but everyone calls me Millie. I boarded at the Royal Pinner School in Middlesex, but thankfully my Aunt Cece arranged for me to attend a finishing school in Poitiers, France. I love their baguettes and cannot stand to think of the Germans taking over that beautiful country."

"Ah, yes, Cecelia Foster, your aunt wrote to me inquiring whether you girls could be assigned here together. She is an old chum of mine and I was happy to honor her request. Well, no fancy bread here, just plain British fare. I despise what Hitler is doing in France as well. That is exactly why we are all doing our part in the Women's Land Army! Carry on and come down for tea when you are ready."

Arriving downstairs in their WLA uniforms, Deacon the butler escorts them to the dining room, where four other girls are chatting around the large oak table. A sideboard bears a warming tray full of boiled cabbage and another with a mushy batch of Brussels sprouts. There is milk for their tea, but no sugar. It seems rationing is part of life here in the countryside as well in London. The thought strikes Sheila that all the newly arrived recruits probably feel as out of place as she does here in this fine country home. She learns the names of her fellow volunteers so they can become a community. They will need each other.

The next day, Aunt Topsy and three of her children conduct an informal tour of the farm with the new Land Girls. Work will begin in earnest tomorrow. It surprises Sheila to learn that the Holcrofts are also hosting two refugee children, and she is delighted to find Greta collecting hen's eggs in the chicken yard. The black-haired orphan brightens as she recognizes Sheila. The two hug as Sheila speaks to her quietly with the few German phrases she had picked up working with the children in London. Greta answers as well as she can in English. This young girl has gone through so much trauma with the loss of her family, and now living in a country that is foreign to her. It is a relief to learn that the child has found shelter for now.

Aunt Topsy has been watching them and comments, "That is the first time since she got here that she has smiled. We have had little Greta and her friend Ingrid helping with the chores of feeding the geese and gathering eggs, but they have been keeping to themselves. Sheila, I remember reading that you were a nanny once. Perhaps you can give us some advice on how we can aid in their settlement here. For now, the girls can join us and help introduce you to the animals on the farm before they must leave to take those eggs into the kitchen."

Greta takes Sheila's hand, and they approach the two geese in the yard. Ingrid speaks a little English and explains that they have named them Hanna and Sofie. Sheila doesn't have the heart to suggest that these birds are destined for the Christmas table in a few months, and the girls shouldn't get too attached.

As the little group rounds the corner of the barn, an English Springer Spaniel bounds towards them; Greta backs away and cowers behind Sheila. Aunt Topsy's son deftly commands the dog to heel. "Aw, don't be afraid. He's a favorite with almost everyone and his name is Montgomery, Monty for short."

The family dog has a beautiful silky black and white coat and soft floppy ears, and Ingrid pets him shyly now that he is calm. Greta still refuses to come anywhere close. The tour continues, and of course, the cows are the final introduction. The cattle are in the field, so the tour members just wave and continue back to the house. At lunch, Sheila asks permission to spend time with Greta and Ingrid in the evenings and on Sundays. She can't help but remember being young and alone with the strict widow, Mrs. Campbell. It is a relief to see that

Aunt Topsy is the affectionate type who will watch over them in their new home. When Sheila next writes to Mona, she will ask if her sister has any extra primers left over from her teaching days to send for the girls. Learning English will be an essential task for these girls.

Reality sets in the next morning for Sheila and Millie as they rise at 4:30 and don their uniforms for their first workday as Land Girls. Ruby, the cook, greets them as they head through the kitchen on their way to the mudroom. Walking quickly over the cold slate floor, they find and slip on their rubber boots from the lineup, each with initials inked on the inside rim. Mist still hangs over the rolling hills, and rosy sunlight tints the horizon. They meet Mr. King, who is the manager of Holcroft Farm. He is of medium height, solidly built, with a weathered face and bushy eyebrows that match his salt and pepper hair. A shy young man who walks with a limp is with him. The veteran farmer eyes the new Land Girls with skepticism, wondering how these inexperienced women could ever replace the men who went off to war. Clearing his throat, he sets out to teach these city girls how to be farm hands.

"How many of you have worked on a farm?" Mr. King inquires.

When none of the women replies, he shakes his head with dismay.

"Have any of you been through training to milk the cows?"

Both Millie and Sheila step forward with Emily.

"We learned the basics at our orientation outside of London," Sheila answers, choosing not to divulge that the exercise was to sit on a stool and pull on a plastic udder the instructors rigged up to simulate the real thing.

Mr. King nods, "Follow me. The rest of you are to follow John out into the fields. There are wheat sheaves to gather in and ditches to dig."

The others groan and look longingly over their shoulders as they walk away from the barn. The old man and the newly appointed milk maids make their way to the cowshed.

Someone has tacked a schedule up on the wall in front of the stalls that states:

5:00 AM   Milk the cows

8:00 AM   Breakfast (about 30 mins)

8:30 AM   Muck out the cowsheds and wash, then sterilize the milking equipment

12:30 PM   Dinner (about 45 mins)

1:30 PM   Bring the cows in from the fields, scrub them down and wash the stone floor

5:30 PM   Home for tea (about 30 mins)

Gasping as they read it over, Millie quips, "Should we pencil in *6 PM Collapse* at the bottom?"

"Farm work is hard, but we are feeding the nation," Mr. King says gruffly.

"We are not afraid of long hours, sir," Sheila replies.

"Glad to hear that, and just call me Charlie. Now let's meet the ladies," he gestures with a faint smile.

He formally introduces Sheila, Emily, and Millie to the cows, with a little commentary on each.

"This is Ethel. You need to watch out for her tail," he cautions. Moving to the next cow, he adds, "Don't be fooled by the pretty name; Daisy cannot abide cold hands. She is likely to kick out if she is unhappy."

The cows' faces have all turned to look at the Land Girls with their huge liquid eyes, and Sheila pats Daisy's soft nose. A loud mooing seems like a demand from the cows to be milked. Three stools and three pails stand ready against the stone wall of the barn. Charlie gives a demonstration by positioning a stool and milking the first cow of many. He stays around to make sure they are getting the hang of it.

Millie mumbles out loud, "Are we ever going to get to breakfast today?" Thankfully, Charlie chuckles sympathetically rather than getting frustrated with the new recruits.

***

Sheila settles into the routine of farm life over the next three weeks. Feeding, milking, and leading the cows out to pasture and back gives a whole new meaning to the phrase "working until the cows come home." Her days include a very different schedule from her life in London. Aunt Topsy gives out certificates when proficiency is shown in certain areas; Sheila earns hers in the Milking category. As she becomes more efficient, she has a little time during the day to tutor Greta and Ingrid, who will start at the village school soon. Ingrid has adapted well to learning a new language, while Greta's grasp of English is progressing, but not as fast. With the help of an English-German dictionary she borrowed from the Holcroft Manor library, Sheila commits a few words to memory each week and includes them in her conversations. When Greta tags along with Sheila, they trade words in each other's language. Her eyes widen at the sound of her native tongue, and she smiles and nods, correcting Sheila's pronunciation when needed.

Another activity that becomes a ritual is walking with Monty. The springer is usually with Will, the gamekeeper, and at first, Greta is terrified by the dog's appearance. Sheila can only imagine what the child might have witnessed in her home country. Perhaps she saw German soldiers with fearsome dogs on leashes. Slowly, she works with the fearful girl to trust the friendly dog who means her no harm. He senses Greta's reticence and stands still while she cautiously pets his soft fur. His large black eyes take in the little one and, with his loyal and affectionate disposition, he serves as her protector when they are together. The three of them sometimes rest in the courtyard, and other Land Girls come over to feed Monty some tidbits from their lunch pails. When Greta's English gets better, Sheila tells her the story of a famous leader of the

Scottish forces who was fighting for independence from England in 1297. He had a very special dog.

"Did you know that a famous Scot named William Wallace would go into battle with his pet dog named Merlin?"

The little girl shakes her head and looks up, waiting for the rest of the tale.

"Well, the story goes that there was a very important bridge that they were fighting over. The soldiers from Scotland did not have as many weapons as the other army. So, William Wallace gathered his men and told them they could win, and that his own dog, who he loved so much, would come along. The other soldiers took heart that their leader would risk harm coming to his cherished pet, and they all fought bravely, winning the Battle of Stirling Bridge. Do you know what kind of dog Merlin was?"

"No, what was he?" Greta asks, still petting Monty, who is sitting quietly by her side.

"A dog just like Monty!" Sheila rubs the dog's ears, and he leans into them both. "So, now you know how brave a Springer Spaniel can be. Aren't you glad to have this fine wee dog as your friend?"

Greta nods in agreement and gives the affectionate dog a brief hug.

***

Rural life has many benefits, and despite the long hours and blackout curtains, it is lovely to see the stars at night in the dusky countryside. It turns out there was another advantage to living on this small farm near Shrewsbury, with the unexpected arrival of a U.S. Army Jeep. It happens when Sheila and Millie hear a cry down the farm lane one afternoon, and they respond to the call for help. They find two American soldiers stranded en route to the nearby RAF Atcham base. A very handsome soldier introduces himself as Major Henry Ostrom, from some place called Indiana. His driver is desolately looking under the hood but is hopelessly inexperienced in motor repair. They are in luck. Since Millie unfortunately received a kick from Daisy the cow, she has become adept at fixing engines while her bruised leg heals. Sheila helps her friend hobble over to the Jeep and watches as she adjusts her kerchief to keep her curly blonde hair back. Sheila holds her tool belt, as Millie takes a rag from her back pocket, and asks if she could have a look. Both men seem surprised.

"By all means, ma'am," Henry says, backing up to give the Land Girls some space.

"I have been practicing on the farm equipment and reading manuals," Millie retorts as she reads the hesitancy on their faces.

Sheila hands over the requested tools as the eager new mechanic dislodges the spark plugs and gives them a wipe. Pulling on wires, Millie finds the problem and adjusts them.

"Try it now, soldier," she calls to the driver, and both girls smile in satisfaction when they hear the engine start up on the first try.

The major removes his cap and bows, sweeping his arm in front of him.

"You saved us. Now let us reward you for your service. Can we come back and pick you both up for the dance at our air base this Saturday night?"

"Arrange for a truck to pick up all the Land Girls who billet here, and we will consider your offer. Of course, my friend and I plan to take a ride in your Jeep!" Millie says matter-of-factly, not to give away her excitement. Sheila squeezes her arm in agreement. They all shake hands, and Sheila helps Millie make her way up the lane as fast as she can, eager to share the news with their friends.

***

Lady Holcroft has mentioned that the Americans took over the Royal Air Force Base as a training facility. This chance meeting confirms the news, and both Sheila and Millie are sure the other girls will jump at the chance to socialize. Because of the demands of farm work and their remote location, they have limited options for entertainment. Daily chores and responsibilities take up most of their working day; in the evenings there is only enough time left to write letters, listen to music on the gramophone, or read before nodding off to sleep.

When the Land Girls arrive for the dance, they find that the soldiers have festooned the dancehall on the base with patriotic posters and a large American flag prominently displayed above the stage. The band is warming up, while others are setting up tables for the refreshments. It thrills Sheila and Millie to be off the farm and out of their Land Girl uniforms. They each wear flowered dresses that are garnering appreciative glances from the servicemen. The petite Sheila smirks as Millie, who is a head taller, searches the crowd for the handsome major she rescued. No doubt he is busy greeting the chaperones.

Aunt Topsy has insisted on coming along to check that there is proper supervision at the event. She takes her responsibility for the Land Girls in her district seriously, but she also likes to chat with the U.S. military officials and then pass on any pertinent information gleaned to her husband. Lord Holcroft has connections with the Royal Air Force contingent that used to be housed at this airbase. The English and Americans are allies, but they don't always share intelligence.

Sheila is looking forward to an evening of music and dance. The soldiers are a mix of English and Americans who have forged a bond in fighting a common enemy. No doubt they are trying to bridge the cultural differences that are sometimes as wide as the ocean that separates their homelands. However, their desire to hold a woman in their arms is common to all.

It is a pleasure to hear and dance to the popular songs of the day played live. Sheila enjoys chatting with her various partners. A tall man with slicked back red hair and a pressed uniform approaches her as a song ends.

"Hello, Miss MacGregor," he says with a Scottish lilt in his voice.

Sheila gives a little gasp as her eyes widen. "Mr. Rennie, whatever are you doing here?"

"Well, it's now Flight Lieutenant Rennie. But at this moment, I am waiting to dance with a lovely woman whom I haven't seen in quite a few years. How do you do, my literary friend?"

She laughs and impulsively gives him a hug. "I'd be delighted to dance with you and talk about books again. It is truly wonderful to see you after all this time. Tell me how a civil servant from Glasgow winds up on this airbase in Shrewsbury."

For the rest of the evening, they spend the time hearing about each other's journeys from colonial Africa to Shrewsbury. Upon their return to England, they parted ways with promises to keep in touch by letter. They both had moved so many times, it was unclear if their missives were still floating in the mail. Gilbert looks fondly at this remarkable woman who could talk about novels and shoot a rifle with equal ease. He remembers well the tenderness with which she took care of her young charge overseas in Nyasaland.

They dance to the last song, and he whispers in her ear, "I have you in my arms at last. When we lost touch, I thought I'd never see you again. Let's make the best of this time we have now." He then pulls her to a quiet corner. Their kiss is long and tender.

"I can't wait to spend the rest of my life with you." She rests her head on his chest and doesn't want to let go. Uncertain days are ahead of them, but she will savor the gift of his presence in her life once again.

Shrewsbury, England 1943

Over words written on a page, Sheila weeps and tries to imagine how she will carry on. It was no surprise when her brother Iain signed up to serve in the Royal Air Force Volunteer Reserve. His theater of war was the Pacific, from which now he will not return. During the duration of Iain's year-long captivity as a prisoner of war, Sheila and her sisters never stopped hoping for his release. They had no way of knowing that, in a hut on Haruku Island, he died of dysentery.

Sheila can only hope that there was a doctor there when Iain was dying to tell him he would see his parents and sister soon in heaven and could leave this hell on earth behind. Mona received the official notification; Sheila reads her letter but scarcely believes the truth. She is grateful for Gilbert's arms to hold her as she cries for her only brother, who died too young.

The war is dragging on, and as she has adapted to work on the farm, her dreams of being a fashion designer are fading into the background. There has been little time for reading, but she keeps up with her sketching. It is a welcome respite when there is time to go into the nearest village and chum around with other Land Girls. Her heart flutters when she sees Gilbert in the local pub, and he comes over to give her a smooch. The more time they spend together sharing their dreams, the deeper they fall in love. Here, there is no distinction between classes, and they maximize their time in each other's embrace.

Her friend Millie is head over heels in love with her American, who everyone calls Bud. What is it about love in wartime, to make them all fools, falling for the impossible? This major has a wife and child back home but swears that the arranged marriage was empty. Millie is the love of his life now and Bud can't live without her. Sheila tries to convince her friend that this man is leading her on, but in a couple of months, they prove her wrong. She can't believe how determined the couple is to overcome their obstacles; when a quickly arranged divorce comes through stateside, they marry.

Sheila and Gilbert have a picnic together before his next mission and share their surprise and joy for the newlyweds.

"Cheers to the happy couple. At first, I thought Major Ostrom would just take advantage of Millie and then return to his wife after the war. I was wrong, and he really proved his love. I'm very glad for them both, but I miss her terribly."

"Every time I see him around the base, he has this broad grin on his face. I'm happy as well that it worked out for them to get married. I will try to keep you distracted now that Millie is no longer on the farm with you," he says, kissing her.

They are together on a blanket and Sheila looks down at her lap and notices that there is dirt under her fingernails. She has washed her hands but, in her haste, has neglected to scrub down to the cuticles. As her cheeks flush, she glances up into the face of her Scottish airman. Sitting carefully on her hands, she hopes the rest of her appearance is enough to keep his attention. Work on the farm has been transforming, as if the soil has baptized her and created a new woman who understands the importance of being close to the earth.

Gilbert extends his large hand out to her, observing how uncomfortably she is sitting. She shifts her roughened hands back to her lap, palms up. He carefully lifts her right hand to his mouth and kisses it.

"Please don't be ashamed of this evidence of the important work you are doing for the war effort. I love you just the way you are."

Clasping his hand, she never wants to release the man who has captured her heart. Pulling him close, she draws him down to the earth. The blanket welcomes them as the shadows draw a cloak over the lovers.

After, they lie close together, whispering. He fumbles with his discarded clothing and pulls out a box, presenting her with a lovely amethyst ring.

"I pledge myself to you, my Scottish lass, now and for always," he says as he slips it on her finger. "I love you. Will you be my wife?"

Sheila feels a stirring in her soul. "Ach, aye, my handsome Scot. I love you with all my heart. Our story is just beginning."

"I have missions to fly, but during my next leave, we will get married. For now, until I can inform my superior, please only tell Millie that we're engaged."

The evening has turned cool, and they stroll arm in arm back to Holcroft Farm. He turns to her and tucks her brown curls behind her ears as he kisses her one last time. Sheila and Gilbert join the Land Girls in the front room. A friend, Sylvia, has her camera out and gets a snap of the happy couple; the propitious moment soon to be a cherished memory.

***

Two months later, Sheila touches her side and winces, trying to ignore the pain and focus on the other source of heartache.

There have been only snatches of news from Gilbert as he has landed and taken off again. Now, it has been a long week and no word at all. She longs to chat with her closest friend, but their schedules are so different now. Millie and her new husband Bud are living in a nearby village, waiting for word of suitable accommodation before they move to a base in Northern Ireland. Sheila gets up and goes outside for some fresh air, still thinking about the rare dessert Cook served at teatime. Ruby's delicious apple crumble with the glorious accent of cinnamon still lingers on her tongue. Surely the sweet dish has not caused her discomfort.

Her friend's presence surprises her as she walks up the lane with crossed arms and lowered head, while darkness falls. Concern shows on the married woman's face, and Sheila knows something is amiss, thinking immediately of Major Bud. Millie envelops her in a loving embrace as she breaks down. Startled, Sheila quickly consoles her friend, calming her tears. While swaying, the new bride shakes her head and eventually finds her words.

"Oh, no, Sheila. It's not Bud. He's safe. We both know that you and Gilbert were engaged, but he didn't notify the Home Office with the change of his next of kin for notification. The Germans shot down Gilbert's plane somewhere over France and the notice of his death went to his parents. They didn't know he had proposed."

Sheila sinks to her knees as grief overwhelms her. The delicate spice in her mouth turns to ash. Others gather around and help her into the farmhouse. Later that night, appendicitis and fever take control and Sheila ends up in a nearby rest-home for wounded airmen. Just as fate has taken her lover, the tiny life inside her also slips from her grasp. The doctor insists that she needs an operation to remove her appendix and a hysterectomy to stop the bleeding from her miscarriage, which means no children in the future. The delicate amethyst ring hangs on a chain around Sheila's neck. Loss and pain weigh on her like a boulder and she cannot move. No Gilbert, no children, no reason to stay calm and carry on. Bereft, she falls into a fitful sleep.

Sheila wakes and finds Millie beside her. They clasp hands and shed tears together. After a week, Sheila will swing her legs off the cot, stand up, and get back to work on the farm, albeit slowly at first. The war is still on and there are cows to milk and children to teach. Life goes on.

Chapter 9 - Meg (January)

> "It is said that truth is far too often eclipsed but never totally extinguished."
>
> *- Titus Livy*

It's a chilly Saturday morning in late January, and I am sitting at the information desk bundled up with a warm sweater, looking into the Sumner Room where the Genealogy Club is meeting.

"I love my job," I sigh contentedly.

My coworker George comes into view and says with a grin, "Well, I'm glad you like working here."

"Did I just say that out loud?"

"Indeed, unless I'm a professional mind reader." He winks.

"Well, it's true. Everyone on staff has been so welcoming, and I'm happy to say that I know most of the regulars and their reading preferences. Especially the older gentleman, Robbie, who is so sweet and a bit of a flirt at his age."

"Ah, yes, he loves his library and is quite the charmer. Did you know that his wife, Marie, is on the library board?"

"Good to know. She is lovely and quite the reader."

"Speaking of our regular patrons, I've noticed that Simon, the sci-fi fan, makes a regular appearance every Thursday just when you are at the reference desk. I used to be his go-to source of recommendations for his next read, but now you have taken over that job," he teases.

"I'm just getting my desk work ready, and I'll be back shortly to take the next shift."

George is gone before I can object to the hint that I'm anyone's favorite. I turn to look at a gentleman who appears to be in his fifties with dark hair cropped short. He is guiding an older woman by the elbow up to the desk.

"Hello, I'm Frederick and this is my mother, Betty. She recently moved into the area to live with my sister. She only has her ID with a Wisconsin address, but would like to get a library card here. The woman at the circulation desk sent us to you. Can you help?"

"Of course. Welcome to our library, Betty. My name is Meg, and I'm the reference librarian. We'll be happy to issue you a library card, but we will need to see some mail with your daughter's address first. Do you have anything official from the government that has been forwarded to your new home … Medicare or Social Security notices, maybe?"

"No. I just got here. All I want to do is borrow some books. They have packed all of mine in boxes. I can't go to sleep at night without a good book."

Betty is flustered and I get her seated in a comfy chair and hand her the library brochure that outlines our programs. Stepping aside with her son, we speak in hushed tones.

"It will probably be best for your sister to come in and check a few items out with her own library card. That is until you can provide the proof of residency for your mom to get registered and have her own card."

"Thank you. I'm only here for the weekend, helping her settle in. It's a big move for us all. My parents lived in Wisconsin all their lives. My dad passed away, and we've concluded mom can't live on her own anymore. She has been getting forgetful and can no longer drive herself around."

"I understand how unsettling it is to move to a new state and to get used to all new routines and places. Our library has some used books for sale. Perhaps I could pick out a couple that might tide her over for now. No charge - I can imagine how disconcerting it would be to not have a book to read. Do you know what genres she likes? Mystery, romance, historical fiction?"

"That's so thoughtful of you. She loves detective novels, but nothing too violent." Then a pause, and he continues, "Here's a mystery for you to solve - I don't mean to be rude, but did you ever live in Wisconsin? You look so familiar to me. I work for a big accounting firm in Milwaukee, and I could swear that I saw you at a company party once. I have an excellent memory for faces."

With an intake of breath, I hope my demeanor doesn't show my alarm. "I'm sorry, but I recently moved here from Minnesota. The Wisconsin countryside was breathtaking on my drive down, but I have never lived in the state." I cut this conversation short by getting up from the reference desk.

Grabbing a couple of novels by Agatha Christie off the used book sale shelf, I try to calm my nerves. I hope that my dye job and shorter hair style will be enough to cast doubt on his recall. If he still works at my ex-husband's firm, I'm worried about my new location getting out. I have tried so hard to keep my new home and workplace off everyone's radar.

With straightened shoulders, I return to the mother and son. "Here you go, Betty. I hope you are a Hercule Poirot fan and that these two books will tide you over."

She eagerly accepts the paperbacks and perks up. I am satisfied to know that I have made a fellow reader happy.

Frederick offers his elbow to his mother. "Meg, you have been very kind. My mistake with the Wisconsin connection. I'm glad you have a cozy library in town. My mom loves to read, and she'll be one of your regulars soon."

As they shuffle off, I turn to clasp my hands under my chin. George comes up beside me. "Are you alright? You look a little pale. You're not coming down with something?"

"No, George, I'm fine. Just tired, I guess."

"Well, take it easy and have a good rest of your weekend."

I head for the bathroom to splash cold water on my face. My first instinct is to text my friend Charlotte, asking if I can see her right away to debrief. Then I think about how alarmed she may get, and I reconsider. I head home to Badger, and we brave the cold and take a brisk walk in the woods. I feel calmer afterwards and reevaluate my situation. This accountant may just forget about the familiar face because he is feeling overwhelmed dealing with family issues. Or he may not. I almost feel like packing my bags, but I am determined to stay put and take a chance for now. Somehow, living in Sheila's farmhouse has given me a sense of security and independence.

Needing a distraction, I check my email and am thrilled to see a response from Sheila's goddaughter, Anna. It has been almost a month since I sent off my email request for information, but I'm relieved that the answer is yes, and her family is delighted that I am researching their Aunt Sheila. Immediately, I dash off a reply with my phone information and ask for times when we can talk. I sit back in my chair and almost want to weep with joy. There are people out there who share my enthusiasm about a project to write about the Scottish woman's life. To create a biography of her, primary sources like photos and memories from close friends or relatives are essential; recollections can be conflicting, but I will work to verify my research with as much reliable information as I can gather. I can't wait to hear from Anna, who served as the informant on Sheila's death certificate. She is the woman who was with her at the end.

This has been a day of contrasts. On the one hand, a man I never want to see again may find out about my whereabouts. The thought fills my heart with an icy dread. Thankfully, it is also brimming with joy, since I am one step closer to knowing more about Sheila MacGregor Beals from Anna, who considered her family.

Charlotte will be excited about all my news, and we will go over the last of the sketches in Sheila's portfolio. We are both sad to have finished our scrutiny of all her artwork. I read again the note from her art professor, who acknowledged her technical expertise and the way she conveyed an emotional connection with her subject matter. He encouraged her to continue pursuing her interest in fashion design. Did she ever see his comments? I imagine that life got so busy with wedding preparations that retrieving her class assignment got put off. Living in the countryside, with no car, probably made it impossible for her to keep attending art college.

This month, I'm focused on a drawing of a Corgi with a black and white mutt (Sheila wrote *Incorrigible Jasper with sweet Snoopy* on the back) and what looks like a 1950s-era sketch of a simple wedding dress. My mind goes back to what Sheila had stated as an occupation on her immigration paperwork - designer. Was this her own creation - a beautiful frock with bell sleeves, cinched waist, a scoop neck collar, and delicate little stitched flourishes at the neckline? I wonder if Anna has a photo of Sheila and Lyndon on their wedding day. Perhaps she also knows who owned Jasper and Snoopy? How am I going to sleep tonight with all the questions that are stacking up like the teetering books in my to-be-read pile beside my bed?

Chapter 10 - Sheila

"In war as in life, it is often necessary when some cherished scheme has failed, to take up the best alternative open, and if so, it is folly not to work for it with all your might."

- Sir Winston Churchill

Kensington High Street, London, England 1947

The London sidewalk teems with pedestrians, yet somehow the old friends exist in a pocket of calm. Their time as London roommates and volunteer stints as Land Girls ended with the war and though they now live with an ocean between them, their shared experiences have knitted them together. They have been apart for three years, and the reunion is sweet for these kindred spirits.

"Oh Sheila, I've missed you so," Millie cries, stepping forward to embrace her friend. Their hug ends up sandwiching a squirming baby.

"And who do we have here?" Sheila asks, letting the infant grasp her finger.

The young mother beams, "Katie, meet your Aunt Sheila. Sheila, this is my daughter, the apple of her gran's eye."

Sheila's eyebrows rise. "I got your letter and could hardly believe you would come all this way to see a surgeon in London about your daughter's eye problem. Do they not have doctors in the United States? Did your mum question how you are spending your time here?"

"My mother was over the moon to meet her granddaughter in person. I barely managed to pry the baby from her arms, but she knows I came first and foremost to seek a British physician's advice. My days visiting family in Derbyshire are complete, and now the rest of my time in London is for Katie and you. Then it will be home to Bud and back to my life as a wife and mother. Let's go for a cuppa. I'm gasping for a cup of real tea, not the kind they brew in Indiana. How long do you have?" Millie says, tugging Sheila's sleeve.

Laughing, they link arms and head off in search of a tea shop. There is so much to say now that they are together again. No crackling and expensive phone lines or carefully crafted missives to impede honest communication.

"You must come to stay with me in Indiana. It is almost like the land of milk and honey and the best part yet - no rationing! I can go to the grocery store and buy whatever I like. However, there is no one I can really talk to with my best friend so far away. Move to America so we can be together again." Millie barely takes a sip of her tea before setting it down as she continues to convince her friend.

"What's keeping you here, my darling girl? Your sisters are well situated, with Mona in Scotland with her loveable Malcolm, and Biddy in South Africa with little Sue and that brave doctor husband of hers. This war has taken its toll on you. I say it's time for a fresh start in the land of opportunity."

Millie waits for an answer while she gently rocks her sleeping baby. Sheila looks her full in the face; she sees only sincerity and wistfulness.

"I hear what you are saying. Perhaps it is time to take a trip."

While considering a future holiday when her budget allowed, it had crossed Sheila's mind to travel across the Pond to visit her friend. Now, the thought of making a permanent move is both frightening and thrilling to her. She has been lonely and restless, and Millie's proposition fills her with hope. Living in Millie and Bud's little house might be just the cozy family home she has been missing, and once she gets a job, she will have occasion to be out and about exploring a new place. Might she be able to revive her dream of being a dress designer with a change of scenery? Surely this Indianapolis where Millie lives is close to New York City and its fashion houses. Even as she entertains these professional dreams, she realizes the biggest draw to move is to be caught up in the whirlwind of optimism that is Millie.

Indianapolis, Indiana 1947

October 1947

Dear Mona,

Hello from Indiana! Now you have my new address here in the grand city of Indianapolis. I have so much to tell you about my new digs. I have a small bedroom on the second floor of Millie's lovely little house and in the summer, I'd often sit out in the back garden that was bursting with flowers. It's autumn now and with the cooler weather there is a beautiful carpet of colorful leaves on the lawn.

Katie, the baby, now has a new playmate. You will never believe the dog Bud bought in England for Millie. Jasper is a pure-bred Corgi with a caramel-colored coat, adorably large ears and squat little legs. His title should be Prince Jasper, for he has an imperious disposition and rules his dominion as if he was royalty. He has little regard for his position as a pet and does not get along with any of the family members. He does not come when called and simply ignores any commands of "Stay." Somehow, with that attitude, he still expects to be pampered and petted. Okay, I give in to that sweet face and end up taking him out for walks.

I will hopefully not be hanging about with Jasper for much longer. Millie's mother-in-law, who is a newspaper columnist, has arranged for a job interview at the Indianapolis News. It's only a secretarial position, but I must start earning a wage.

In good news - I have found a wonderful art school which offers night classes. Perhaps now is the time to put together a portfolio and launch my career as a fashion designer? For now, I am completing a class assignment of drawing subjects that reflect stages of my life story. I hope the instructor will understand why there are several dog portraits. (How can I choose to draw just one? They are all my favorites!)

More good news - there is a group of English war brides, who have bonded together for mutual support. Millie let me tag along to one of their luncheons, and I am ever so thankful to join in and hear those familiar accents. Some of these women had tried attending meetings of the Daughters of the British Empire which was (and I quote from the brochure) "founded in 1909 and organized to stimulate social and intellectual intercourse, good fellowship, and philanthropy among women of British birth or ancestry, and to promote good feeling between England and America."

You can imagine that meetings of this proper organization were rather stuffy! Millie told me that after one particularly dull session, they all decided that if they had their druthers, they would rather meet at each other's homes and sip sherry. So, they formed a group called The Druthers, and I am happy to be counted among their numbers. I'm grateful to have gained some more friends who know what it is like to be far from home.

Jasper is begging to go for a walk, so I'll sign off. Love to Malcolm and your dogs. Write soon.

Fondly,
Sheila

Just before Sheila starts her clerical job at the newspaper, Millie drives her to one last meeting of the Druthers; as a working woman, she won't be able to attend their daytime gatherings. Sheila's heart always felt lighter whenever they met and sipped their sherries together. She listens today as they talk about the prejudice of many American women, who feel resentful of the foreign war brides who stole their soldiers. The English women all agree that love just happened in the intensity of wartime.

She and the other members of the Druthers are all women who are far from their native shores, and far from family. Although Sheila is neither a wife nor a mother, she listens as they chatter about taking care of their husbands and raising their children. They are trying hard to understand the way the local wives and mothers conduct themselves. Most of the neighbors let their children run wild when they get home from school, playing across the yards and tossing balls. Millie and her new friends have known more orderliness, growing up with their emotionally distant upper-class parents. Children were to be seen and not heard. Nose to the books to get grades that would please their elders. Sheila and many of these women have been to boarding school, and their experiences were a whole other kettle of fish. Months away from home with the strict discipline of school masters and form leaders. She understands it is hard for them to let their own children loose to play with the local hoodlums, as that is what it feels like they would be doing.

The conversation turns to the experience of going into a grocery store and finding aisles and aisles of foodstuffs. So many choices after the years of rationing are overwhelming for most of them. It seems impossible to get the familiar British brands of tea, biscuits, and cooking supplies. One member, Irene, complains that for weeks she had searched for corn flour, until she found out the cooking essential is called corn starch here. Millie says that she has yet to find a neighbor, who, upon inviting her over, has offered to serve her tea. If she asks for tea instead of the proffered coffee, the hot drink that is served comes nowhere near a proper cuppa. They all nod in agreement.

***

The next week, Sheila starts her work as a newspaper clerk in downtown Indianapolis, Monday through Friday. The typing is routine, and she looks forward to getting out of the office, when the weather allows, to walk the short block over to University Park to have her lunch. She loves to sit by the beautiful fountain with bronze adornments of dancing children and leaping fish encircling a toga-clad woman. Sheila is also quite fond of a statue of Abraham Lincoln, one of the most beloved presidents of the United States. He has such a benevolent look on his face.

One day she walks briskly south down Meridian Street to view the impressive Soldiers' and Sailors' Monument. Sheila buys a postcard to send to Mona so her sister can marvel with her at the amazing feat of engineering. It reminds her of Trafalgar Square in London. At the Central Library branch, she learns that the massive stone structure with intricate carvings is almost as tall as the Statue of Liberty in New York City. Sheila remembers when they processed her immigration paperwork at Ellis Island; Lady Liberty was in the distance, welcoming foreigners to her shores. America, with its iconic monuments, is her new beginning, but she still misses the wild heather on the hills of Scotland.

November 1951

Dear Mona,

How are you and Malcolm doing? I was sorry to hear that rationing is still in effect and am happy to slip in this little cheque to help you out. It may not buy you more eggs and meat, but you can at least get a nice bottle of whisky to warm you up at night. I don't have many expenses myself because of the kindness of Millie and Bud.

It will surprise you to hear that I have an appointment to meet a gentleman who is another newspaper employee for lunch next week. Millie's mother-in-law, who goes by "Miss M." is a columnist with a byline under her maiden name. Well, Miss M. knows this fellow from the Indiana Historical Society meetings. She will make the introduction. I don't know what to expect, but at least I'll get a tasty meal. I can hear you chuckling and saying to yourself: <u>there is no such thing as a free lunch</u>! We will see about that.

In doggie news, Jasper's temperament has worsened with the addition of a sweet black-and-white beagle mutt. The children have named him Snoopy after a cartoon character from the newspaper's funnies page. I found him wet and shivering on a cold evening, huddling in the street. He had no collar and looked like he was starving, so I couldn't resist bringing him home. The children fussed over him, wanting to give him a bath, scurrying around to set out food and finding him a nice place to sleep. You can imagine that His Highness has taken exception to an extra pet in the house. When I am home, Jasper behaves like a proper representative of the British Monarchy; yet while I'm away at work, he considers himself free to terrorize Millie and run wild with the young girls, who giggle at his naughtiness. Then when I get home, he clings to my heels and enjoys every minute of our perambulations around the quiet Indianapolis neighborhood where we live. Is he Jekyll or Hyde?

Tune in for the next exciting episode of "Jasper Rules" in my next letter!

Fondly,
Sheila

On her first meeting with Lyndon, Sheila takes in a tall, well-built, and middle-aged man who carries himself with a physicality that seems to fill the room when he enters. His broad smile encompasses each person he passes as he strides towards her in the downtown Tea Room on the 8th floor of the L. S. Ayres department store. Lyndon seems to bask in the attention he garners, confident of his own charm. Sheila directs her focus to the well-groomed, mature woman on his arm who is Millie's mother-in-law, a newspaper maven with her own column. Miss M., as she is known, is at home in the elegant surroundings, which include chandeliers and crisply uniformed waitresses. Thank goodness Millie had warned her friend to wear gloves and a hat with her best tailored suit for the occasion. Sheila is also grateful for the extended lunch hour Miss. M. arranged for her.

"Miss MacGregor, how lovely to meet you at last. Imelda has told me so much about you. When I heard that you've only made friends with ladies who were war brides, like my daughter-in-law, I just knew that I needed to introduce you to more suitable single people."

"Pleased to meet you, Mrs. McWhirter. I arrived early, and they showed me to the table. I hope you don't mind that I sat down before you."

"Oh, we don't stand on ceremony here in Indiana, and please call me Miss M. Everyone does. May I introduce you to my fellow historian, Mr. Lyndon Beals?"

He shakes her hand. "I am Lyndon, current president of the Indiana State Historical Society. Miss M. and I share a passion for all things historical."

With introductions complete, Lyndon orders the house specialty for the ladies. Sheila enjoys her serving of chicken salad served in a carved-out pineapple, with pumpkin bread and cream cheese finger sandwiches on the side. She also savors a perfectly brewed cup of Earl Grey tea. With her meager resources, this sort of treat is rare. They chat about the weather and common interests, passing the time in a pleasurable enough manner. The older woman looks at her watch and coughs softly, explaining that she has an interview for a column she is working on. She excuses herself and Sheila cannot help but notice how she gives Lyndon a gentle pat on his shoulder as she rises to leave. He gets up quickly, as befits a gentleman, and sits back down only when she is out of sight.

He invites Sheila to an upcoming concert, and she admits she is available to attend. They walk back to the Indianapolis Star newspaper office and plan to meet up after work the night of the recital. Thus begins her courtship.

***

The months to come are a whirlwind of activities. Millie jokes how her friend seems to receive more phone calls than she does. Sheila enjoys the church music and services at First Methodist Church, where Lyndon is the choir director. She feels pampered when they have an extravagant dinner in the tastefully appointed Travertine Room at the Lincoln Hotel.

They both appreciate a glorious Indianapolis Symphony Orchestra performance at the Murat Theatre. Afterwards, the couple stroll arm in arm downtown along Mass Ave. The glowing streetlights make the evening feel magical.

Lyndon shows off all the attractions of his Midwest city in case Sheila has the idea of moving to New York City in pursuit of her dreams of being a fashion designer. Her suitor wants her to appreciate Indiana as a vibrant place to live and settle down.

He gives her a tour through the Indiana State Museum's pioneer collection, unfortunately housed in the dank basement of the Statehouse. As a prominent member of both the Pioneer and State Historical Society of Indiana, he tells her many details of his family's past. He proudly shares that his maternal grandfather still lives on a farm that has belonged to the Lindley clan for over one hundred years. Sheila survives the tour and gratefully gulps the fresh air outside when they exit; Lyndon is oblivious to her discomfort, his mind still on the ins and outs of historical farming tools.

After the museum experience, Sheila suggests they explore woodland trails next. They truly enjoy attending Hamilton County Nature Study Club meetings together. Lydon has mentioned several times that he is a founding member of the organization. The group meets in different homes where members give talks on various subjects. She has an idea for her own presentation and plans to do research at the library. She is grateful to spend time with kindred spirits who love learning about butterflies, trees, and exotic animals. The club's annual spring wildflower hike will be a highlight for her.

Home from a day's tromp in Forest Park in Noblesville, Sheila looks about her small bedroom in Indianapolis, appreciating the kindness of Millie and Bud in providing her a place to stay these past four years. Yet quarters are getting tight for the Ostrom family in their cozy house on 53rd Street. Now that there are three children who need their own rooms, she must find a place of her own. Is Lyndon's farmhouse with its beautiful surroundings the answer? Is the spark of affection enough? Sheila ponders the possibility of marriage to the successful gentleman.

The practical woman marvels at how many interests she shares with Lyndon: music, history, and nature. There is but one exception. He does not take kindly to dogs. Will this be a hindrance in their relationship?

March 1952

Dear Mona,

I'm engaged!

Yes, I know I should start this letter with the usual - are you both doing well? - but I thought you would want to hear the news first off. We plan to be married in April. I know you can't afford to travel all this way for the wedding. Also, I know Malcolm is proud to declare that he hasn't been south of Edinburgh since 1930, so I wouldn't want to spoil his record by insisting you come. It is my hope that Lyndon and I will visit you in Scotland next year so you can meet him in person.

It's curious that when I sensed he was leaning towards a marriage proposal, I had formed a simple response in my head - "I will have to give it some thought!" However, that was before I saw his farm with its glorious woodlands. Is it odd if I say that I first fell in love with the forest and the little farmhouse that is tucked away up on a hill? Even though I hardly know this man, my answer to his proposal was, "Yes, of course I will marry you!"

At this time of my life, I think it is a wise move to marry Lyndon and make a home of my own. We have our differences, but I am sure we will sort these out in due course. We both have hinted at our disappointments during the war. I will never forget my lost love, but I will say Lyndon's name clearly when I declare, "I do." We set the date for April 26th at the Tabernacle Presbyterian Church here in Indianapolis with my pastor, Rev. MacDonald, officiating.

I am working on my wedding outfit and have included a sketch with this letter. I am happy that some of my friends from the Druthers group will be there to wish us well. Hopefully, someone will take a photograph so I can send it to you.

On a final note, I must report that Jasper has not taken well to my upcoming nuptials. It's not that he is my dog, but my involvement with Lyndon has taken away from my time for walks and ear rubs for His Highness. He will have nothing to do with Lyndon, cannot even stand to be in the same room! The children have tried to fill my shoes, but the poor doggie seems miserable and intractable. Millie finally has found him a new home with an older couple who will appreciate his pedigree and have more time to lavish their attention upon him.

My wedding day will also be a farewell to Snoopy; I shall miss them both. Perhaps Lyndon will agree to adopt a dog to keep me company when he is at work? What a fine wedding gift that would make.

Lovingly,
Sheila

Sheila steps from the Ostrom home in her short-sleeved, cream-colored wedding dress; she is clutching her bouquet of dusty pink gillyflowers and delicate white *Stephanotis*. The birdcage veil on her capulet shakes slightly in the breeze. The bride takes a deep breath in and smells the fresh spring air. April has come, and the sun casts her in a benevolent glow. Bud and Millie drive her over to the beautiful red brick Tabernacle Presbyterian Church building, which has been her church home for the last five years. She is sad not to have Mona by her side, squeezing her elbow and whispering that all will be well. Instead, her closest friend Millie is there for moral support and Sheila supposes many will consider her a war bride, even though she had met her groom after the war.

The ceremony is simple and beautiful, followed by a small reception in the church parlor. Sheila now stands beside her new husband to greet their guests. Once they pick up her trousseau, which she has packed carefully into a suitcase at the Ostroms, friends from The Druthers gather around the couple to see them off.

Carnation in his lapel, Lyndon has his arm possessively around her waist. She attempts a smile to match his huge grin as the camera clicks. Soon Sheila will start her new life on the Beals farm in Westfield.

Chapter 11 - Meg (February)

"Yet nothing delights the mind so much as faithful and pleasant friendship: what a blessing it is when there is one whose breast is ready to receive all your secrets with safety, whose knowledge of your actions you fear less than your own conscience, whose conversation removes your anxieties, whose advice assists your plans, whose cheerfulness dispels your gloom, whose very sight delights you!"

- Lucius Annaeus Seneca

Charlotte and I settle into wingback chairs in what I call my *room with a view*. Late afternoon sunshine filters in and the scene out the back window is of snow-laden branches tinged with rosy hues. We are having a cozy overnight, just the two of us. Raffi agreed to this getaway for his wife when I offered to host their girls for a sleepover on Valentine's Day. I'm still jittery from my library encounter with the man who thought he recognized me.

"I'm sorry I've been so busy, but I'm thankful for this time to catch up. How's work and are you making any progress with your research project? With these wintry days, it must be easy to stay in and search for more info on Sheila. You mentioned that you may have found someone who knew her, but you wanted to tell me in person?"

She nudges my foot when I don't answer, and I look over.

"Oh, sorry. Yes, work is great. I enjoy working at a smaller library and the staff are friendly. There's a wonderful community feel and the Friends of the Library group of volunteers are very supportive." I hesitate.

"But ..." she prompts.

"Everything was going really well until a couple of weeks ago." I pause, anticipating her negative reaction to the next piece of news.

"You know how I've tried so hard to keep a low profile. A man from Wisconsin came in with his mother, who has just moved to the area. He mentioned he works at an accounting firm in Milwaukee, and then he asked if he'd seen me at a company party a year ago. I lied and told him I moved here from Minnesota. If he tells the guys at the office that he thinks he saw Trent's missing wife in Indiana … I'm afraid that my ex may soon know where I have landed. I really don't know what my plan should be."

She sits upright, almost spilling her wine. "What? … Why didn't you tell me right away? That's it. I am bringing in the police. We can't take the chance that Trent discovers your whereabouts. Is that thumb drive with proof of his tax evasion still in a secure location?"

My friend, the lawyer, is the fiercest when she sees the possibility of harm coming to her family or friends. I love that about her and feel protected at this moment.

"Maybe this is not as serious as it seems?"

"It absolutely is. We must do everything we can to make sure that man does not find out where you live. We both know that he is currently sitting in a Wisconsin jail cell, but who knows if he will try to use his connections to get an early release? Where's your copy of the restraining order? I know I've had distractions at work, but I should have insisted we go to the police sooner. You and I are going to make an appointment with the County Sheriff's office. I want to make sure that the police are on alert for any of that jerk's associates."

"I'll find it and look at my work calendar for a time to go in. What if that guy who recognized me forgets all about seeing me?" I shudder as I get up to find my folder of documents.

"Being prepared is better than being surprised," she rejoins.

I hand over my folder and refill her wineglass. "Do you want to hear about my latest research breakthroughs?"

"Don't you be changing the subject so fast. First business, then yes, I do want to hear about your mystery woman who lived all alone in these woods. Was she hiding from a shady past as well?"

My best friend has moved to the kitchen table and pats the chair beside her; we settle in to look through my legal forms from Wisconsin.

After sorting my paperwork to take to the police station, I launch into my research report, hoping to lighten the mood.

"You won't believe this, but I found someone who considered Sheila as part of her family. When I started a whole new line of inquiry into Imelda, I found the names of her daughters who still live in the area."

"Wait, who is this Imelda and what has she got to do with Sheila?"

"She was a friend, and Sheila lived with her when she first arrived in Indiana. I found her name listed as Sheila's matron of honor on her wedding notice. Digging deeper into Imelda's family, I struck gold with a wedding reference to a daughter named Anna. A newspaper also lists Anna as a survivor in Imelda's obituary. I recognized her name from where she was listed as an informant on Sheila's death certificate; Anna notes her relationship to the deceased as a goddaughter. I knew then that I was on the right track."

Charlotte has leaned forward and is sitting on the edge of her seat.

"So, I have this potential source with quite a personal connection to Sheila and start looking into information about Anna online. She has a Facebook page, and I sent her a DM but didn't get a response. As she hasn't posted in a couple of years, I looked at her children's pages as well. Turns out that one of her daughters works at a school, and I found her school email. I emailed Anna's daughter with the heading: *Researching Sheila MacGregor Beals - would love to talk to your mom.*"

Charlotte interjects, "And did Anna or her daughter contact you?"

I continue, gesturing animatedly, "Yes, and I did a little happy dance. Anna's daughter sent back a reply: *Yes, my mother would be happy to chat with you about your research.* It was tempting to call you, but it was the middle of the night."

"This is amazing news, but I'm grateful you didn't phone me at an ungodly hour."

"Let me show you the first email I got from Sheila's goddaughter."

I look over her shoulder as Charlotte reads my first response from Anna, who writes that she is so thrilled to hear about my interest in her Aunt Sheila. She plans to call me soon.

"And look, she even sent scans of photos that show Sheila with various dogs. As well, there is an attachment of a charcoal drawing featuring Sheila's Irish setter with his fur blowing in the wind in front of this farmhouse. It is almost as if this dog, who she named Paddy, is smiling."

We both admire the pictures and her sketch, sensing Sheila must have loved this pet very much. Charlotte speaks first and breaks the spell.

"I'm impressed with her attention to detail. Her artwork really draws me in. I want to hear more about this woman."

"I'm so happy to see that Sheila continued her sketching. Now my goal is to fill in some gaps in her timeline, like how she met Lyndon in London and how long she had been friends with Imelda. It will be exciting to hear some family stories."

I take a breath, and my friend gives me a hug.

"Wow, Meg. All your detective work is paying off, and it's amazing that you get to talk with someone who actually knew your Sheila."

How is it that Charlotte can sum up in one sentence something I take a paragraph to explain? It's truly comforting to know that she values my dogged determination to find out more about Sheila, even if I get a little wordy in my descriptions. I can't wait to talk to my source by phone and then report back to my friend. Also, I appreciate she will make time to come with me to the local police station for an appointment I've been putting off since I arrived in town. For all that I have learned so far, I'm certain that Imelda and Sheila had this kind of genuine friendship as well.

Chapter 12 - Sheila

> "If you don't have a dog, at least one, there is not
> necessarily anything wrong with you, but there may
> be something wrong with your life."
>
> *- Roger A. Caras*

Westfield, Indiana 1952

Sheila wakes in her new double bed and feels the warmth of sunshine on her skin. She throws the sheets to one side and lowers her feet onto worn wooden floorboards. Lindy has already gone downstairs and started the coffee in the percolator. Early on, her husband let her know Lyndon was the name his mother had used for him; all his friends from the Army shortened it to Lindy, possibly because of his moves doing his favorite dance, the Lindy Hop.

Sheila understood when he said there was little money for an extravagant honeymoon. She was just as happy when he took a few days off work, and they rented a rustic cabin in the Brown County State Park. The trails had glorious vistas of wildflowers blooming on the hillsides. He even surprised her with a drive over to the little village of Scotland so she could buy postcards to send to her sisters, writing *"Hello from Scotland, Indiana."*

She dresses quickly and joins Lindy in the kitchen to make his breakfast. With a contented sigh, she watches him drive away on the short gravel driveway leading down the hill.

He is off to work in the city, and the day is her own. The quiet of her new home does not disturb her; it is a welcome change from the hubbub of Millie's household with children afoot, although she misses their hugs. Nestled in the magnificent woods, her farmhouse needs a thorough spring cleaning. A higher priority, however, is the various paths that beckon her into the surrounding land which is now hers to explore at her leisure.

Sheila grabs a flannel jacket and steps out to follow a familiar trail that leads into the forest and along the perimeter of the property. She is alone, yet there are creatures in the woods that greet her, chirping and chittering. She finds peace in this place where there is no noise of traffic or horns or people. Sheila feels welcomed and sheltered with nature around her, as she did in childhood.

On her hike, Sheila admires the vivid blue sky and the springtime flowers that carpet the ground. Delicate little white blooms are making an appearance and Sheila wants to learn all their names. When she has circumnavigated the entire property, she returns to her porch. She eyes the ground in front of the house, imagining the design of her own English garden. She will have to ask Lindy to take her to the library to get some horticultural books so she can make a list of flowers that will grow in this Indiana soil.

Perhaps she will ask Millie if she could divide some of her perennials to aid a fellow gardener. She will plan a special meal tonight and propose this plan to leave a little early in order to drop her off at Millie's house. Sheila can get a ride into Indianapolis with Lindy, even though it will be out of his way to the office. Pen in hand, she dashes off a note to her friend to arrange a day that will suit them both, and then begins her weekly missive to Mona.

May 1952

Dear Mona,

How are you and Malcolm? Please congratulate him on being named president of Elgin's Salmon Fishing Club. No angling here in the two little shallow streams that run through our property.

All is quiet this spring, but I am slowly making new friends. Millie is faithful to come and pick me up for the get-togethers with the Druthers. I don't want to miss a meeting with these mostly English friends - they all have such interesting stories to tell about their journeys to America and their experiences of living as immigrants!

As always, I love to attend the Hamilton County Nature Study Club meetings. Lindy and I plan to host a wiener roast at the farm this summer and we think most members will attend. Fingers crossed for no rain that day - it would be something to cram everyone inside our small farmhouse! For most of the meetings, a member will deliver a talk on a certain topic. Work has begun on my first presentation about the history of the English Garden!

My dream is to plant some perennials in front of our home and start my garden. I hope to find club members who will gift me some of their lilies and primroses. The public library must have a book about native Indiana plants I can borrow, and I will look up plants that will grow well in this soil. Then I can tell you all about the new flowers that will brighten my corner of the world.

My life is full, but I can't help but think about how there is one last thing to complete my happiness. I need a dog.

I miss you.

Fondly,
Sheila

Early one morning, the sound of barking in the distance startles her. Not quite barking, more like yelping. The sound of a car taking off with tires squealing also catches her attention. Sheila flings on a jacket, fills a thermos with water, and heads down the hill. With the sound of a dog in pain, she quickens her pace, knowing the main road is about a mile away.

During the war years, there was so much suffering in the world. When she is able, Sheila responds like an avenging angel to a call for help. At the bottom of the drive, she sees a flash of red on the gravel up ahead. A young male dog, possibly an Irish setter, lies on the ground panting. As Sheila approaches, the dog is instantly on his guard. With soothing words, she edges closer, trying to examine his body without touching. A dog's eyes convey so much, and he looks at this woman with distrust and exhaustion. Sheila kneels and pours water into her hand, showing she means no harm. Thirsty and probably hungry, the dog's pink tongue comes out and laps up the offering of kindness. She waits patiently for this lovely creature to relax so she can try to convince him to take shelter here, in her forest.

Sheila decides she needs to entice him away from the busy road and up to the farmhouse. Does she have anything in her fridge from last night's meal? She figures that a juicy piece of pot roast would do the trick. It doesn't take her long to trek back to her kitchen and return to the scene of the crime, but Sheila is relieved to find him still there licking his wounds. The injured animal glances up and sniffs. Yes, that roast beef has his attention, and she lets him lick the gravy off her fingers, then coaxes him to follow her. The dog lifts himself painfully to standing, a little unsteady on his paws, but he follows her with a hopeful look. Halfway, before they do the climb up the hill, she rewards him with a nibble of meat.

"Oh, you poor wee doggie. I'll get you fattened up, but first you need a name."

He looks up and woofs.

"You look like an Irish setter, so how about Paddy? I'm sorry you were with those horrible people, but you'll be safe and loved now."

Slowly, she offers him another taste of beef. Paddy licks his chops. It will take more time to win him over, but it's a start. For now, he limps his way up the hill and on to the porch to finish what seems like his first meal in days. Sheila is content to monitor him from the living room window. A warm house might entice him to come inside, but it will take months before he forgets the harsh words and blows received at the hands of his previous owners.

Sheila looks out at the scruffy red head that is nestled into the old blanket and is relieved to see those even breaths. She puts half the pot roast aside for Paddy, and then she whips up a beef stew thick with potatoes and thin on meat. Sheila thinks warm biscuits will take Lindy's mind off the less than hearty meal, and she sets a bowl on the counter and reaches for the flour canister. As she mixes up the dough, it suddenly occurs to her that Lindy may have never owned a dog.

When he gets home, Sheila will insist that she needs a guard dog in case anyone strays onto the property. During the upcoming Nature Study Club gathering, she will make certain to inform everyone that he was the one who came up with the idea to adopt a dog. He enjoys taking credit for excellent decisions that showcase his role as a protective spouse. Paddy is all the security she needs, and this dog is here to stay.

***

It is turning out to be a sunny day in May, and Sheila steps out of the farmhouse donning her gardening gloves, Paddy at her side. Yesterday, Lindy had done the heavy lifting and turned the soil in the front yard, expanding the small garden bed that now brims with potential. She looks for any signs of life poking up through the ground, not expecting this earth to contain any flowers.

According to Lindy, the previous residents on the farm had gone through hard times during the Depression and World War II. Those years hardly left time for something as frivolous as growing flowers. It would have been nice to inherit some plants, but Sheila appreciates the chance to start from scratch. She has a few flowers she picked out at a local nursery and has carefully drawn a design for her own English garden.

Sheila thrusts her trowel into the ground but pauses as she hears car tires on the gravel driveway. As the honking begins, Paddy barks madly, and she is astonished to see her friends from the Druthers group pull up in several cars. Her good friend Millie leads the way as Donna, who is an amazing horticulturist, follows close behind. The women carry gifts of perennials freshly dug from their own gardens. The rest of the ladies arrive and some stop to fuss over Paddy, the now healthy guard dog, and stroke his silky chestnut red fur.

"Welcome to the farm. I am so surprised, ladies. How can I ever thank you for these gifts?" Sheila exclaims, looking at everyone in amazement.

"Oh Sheila, when I got your note about digging up some flowers from my garden, I had this fun idea to ask our group if they wanted to contribute to your garden as well. The Druthers always gather round when someone asks for help, and here we are to share from our bounty. What you need right now is to show us where to plant these beauties," Millie replies.

Evidently, she coordinated what flowering plant each would contribute, so there is a variety. Sheila smiles as she inspects each offering, laughing at Glenda's gift of a tomato plant. This member of the Druthers and her husband grow tasty fruits and vegetables on their farm. Some of these ladies are not gardeners and they carry baked treats and, of course, the requisite sherry.

"Just think of us when the flowers bloom," says Betsy.

"And there are more where these came from when you want to add more," notes Susan.

Sheila stands amidst this group of friends for a moment, soaking up the camaraderie. Millie takes charge of organizing her gardening recruits.

"To work everyone!"

They consult Sheila on how she wants to arrange the proffered plants. This peony needs a place, so it gets the full amount of sun it requires for blossoming. Those hollyhocks need to be placed at the back up against the house. Eloise produces a trellis which will support the climbing rose.

The afternoon progresses with irises tucked in and the primrose carefully positioned beside the porch. They plant lavender under the window so Sheila can appreciate its fragrance inside. Black-Eyed Susans and echinacea go in a space big enough for them, as they will spread quickly. Someone has brought mulch to spread around to discourage the weeds. The tomato plant has its own pride of place with a wire cage surrounding it. Satisfied with their labor of love, it's time to wash the dirt from their hands.

They set chairs and a blanket on the grass, pass around finger sandwiches, and sip sherry. Sheila looks around at Millie and her sidekicks, who have shown up for her.

"You must all come back to see how everything is growing," she declares with a smile of appreciation. "I can't thank you enough for your kindness."

She watches them pack up and drive off in their cars. As a child, her caretakers told her to not express emotion and maintain that "stiff upper lip" countenance. Right now, she is near tears with the immense gratitude swelling her heart to bursting. Reaching down to ruffle Paddy's fur, Sheila calms herself, knowing she will remember this afternoon for a very long time.

August 1952

Dear Mona,

Hello from Indiana. It is summer here and my garden is coming along nicely, mostly thanks to my friends from the Druthers group. They were very kind to come over and bring flowers from their gardens. So lovely to see my English garden blooming!

I am feeling less lonely on the farm, for now I have new friends to pick me up for meetings of two new clubs I've joined. As much as I love my dog, Paddy, he can't hold a candle to the ladies when I am talking about clothes or other interesting topics. One group has such a fun name - The Hinklettes - named because most of us live close to Hinkle Creek. This is one of the original Home Demonstration Clubs the U.S. government started back in the Depression. The original goal was to encourage rural women to expand their domestic skills and socialize. Now we have a variety of topics each month. Last week, I showed the ladies how to wear a Scottish tartan and shared the history of the MacGregor clan pattern. Then we had what they called a "carry-in lunch" - I wonder if I should introduce them to the ploughman's lunch?

The other club I attend as a regular member is the Westfield Women's Club, where the expectation is to "dress to the nines" for the meetings. They have a variety of interesting educational presentations. Last week they presented information on this season's fashions, with tips on accessorizing your outfit. They are also involved in supporting charity events for the community. Oh, don't worry that I've gone "la de dah" on you. Never fear, most days I am mucking about the farm in my dungarees, Paddy at my side.

With love,
Sheila

Well into the fall, her garden flourishes, as does the connection with her dog. The two become inseparable, as if life has made each a place that only the other could fill. Lindy does not understand this connection and often grumbles about having a smelly dog underfoot. Paddy knows enough to stay well away from this towering man, but close enough to have his mistress in sight. Early in the morning, regardless of the weather, Sheila and Paddy hike the path that leads away from the farmhouse and down the hill to the creek.

Crossing the stream is no issue, as her resourceful husband has constructed a little bridge for her. Paddy goes straight through the brook, and she laughs to see the Irish setter up to his haunches in the cool water. Then Paddy shakes his whole russet colored body and Sheila gasps in shock as the droplets hit her skin. Often, she talks about her plans for the week, but just as frequently, they saunter through the forest with only the sound of birds to keep them company. When they stop at the crest of the trail, Sheila pats his head, and he casts his dark eyes up in adoration. The feeling is mutual; this dog provides a loving companionship that enriches her life.

The weekend comes when Lindy is picking up some antique farm equipment with his old truck and decides that Paddy should accompany him. Sheila has her doubts but thinks this could be a welcome opportunity for her husband to bond with their dog. Paddy looks a little apprehensive at the time of departure but seems excited to sit in the passenger seat and hang his head out the window, feeling the rush of air in his face.

"Keep Paddy with you the whole time. Here is his leash for when you are close to the busy road."

He shrugs her off with annoyance at her request.

"We'll be fine."

She waves them off and goes inside to resume her sewing project. Sometime later, Lindy returns, his face ashen. Sheila listens with dread as she looks behind him for Paddy.

"I had finished my errand and stopped to chat with Dave at the farm just across from here on State Road 38. Paddy must have realized how close we were to home and jumped down from the truck. He took off before I could stop him - stupid dog crossed the road, and the approaching car had no time to apply their brakes. We heard a thud ..." Lindy pauses. Sheila utters no words.

"We loaded your dog in the back of my truck. I will bury him, or I can take him away."

She goes to the shed and gets a shovel. Walking to a place by the stream, she plunges it savagely into the earth.

"Let me know when you are done," she murmurs in barely a whisper.

He nods morosely, "I'm sorry."

***

A bereft Sheila is in her bedroom, the door closed, and she sits with Paddy's collar and an open jewelry box in her lap. With one hand, she lifts an amethyst ring and brings it to her lips. She strokes the soft leather of her beloved pet's neckband with the other hand.

"My boys," she whispers. "Isn't it the way of life that you get attached to someone, or something, and then that object of your affection is snatched away?"

She remembers her father, mother, and older sister, then Iain and Gilbert, all dying so young. Now Paddy. Her losses pile one on top of the other until the weight of grief seems too much. With a deep breath in, she tucks the ring case and collar into a larger box that has the penny her father had tossed in the air for his dancing daughter. She places her mementos at the back of her dresser drawer. Sheila also firmly gathers the images of her loved ones into a sacred alcove in her mind and gently closes the door to that compartment. Not that she forgets about those dear to her, only that she cannot bear to carry the heartache at the front of her mind. However, their memories are tiny precious jewels, carefully tucked away in her soul. Sometimes she brings these talismans to mind and remembers, then delicately returns them to their place next to her heart. She was not prepared to add another jewel on this fateful day - but then, one never is.

She doesn't speak to Lyndon for some time. Oh, and she can't bear to use the nickname of Lindy anymore. That moniker reflects affection and friendliness. Sheila feels little of either.

Westfield, Indiana August 1954

The little fan only pushes the hot air around Sheila's sewing room as she works on a cinch-waisted pale peach suit ensemble to wear to a family wedding. As she pins a seam, she recalls how much money she has saved sewing her own outfits. Just before their nuptials, Lyndon stated one primary directive: he would be the head of the house and would manage all the finances. It rankled Sheila at first, but she has dealt with his domineering attitude. She is and will always be her own person.

At first, with no car and no driver's license, he takes her to the grocery store on Saturdays and pays for the food she picks out. On these trips, he gives her a little extra cash and calls it her "pin money" which Sheila squirrels away. Sheila knows Lyndon wouldn't approve, but she arranges with Millie to send a money order to Mona and Malcolm. The slump in the Scottish economy had made for hard times for her sister.

The major gift Lyndon purchases for Sheila on their first anniversary was an electric Singer sewing machine with a foot control. What a beauty it is, with its ebony body and lustrous wooden case. Sheila is an accomplished seamstress and designs her own outfits; she has a substantial allowance to spend on clothes, patterns, and material, which she orders by mail from catalogs. She also pores over her fashion magazines, Vogue, Charm, and Harper's Bazar, for inspiration. Lyndon likes her to dress well in social situations where she appears by his side. It works well for them both that she endeavors to look the part of a fashionable and supportive spouse, while having the budget to indulge in a stylish wardrobe.

She nods with satisfaction as she tries on her newest creation, knowing that this event is special. Her suit is elegant but understated, and she will wear her pearls. Lyndon's eighty-year-old father, who cannot manage on his own on account of his failing eyesight, hired a nurse named Ruth to assist him. Now, after a year, Mr. Beals, Sr. has just informed them by letter that they are planning to have a quiet wedding ceremony at her church. Sheila thinks back to how she stood in the kitchen with her cup of tea and observed Lyndon slump down into a chair after reading the wedding announcement, speechless. That was new, and she waited for him to utter something.

Finally, he huffs, "Well, this was unexpected."

Sheila just pats him on the shoulder.

"It'll be nice to see your brother and his wife. I assume they will attend. It's a rare occasion when the entire family is together."

Now that she thinks about it, she and the newest family member have a lot in common. The two women will have married for the first time later in life. They both served in a women's division of the army: Sheila in the Women's Land Army in England, Ruth in the American Women's Auxiliary Corps. They will both be Mrs. Beals. Sheila considers how strange it is to think that her father-in-law's new wife is only three years older than Lyndon.

Sheila has discovered her husband's true nature after two years of marriage. She now knows that Lyndon primarily wanted to be married for the respectability in society it affords him. She has learned that his father, Homer, was constantly away as a traveling salesman, so his mother took charge of her sons' upbringings. Lyndon was proud to tell her that his mother, Mabel Clare Lindley, graduated from Purdue and also got her Masters from Indiana University - an amazing feat for a woman at the turn of the century. Lyndon grew up with a mother who strove for education, excellence, and social status; he is following in her wake. His brother Thomas escaped those maternal influences early and moved to another state, yet he settled in with an independent woman who owns her own business. The eighty-year-old patriarch is marrying a forty-eight-year-old spinster who will continue to be his nurse and companion. It strikes Sheila that the father and his two sons apparently need capable women to attend to their needs. In some ways, she would love to get the wives together and share stories.

After the wedding, she and Lyndon entertain the newlyweds for dinner. Sheila gets along well with Ruth and notes that Homer, her father-in-law, is a cheerful man. Sheila playfully considers taking Lyndon's charming new stepmother with her when she goes to the animal shelter to get her next dog.

Chapter 13 - Meg (March)

"When you take a flower in your hand and really look at it, it's your world for the moment."

- Georgia O'Keefe

It's late March, and the weather has been unseasonably mild. Some wildflowers in the woods are coming out early. Charlotte and her daughters have come for a walk along what I consider Sheila's trail. They will stay for supper and a sleepover. Badger recognizes the girls as friends and loves frolicking with them and appreciates their belly rubs.

Five-year-old Tara has a disarmingly sweet smile, yet she can be downright sneaky when she wants something. Her dark curls bounce as she sets off down the path, eager to give Badger a run for his money. She seems fearless, taking life head on.

Her older sister, Maya, is eight years old and walks at a slower, more determined pace. She stops and squats down to look at the patch of Mayapples, a beautiful flower native to the Midwest. The plant has a large leaf that resembles an umbrella, and just underneath a white bud hangs down in the shelter provided. It's one of my favorites here in the forest and I crouch down beside her to show her the hidden blossom. We pause in wonder.

"What did you think was underneath that big leaf, Maya?" I prompt.

"Nothing, so it surprised me to see that flower," she admits.

"Isn't it interesting to find something you weren't expecting?"

Maya nods in agreement. We stand, and she takes my hand. Tara is charging ahead to catch up with Charlotte, but Maya and I are scouting for more hidden treasures.

"Slow down, Tara, or you may get hurt," she calls out.

Maya is the older child who, despite her age, feels the responsibility of looking out for a younger sibling. I am once again pondering the road not taken. No children, my husband had insisted. Too messy and loud for our beautiful home. As usual, I had gone along with the decision but now feel regret in a moment like this. I'm grateful for time with these young explorers and consider how I can encourage more trips to the farm while I am still here. We catch up as Charlotte is helping Tara cross the stream.

It seems as if the forest has put on a new emerald cloak, and it is all I can do not to burst into song with *The Happy Wanderer.* I take out my phone and capture a photo of the girls running, backlit by the fading sun amongst the verdant new springtime leaves.

"It's almost time to eat, but we have one last discovery to make." I lower my voice and cup my ear, alerting them to be quiet so they can discover something incredible by listening first.

We come up the hill where the path leads through a vast meadow. The barrage of an almost deafening chorus from a patch of wetlands accosts our ears - spring peepers. I'm thankful for the boardwalk that Bruce and his crew have installed. Otherwise we would all need boots to transverse this boggy area. The wooden walkway allows us to continue forward to see if we can pinpoint the source of the racket. As we come close, the froggy din stops all at once. Total quiet ensues and we freeze like statues, the children still in mid-step. The noise begins again.

The adults whisper in little ears, "Let's see if we can spot the spring peepers, shall we?"

We scan the water, looking for the slightest ripple, and then we spot our first tiny frog. Maya points one out and Tara is eager to find another. How is it that these miniscule creatures can make such a racket?

Suddenly, Badger comes along and is ready to leap into the marshy wonderland. Just in time, I grab him by the collar and wrangle him past the viewing platform and the budding biologists. The dog doesn't realize that we need quiet to observe our choir of amphibians. The girls giggle over their ability to stop and start the pond music with their movements. Sheila feels close by in spirit, listening to the echoes of other children who have explored these woods with her. We all feel the breeze caress our cheeks and savor this moment of connection with nature.

After their favorite meal of spaghetti and meatballs, the girls are upstairs in their sleeping bags, and I read them the picture book, *Linnea's Windowsill Garden.* They nod off quickly after all that fresh air and activity; I head down to share a glass of my favorite Merlot with Charlotte, who is sitting contentedly in the wingback chair.

Badger settles in at our feet with a contented woof.

My friend asks, "Why is it we need the girls to show us how extraordinary life can be?"

"Like finding a flower in the forest, or coming upon a cacophony of peeps created by these tiny frogs?" I laugh at the recollections.

"Amazing, isn't it? How life is such a rush of activity, and yet we miss the small things sometimes?" she sighs then adds, "However, speaking of big deals, you do not know how relieved I am to know that the police are now aware of your situation with that wretched ex-husband of yours. It was no trivial thing to gather your courage and reach out to the authorities."

"I couldn't have done it without you prodding me to action and going with me to the sheriff's office. Thanks again for looking out for me."

"Well, from what you have told me so far, are we not much the same as Sheila and Imelda? Friends through thick and thin? Didn't you tell me that according to old Indianapolis phone directories, Sheila was living with Imelda and her husband for five years when she first arrived in Indianapolis?"

"Yes, and I now know, according to her daughter, that Imelda was called Millie by her friends and family."

"Oh, that sounds much more down-to-earth than Imelda. Let's get some of that delicious dessert I saw in your kitchen, and you can give me an update on Sheila and her friend Millie. I'm dying to know what else you've found out."

"Yes, the cake is to celebrate my breakthrough. I had several phone calls and email exchanges with not just Anna but also with her older sister, Bea. Both are so enthusiastic about my writing project. I now have confirmation that Sheila and their mother were best friends who met and worked together in London during World War II. Evidently, they moved to the country to work as Land Girls when the Blitz started, as they were tired of spending their nights in an air raid shelter. They told me the story of their mother meeting a handsome American major when his jeep broke down near the farm where she was working. Evidently, Millie repaired the problem and things progressed from there. Within the next year, she was a war bride who emigrated to Indiana. Sheila followed a few years later."

I serve out two pieces of carrot cake with cream cheese frosting from the Cake Bake Shop in Carmel - a splurge worth every delicious bite.

"Mmm, this cake is so good! Tell me more of what the sisters said about the woman they called their Aunt Sheila."

"It's almost too good to be true that I now have two women who considered Sheila a part of their family, with first-hand recollections of her. Anna called me and she gave me her sister's phone number as well. I've learned so much, like how the sisters would visit the farm as children, especially during the summer. I heard about how Sheila rescued stray dogs, and how much she loved walking every day with them around the perimeter of the property. Anna called Sheila a woman of nature who did not suffer fools. Bea was straightforward in relating how she remembers events. She didn't like the way Lyndon was, in her words, keeping her aunt isolated on the farm. Finally, tired of Sheila not having a driver's license, Bea and her fiancé took her out and taught her to drive. I couldn't stop laughing at the thought of this fierce young woman standing up for her aunt."

"They sound like dedicated goddaughters."

"Yes, Anna looked out for Sheila, right up to when she died. The sisters honored her wishes to not let the developers turn her forest into a subdivision. Bea says that she resembles her aunt in how she calls a spade a spade when describing people. In contrast, she said her sister took after Sheila in her artistic abilities. Anna designed the beautiful sign that they will install at the park entrance. Here is another charming tidbit: Sheila and Millie were part of a social group of friends, most of whom were war brides from the UK. They called themselves *The Druthers,* which was from an expression that goes: *If I had my druthers, I'd rather be …* and in their case the phrase concluded with … *sipping sherry with my friends.* They eschewed the high society meetings of the *Daughters of the British Empire* and instead met monthly in each other's homes. Their club goal was to encourage each other, as they were all so far from kith and kin."

"Wow, you've probably been busy recording all these accounts. Do you have plans to meet up in person?"

"Yes. We have lunch scheduled for when they both come back to Indiana for the summer months. I have so many follow-up questions and it will be great to fill in the gaps I have in Sheila's timeline. I'm so excited to hear about the details of how Sheila and Lyndon met during the war as well. Do you suppose that they might have heard Sheila talk about her time in Africa? I'm hoping that they can give me clues about what some sketches represent."

I rummage through my notes and find Sheila's art portfolio.

"Did I show you the scans and photos Anna sent this month? There is one sketch with a friendly dog in front of an old shack in the woods. Another is a black-and-white photo with a farm truck with some tow-headed children and a couple of dogs in the back bed. I imagine it might be Anna and Bea in that one. Just think, they might remember the names of some of Sheila's beloved pets. I don't want to cause any damage to

Sheila's artwork, so I will take photos of some of her sketches on my phone and pass them around when we have lunch. Since they seem to be the executors of her estate, I will pass on the portfolio to them. For now, I want to hang on to it just for a little while longer and get high-resolution digital scans of the original artwork."

Charlotte smiles but stifles a yawn. "I'm sure they will be ecstatic to see the art that Sheila left behind, but hopefully will realize that it is in excellent hands for the time being. We should get some sleep, as those two budding naturalists will be awake early and wanting another expedition in the morning."

She adds, "You no doubt will stay up longer to make notes and add questions to your notebook. Don't be too late. Remember, we promised the girls that we would make waffles for breakfast."

Chapter 14 - Sheila

"In this very attitude did I sit when I called to him, rapidly stating what it was I wanted him to do … Imagine my surprise, nay, my consternation, when without moving from his privacy, Bartleby in a singularly mild, firm voice, replies, *I would prefer not to."*

- Herman Melville
Bartleby, the Scrivener: A Story of Wall-Street

Westfield, Indiana 1959

At Homer's funeral, Sheila overhears the newly widowed Ruth telling Lyndon that she is choosing not to stay in the family home. When the couple arrives back at their farmhouse, the quiet of the place is calming after the commotion of family conversations. She offers her husband a drink and gets one for herself.

They come out onto the front porch and settle in to watch the light show of fireflies dancing on the front lawn. It is magical. The summer flowers in Sheila's garden give off a fragrance that soothes her soul. Her dogs, Hamish the sensitive collie and the loveable black cocker spaniel mutt named Gordon, rest at her feet, both snoring contentedly. The evening is perfect and then Lyndon clears his throat.

"I have been thinking about my childhood home in Noblesville. Father is gone, and his widow wants to live closer to her relatives. My brother Thomas lives in Maryland, so he has no interest in the old place. I know that there are renters living upstairs, but we can choose not to renew their lease."

"There's no rush to force that couple and their children out of their home," Sheila comments.

The two-story brick house is in a historic part of Noblesville, on a quaint street that is cobbled in the old-fashioned way. Majestic trees line the neighborhood roadways. The residence certainly is larger than their farmhouse, with more access to shops and closer to Indianapolis where Lyndon works.

"I am determined to move back to Noblesville and live in that house. It makes perfect sense to me, as the commute to work will be easier, especially in the wintertime. Just think, you would be closer to Millie and your other friends." Lyndon's tone is persuasive in the way an adult might explain a logical outcome to a child who has a decision to make.

"I would prefer not to," Sheila responds with a literary quote from Herman Melville that Lyndon is sure to recognize. She speaks in a firm but quiet way that brooks no argument. It is impossible for her to leave her forest walks and the trail where she and her dogs love to ramble. Lyndon stands up quickly with a set to his jaw, and the dogs rise to their feet as well, assuming defensive positions. Without another word, he enters the house and slams the screen door. She will sleep in the guest room tonight. It is the first time that she has stood up to her husband about a major issue other than having dogs in the house. She suspects it won't be the last thing he will say about his desire to move.

Lyndon packs a bag and leaves the next morning for work. He doesn't return home at night. The silence cloaks her in peace and allows her to contemplate a solitary life. What if Lyndon decides to leave her? Sheila is grateful when a couple of days later, Millie drives over to pick up Sheila for a meeting of the Druthers. They have a lot to discuss on the way to their monthly gathering.

"What do you mean, Lyndon plans to move down to his childhood home? I suppose if you lived in Noblesville, you would be closer to me."

"Like Bartleby the Scrivener, I responded to Lyndon by saying *I would prefer not to*."

"Is that a quote from a famous book I have not read yet? You really told Lyndon that you won't move?"

"Exactly. It is a line from a short story by Herman Melville. I believe it fully reflects a person's statement of defiance. I love living in my farmhouse in the country. It is peaceful there without cars rumbling past like in the city. I'd miss taking the dogs out every day for our walks in the forest. Lyndon has moved out, but I am staying put."

"Well, I'll take you to buy groceries on the way home and check in on you in a few days. If only you had a telephone, you could call if you needed help."

Sheila and Lyndon are currently without telephone service on the farm, although they will have a party line connection in the next year. Millie is true to her word and comes by to see how things are going twice a week. She finds out that Lyndon has come back home to drop off his laundry and get clean clothes.

"He is adamant in his desire to leave the farm and complains that people in the neighborhood keep dropping by and asking about when I will join him," Sheila reports. "His friends have been noticing him dining at restaurants after work, and he is struggling to come up with excuses for why he is on his own so often. The whole situation is causing him embarrassment, and he threatens to lay the blame on me for his final decision."

In the end, Sheila is resolute, and Lyndon cannot imagine the damage to his reputation if they continue to live apart. Lyndon's social circles frown upon divorce, so he locks up the charming old house and comes back to the farmhouse, pretending that his time in Noblesville was only until the renters vacated the premises. He never returns, neglecting his childhood home and letting it fall into disrepair; if Lyndon can't live there, he swears that nobody will.

Westfield Indiana 1968

As much as Sheila doesn't want to admit it, living in Noblesville would have given her more freedom. She doesn't have a driver's license, and besides, Lyndon takes their only car to work; she would like to run errands or make her way to club meetings on her own. Millie's daughter, Bea, who is herself an independent young woman, senses her frustration. She and her fiancé, Norman, come over during a day when their college class schedule allows and they teach her to drive. After a few weeks of practice, Bea tells her aunt that she is ready to get her driver's license.

"It will be such a surprise for Uncle Lyndon when he finds out what we are doing," Bea says mischievously.

"I take it you would like to be here to see the look on his face when I get in your car and take you for a spin?"

"Why Auntie, I thought you'd never ask. It would be an honor to have a front-row seat to that show. Unfortunately, we can't stay late today."

"There is only one problem. I really don't feel comfortable driving the old farm truck that we have for my road test."

Norman clears his throat. "Did you notice we came in two cars today? We hope you don't think us presumptuous, but we made an appointment for you to take your driver's written exam this afternoon. You can use this smaller car to take your road test. Try it out and see if you like how it drives."

Sheila climbs into the sky-blue Ford Pinto and settles in. She remembers as a Land Girl, everyone on the farm eventually got behind the wheel of some vehicle. In America, one hitch is that she is used to driving on the proper side of the road, meaning the left. Before getting behind the wheel, she inks a tiny arrow, pointing to the right just below her left thumb, as a little reminder. Bea takes a seat beside her and off they go down the hill. When they return to the farmhouse, Sheila hands the keys back to the grinning couple.

Bea exclaims, "No, the car is for you!"

"Anna and I bought it with help from mom and dad. Our cousin gave us a deal since it was secondhand and they no longer needed it. When you get your license, we will handle the transfer of car ownership at the same time. All you owe us is one dollar to make it legal."

This act of kindness astonishes her; Sheila can't wait to thank Anna in person and tell Millie about the generosity of her daughters.

"How can I thank you both for looking out for me?"

Bea gives her a hug. "By getting your license, you will be free to explore the countryside. Get off the farm and go places! Get a job or take a trip!"

"Well, I might just do it all, my dear Bea."

Sheila proudly claims ownership of the used Pinto and a valid driver's license, even though Lyndon dismisses it as her new hobby. Weeks later, she overhears him telling his friends at a party that he had encouraged her to get her license. She will not amend the account of how she has gained her independence. All that matters is that Bea told her she can come and go as she pleases. She calls her car Clyde, inspired by the Clydesdales, that distinctive Scottish workhorse. Sheila is preparing for her inaugural solo adventure - a visit to the Westfield Public Library to discover new books.

It's a lovely weekday, and Sheila delights in driving to town without Lyndon having to drop her off at his convenience on Saturdays. She pulls into the library parking lot and steps out to admire the brick building, built back in 1910 with a grant from the philanthropist, Andrew Carnegie.

Walking in, Sheila returns her library books and spends the next hour just browsing the shelves at her leisure. She then takes her stack over to a comfy chair in a sunny corner of the reading room. An avid reader, she reads from the beginning of each novel, discarding any that doesn't capture her in the first ten pages. So many books, so little time! The librarian at the check-out counter smiles as she stamps the due date cards and slips one in the back pocket of each book. They have a quiet chat together about the books they have read recently. As a final note, the friendly librarian informs Sheila about the opportunity to volunteer if she is interested.

That same librarian will mention to the library director, Mrs. Cora Beals, that Sheila, being so well read, would make an excellent volunteer. She also suggests that Mrs. Lyndon Beals could be a replacement for their coworker who is thinking about retirement in a year or two. Little does Sheila know they are talking about her! Carrying her literary finds in her canvas book bag, Sheila has a huge smile on her face and a new dream in her heart. Within the month, she is a regular volunteer. When the library has a vacancy the following year, they hire her as an assistant librarian, with half-day shifts from Monday to Friday.

Westfield, Indiana 1974

When she began working at the library in 1971, she had wanted to open a separate bank account. However, she believed that the requirement for her husband to cosign defeated the purpose. The law eventually changes, three years later, granting her the ability to open her own account in just her name.

As she fills out her forms, the bank clerk remains puzzled about her decision to exclude her husband's details from the registration card. Sheila straightforwardly mentions that Lyndon has his own account, therefore he doesn't need to share hers. The manager looks askance but sets up her paperwork, shaking his head and muttering about the women's liberation movement.

Sheila admires her bank passbook and tucks it carefully into her purse. She has her own money for the first time in almost 20 years and has ideas on how to spend her well-earned dollars.

It's obvious that her trusty Pinto, although having a stout mechanical heart, won't last much longer on the icy Indiana country roads. Fortunately, a neighbor agrees to sell her a sturdy but not necessarily attractive automobile. The recent acquisition resembles a station wagon, but it's equipped for off-road expeditions. The boxy canary yellow American Harvester is perfect for Sheila. She might even, in her eagerness to get to work, simply take off across the frozen farm fields rather than down the icy hill. With room for Millie's children, she can pick them up so they can explore the countryside together, looking for different nature trails. The one drawback is the unavailability of parts; however, Sheila is in love and quite proud to turn heads when she pulls into the staff parking lot at the library. She chooses the name Scout, inspired by the brave and inquisitive protagonist of Harper Lee's novel *To Kill a Mockingbird*, a book she frequently recommends to library patrons.

After a morning of work, she will pat the steering wheel and say, "Where to Scout?" If she has enough time, she will drive to a new town, in search of shops that have material for a current sewing project. For her, finding fabric with unique designs, colors, and textures brings immense joy. Yesterday, she drove to Oxford, Indiana, just to buy a postcard for her collection of mementos from towns with quirky geographic names. Sheila never tires of imagining the pioneers who, missing their homelands, named a new settlement after far-off cities or countries dear to them.

Today's plan is a familiar ramble through the trails of the Nature Study Club. She drops by the farm to collect her dog, Sherlock, who loves riding in the passenger seat with his head out the side window. Making sure she has her thermos of water and a doggie bowl, Sheila looks at the steadfast Basset Hound, who bears the name of the renowned British literary detective. The rescue of this dog was a fortunate occasion of being in the right place at the right time. With the freedom to come and go where she pleased, she developed a monthly habit of checking in on her local humane society to see what dogs needed a new home. That's where she found Sherlock, with his floppy ears and baleful eyes. Someone had left the forlorn pet in a box, hungry and shivering, on the doorstep of the animal shelter. One look at him and the thought of adopting him was elementary. In her soft Scottish brogue, she beckoned, "Come along, Sherlock, the game's afoot." The grateful pup had followed at her heel, happy to have found a sympathetic mistress.

They reach the clubhouse in Noblesville, and the dog stands guard as Sheila pulls on her wellies. Although there may be some muddy spots along the way, they embark on the trail together, exploring the hills and ravines. This peaceful walk is a balm to their souls.

***

As Sheila opens the library one morning, there is a shaggy individual waiting on the steps. It's brisk outside and the young man, head down, is rubbing his hands together in anticipation of the warmth of the reading room. She welcomes him in, noting his slight limp as he passes her. Her opening routines begin: hanging the day's newspapers on the racks and arranging the check-out counter with cards freshly stamped with due dates, ready to be placed in the back pockets of library books. As the librarian in charge, she greets the regulars and falls into her pattern of collecting a variety of books, ready to recommend to them. The retired gentleman will want the latest in spy thrillers, while a young mother, whose children are in school, is reading "The Russians" and will pick up her inter-library loan request, a novel by Aleksandr Solzhenitsyn. Another patron is looking for the latest novel by her favorite author, Agatha Christie. The morning is passing pleasantly when a woman comes to the counter.

"Mrs. Beals, I wanted to alert you to the man sleeping in the reading room." She points behind her to the bowed figure in the corner chair. "Really, this is not a place for such a thing. He shouldn't be here." She sniffs with distaste.

"I'll see to him, but the library is a place for everyone who needs a quiet place and a good book," Sheila speaks soothingly with the air of someone who has everything in hand.

She approaches the slumbering form with a cough loud enough to awaken him.

"I understand how some novels that aren't very riveting can put someone to sleep." She points to the book that has slipped down to the floor.

The young man looks embarrassed and sits up straight. He retrieves the paperback with a wry smile and moves to open it to the place where he left off.

"If you're looking for a more engaging read, please let me know. I'd be happy to suggest another that might keep your attention. Do you like science fiction? My favorite authors are Ray Bradbury and Isaac Asimov."

With a shake of his head, he sets down the library book, picks up his duffel bag, and swiftly departs. Sheila is unhappy about scaring him away and resolves to find out more about the stranger. After talking to the local police, Sheila discovers that the drowsy patron is an army vet, and he goes by Wally. Sadly, his mother died when he was serving in Vietnam. According to the sheriff, his stepfather, who used to live nearby, has moved to Ohio. Currently, the young man is searching for a job and staying with family friends since he doesn't have a home. The veteran of an unpopular war, he is trying to sort out his new life stateside.

Sheila welcomes him back to the library on his next visit and strikes up a conversation with him.

"How very nice to see you again. May I ask what your name is and whether I might sign you up for a library card?"

She continues, "It was one of the first things I did when I first arrived in Indianapolis after the war and was staying with my friend Millie. The library was my destination to look for a good book and then find a quiet corner to read during my lunch hours. The house where I was living had a couple of wee ones who were always clamoring for my attention as soon as I stepped inside from working all day. You also look in need of peace and an excellent novel."

He smiles shyly and nods. "I'm staying with friends. Can I use their address?"

"Yes. Here, let me give you an application and we will get you that key to magical worlds. Of course, I'm referring to your very own library card. We librarians are proud of what books can offer to those in need of a bit of a getaway from their regular life."

"My name is Wally Hodgins."

"Pleased to meet you. I'm Sheila Beals." They shake hands and a new friendship begins.

Sheila returns home that afternoon with an idea. There's a small shack on their property and with a bit of carpentry work, it would be habitable in no time. It might serve as a place of shelter for a soldier at loose ends. In her opinion, Wally could benefit from the healing solitude of the forest. She has concluded that he needs time to put his life in order.

After a hearty meal of roast beef and potatoes, along with Lyndon's favorite pie for dessert, Sheila broaches the topic foremost in her mind.

"We have a new patron at our library, and he may be your distant cousin's son. He's back from Vietnam and in need of a place to stay."

"He should check out the American Legion post in Noblesville. They might have information on temporary accommodations, as well as people who can help with his paperwork. It can be such a rigmarole to sort out his benefits. Oh, the Vietnam War! We should never have gotten involved."

"That may be the case, Lyndon, but these young men coming back need our help. His mother died when he was away serving his country, just like you. I thought it might be a good idea to have Wally move here to the farm. The two of you can fix up that rundown shack in the woods. It could serve as a temporary home for him as he transitions back into civilian life.

"Absolutely not! How absurd that you would think of such an arrangement! He could be violent. You know nothing of what he's been through."

Sheila looks him straight in the eyes and replies, "Ach, but you do. You know the toll war can take on a young soldier. Coming back here, you had a home waiting for you and family to welcome you, whereas Wally is alone in the world. He needs the forest and nature to be a healing place for his soul. The hut restoration could be a group project that you could present at one of your historical society's meetings. You can even use some of those antique tools you keep in the garage. The work will do you all some good, and you can gain a new appreciation of how your ancestors started their new life on this very land."

"Let me think about it. When you put it that way, this project might just appeal to others in the Hamilton County Historical Society. Imagine - a replica of a pioneer cabin on my property."

Lyndon softens his tone. "Really, Sheila, you have some outrageous ideas in that pretty little head. First, getting a job at the library, and now taking in a stranger. Don't we have enough rescue dogs without taking in another stray?"

"You'll be happy to know there will be one less canine in the house soon. I decided the young man will need a dog to keep him company in the woods and Buddy, the labrador retriever, will be the perfect fit for him. Also, I've researched some old recipes so I can make hearty meals for your work crew …" Sheila pauses, "… and speaking of food, Wally is coming over for supper on Sunday." She quickly clears the dishes as Lyndon sits back, stymied. He mutters to himself as he leaves the table and wanders out to his workshop in the garage to assess his tools and the building supplies he might need.

Westfield, Indiana 1977

The dinner party is going well. Their friends discuss topics ranging from gas prices to vacation plans to President Jimmy Carter's inauguration.

Fred, a newspaper friend of Lyndon, is getting worked up.

"I can't believe the new president is granting unconditional pardons to so many draft-dodgers."

"Now, now, let's not get into politics," chides Joanne, his wife.

Mary, who lives on the neighboring farm, chimes in.

"Whatever happened to that hermit you had living in the old shack out in the back forty? He was a Vietnam vet, wasn't he? I haven't seen him around lately while I am out riding. I often saw him and that old dog of his tramping up and down the hills at all times of the day."

"Wally moved on about a year ago. He is trying his hand at carpentry down in Brown County. The experience of rebuilding the shack with Lyndon and his team must have sparked a love of working with his hands. He worked as an apprentice to a carpenter in Cicero and later got a job as a handyman at the State Park. He is now responsible for the maintenance of the cabins and the lodge. I got a letter from him the other day and he is quite happy living in the woods," Sheila reports with satisfaction.

Her husband smirks. "That's where he belongs, deep in the forest."

Lyndon is in a strange mood.

"My dear," he tells his wife, "everyone has finished eating. Is dessert coming?"

The other couples around the table chime in with compliments about the meal they had just finished. Sheila served an excellent pork roast and vegetables with flaky biscuits. The Dutch apple pie she brings to the table smells heavenly and Lyndon moves to cut pieces for everyone.

"What do you think about telling everyone about the first time you met your spouse? It should make for some entertaining stories, don't you think?" he prompts, passing dessert plates around hand to hand.

Seated at the table are friends from the neighboring farm, from Lyndon's work, and fellow members from their Nature Study Club. They are people Sheila is happy to have in her home; she appreciates their friendship and is curious about their responses.

Laughter ensues as each spouse eyes the other with smiles, while some show expected embarrassment. Sheila imagines them considering their version of the truth - *How would revealing we met in a bar go over? Would it be better to say we met at church?*

Each couple takes a turn to explain the time and place when they had first laid eyes on their beloved. Chuckles follow stories of unusual encounters, and they progress in a circle.

When it comes back to Lyndon, Sheila quietly wonders how he will embellish the first time they met at the famous L.S. Ayers tea room in Indianapolis.

It shocks her to hear him say, "It was wartime and bombs were going off every night. As officers stationed in London for a time, we had to rely on the Transport Mechanized Corp for rides between the bases. A volunteer driver would show up in her car and deliver us safely to our destination. The first time I heard Sheila introduce herself with that distinctive accent, I exclaimed - *ah, look at the pretty little Scotch lass I've found.* It was love at first sight and I knew I needed to bring her here to Indiana and make her my wife!"

Sheila cringes but allows this story to stand. Lyndon is misremembering, or perhaps he is thinking of his time at Fort Breckenridge, where he arranged dances at the military post? He even wrote in a newspaper article in 1943 for the Noblesville Ledger about life on base and related the time when he met a woman from Scotland. He recalled declaring out loud: *ah, a bonnie Scotch lass, I see!* Did he have a romantic encounter with this nurse named Virginia MacDougall, and is he thinking of that incident?

It isn't worth the trouble of correcting him in front of their friends and neighbors. Besides, he has had a little too much to drink and will probably not recall the fabrication in the morning. Their first meeting took place over twenty years ago, and he has not been feeling his best in the past few weeks. It's time for him to see his doctor just to get checked out.

Chapter 15 - Meg (April)

"If you look the right way, you can see that the whole world is a garden."

- Frances Hodgson Burnett

The month of April is my favorite, with all its promises of spring. Here in Indiana, it's as if the farm is shaking off the cold cloak of winter, as evidenced by little green shoots peeking through the carpet of fallen leaves in front of the farmhouse. While examining the area where I imagine flower beds used to be, I also sense Sheila's presence. The first turn of the soil is special to gardeners, and it's a thrill to feel an awakening of the patch she probably tended. The weeds have almost gained the upper hand, but hours later, my diligent overhaul reveals the pattern of a carefully planned English garden. Among the plants making a comeback are classic favorites like peonies, hydrangea, bleeding heart, and hollyhocks. With some attention in the coming months, I hope to make Sheila's garden thrive and bloom again for at least one more season.

The wildflowers growing in the forest surrounding the farmhouse have got me thinking about a sketch that Anna came across. It's one of a Basset Hound, with those long droopy ears, who looks like he has decided to take a rest in a patch of wildflowers on a hillside. Anna noted that the words *Hamilton County Nature Study Club* were on the back. I have found multiple references in the newspaper archives concerning their meetings and an annual wildflower walk along their White River property. The old articles talk about Lyndon and Sheila as presenters or hosts who organized a yearly wiener roast at their farm. Another item for my research list - to see if I can find if the nature study club is still around.

Although I've been treating Sheila's place as my own, I know that eventually I will have to find a home of my own when my rental agreement ends. The White River runs right through Noblesville, so while I am searching for the club location, I might as well check out some housing options. I am especially drawn to the charming homes in the more historic part of town, and with the address for Lyndon from a 1940 U.S. census record, I turn down that street. Curious about his childhood, I drive by Lyndon's old home and discover it's a lovely brick house on a cobblestone street close to the downtown square. Rentals in this neighborhood are probably out of my price range, but I'm happy to see the place where Sheila's husband lived with his family.

Back to scouting out the nature study club location, Badger and I get sidetracked and end up exploring the sprawling Forest Park with a delightful antique carousel and shady trails. We don't find a clubhouse, but up the road and running alongside the White River, we discover a beautiful tree-lined walking path with a century-old covered bridge at the trailhead. Potter's Bridge Trail is a lovely place to stroll and we greet lots of other dog walkers. There is even a little beach area where I admire the reflection of the trees in the flowing water. I appreciate the profusion of wildflowers along the path.

On our way back to the parking lot, I pass a friendly county park worker who is busy digging up what looks like common honeysuckle growing along the side of the path.

"Wow, you are really going to town with those bushes," I observe.

She keeps hacking, "This here is Tatarian honeysuckle that was brought to North America as an exotic plant, but it doesn't belong in Indiana. The bush grows wild and smothers out other plants."

"I admire your effort to protect the native plants. These wildflowers are amazing. I'm glad you are making room for them to flourish. I'm usually on the lookout for trilliums this time of year."

"Oh, we have prairie trilliums on this side of the White River. They have tall, slender stalks with purple flowers."

She points one out for me and I bend over to admire the delicate three-petaled blossom.

"If you want to see the Trillium Grandiflorum White variety, attend the annual wildflower walk put on by the Hamilton County Nature Study Club. It is a private association, but every year they open their grounds to the public. On that one April weekend you can see the glorious but ephemeral display of wildflowers that bloom and fade quickly just as the forest awakens from its winter slumber."

She sighs, "Ah, I always get a little poetic when I talk about springtime in Indiana. Anyway, their property is about ten miles north of here on the west side of the river. They don't have much of a presence online, maybe a Facebook page? They put out signs along Highway 37 to show you the way, but go early as parking can be challenging. I think maybe the city of Noblesville might have the date on their community events calendar."

"Thank you for the poetry and the information. That's great news. I've been looking for the nature study club."

Waving, I continue on my hike with Badger. I think to myself - so close. It will be exciting to get more details online when I get home. Maybe Charlotte and the girls will want to come with me?

There are friendly people everywhere, I remind myself. Since I had an awful experience with Trent, it's hard for me to believe that others can be considerate. In keeping with people being good at heart, I get a response to the message I sent to the nature study club's Facebook page. Their president sends a photo of the roster from 1960, which lists Lyndon and Sheila as members, and suggests that I try talking to a longtime attender who might have known the Beals. I also received a warm invitation to attend their annual Wildflower Walk.

***

Unfortunately, Charlotte and Raffi are out of town, so they cannot join me. I'm normally shy about going alone to a new place, but this is my opportunity to see another spot that was dear to Sheila's heart. Despite the iffy forecast for the day, I set my GPS and drive. The winding road off the highway leads to a gravel parking lot in front of a weathered clubhouse, more like a camp building than anything else. Beyond is a forest almost as beautiful as the one in my backyard. There are people greeting newcomers and I explain my contact through Facebook.

"Hello, I'm very excited to be here this afternoon." I begin, "I'm a librarian doing some research on a local couple who were members of the club in the 1950s. Any chance that Mrs. Gloria Smith is here for the walk today?"

"No, I haven't seen her this morning."

Trying to hide my disappointment, I say, "Well, no worries. I would like to join the club. Your meetings sound so interesting, and I'm a nature lover."

They are happy to pass me an application form and I hand over the cash for the membership fee. This is an investment in my research and a place that I'll be happy to explore again, so it seems like it will pay off. I'm directed outside so that I can join a group heading off to identify the wildflowers that grow along the trails and on the hillsides.

I approach the leader with high hopes.

"Excuse me, have you seen Mrs. Smith? I've heard that she is your oldest member, and I'm hoping to hear some of her memories of the Club."

Our guide shakes her head.

"I don't think she is coming today. Parts of our trail are too steep for her to manage."

She turns to make sure that everyone in our group has a flower guide. We are ready to begin when I notice a middle-aged woman with an older beagle coming up behind us. Her appearance makes me think she might be a professor. To protect herself from the cool spring air, she has bundled up with a scarf wrapped several times around her neck and sports a Tilley, a popular Canadian brand of hiking headgear.

"Hello," she calls with a wave in my direction.

Surprise and delight must show on my face as I tip the brim of my hat in her direction.

"My name is Meg and I'm always happy to meet another person wearing a Tilley. I'm originally from Canada, and this hat belonged to my father."

She nods and points to her head.

"I purchased mine while on a hiking trip in the Canadian Rockies. One of the best on the market and it brings back such wonderful memories when I wear it."

She hesitates, "I couldn't help overhearing that you were looking for Gloria Smith. I think I can help you with that. I'm her daughter, Vivian."

The volunteer directs her group around us and heads down the trail, having evidently decided that she can proceed without us.

"If it's okay, the two of us can walk the trail together and chat. The speed at which my old dog, Ranger, walks is quite slow. This will be a leisurely stroll, which should give me enough time to answer your questions," she suggests.

"That's so kind of you. Did I mention that I'm a librarian doing research on Sheila and Lyndon Beals? I've been looking for people who might have known them personally, and this nature study club seemed like a promising place to try."

"I was just a young girl, but I definitely knew Mr. & Mrs. Beals, and my parents were friends with them too," she states in a matter-of-fact tone.

Overjoyed with this opportunity, I begin.

"What were your impressions of Sheila and Lyndon? How would you describe their personalities?"

She takes a moment to think.

"Even though I was just a kid, Sheila always took the time to chat with me and ask how I was doing. She spoke with the most beautiful accent and was really very attentive, listening to my ramblings about nature observations. In contrast, Lyndon was, how shall I put it? Austere. His focus was primarily on interacting with people he considered more important."

Vivian continues, "You know how there are some adults who solely want to relate to other adults? Kids aren't worth their time. It seemed like he only wanted to talk to his friends and exchange accomplishments with them. Mr. Beals was very proud of the fact that he was one of the founding members of the Club, and he often mentioned it to anyone who was new. Sheila wasn't boastful; she was just happy to talk about her walks in nature with her dogs. Even though it was sixty years ago, I still remember the first talk she gave about the history of English Gardens. There are filing cabinets in the clubhouse's basement where they have copies of the presentations going way back. I got a hold of her notes last week and transcribed them. If you give me your email, I can send you a copy."

"Wow, that would be amazing to read."

She has been talking while we progress along the woodland trail and from time to time we pause and call out the names of wildflowers we recognize. We toggle back and forth in our conversation, from the past to the present. I recount how, as a child, I was always outside, riding my bike and visiting my woodland haunts. Growing up in Toronto, it was always a highlight for me to find the first wild blooms of spring in my neighborhood park, especially those of the official provincial flower - the trillium.

Vivian grins and says, "Just wait until we come down into the next ravine."

As we round a bend in the trail, there they are. A glorious stretch of the white beauties.

"How wonderful to find a patch of my favorites, here in this nature preserve. This sight brings me the same joy I experienced as a little kid."

We crest the top of the next hill and come out to a level area with a bench overlooking the White River. The view is beautiful, so Vivian and her dog pose for a picture, companions like Sheila and her cherished canines. Ranger, who is a little tired from the hike, lays down, and she pours out water for him. We both feel accomplished and I'm especially pleased about gaining not only information, but perhaps a new friend.

Exchanging emails and phone numbers, Vivian promises to coordinate a time when I can talk with her mother. She also mentions that she found some club photo albums and she can send me some digital scans that feature Sheila. One such photo is of Sheila with her German Shepherd on guard in front of the farmhouse. An amateur photographer went around to the homes of all the older members and took pictures of them in their gardens. Vivian has a similar shot of her parents at their home. We say goodbye and I thank her again for all the material she has gathered.

When I'm about to leave, the club volunteers inform me I can now hike on their property whenever I want as a member. If I move to Noblesville, I will have forest trails close by and a connection to a special place that Sheila loved. Badger is going to love this place and I look forward to attending club meetings where I can meet people in my area who appreciate nature as much as I do.

With the prospect of getting those scans plus talking with Mrs. Smith and hearing her reminiscences about Lyndon and Sheila, I drive home in a great mood.

***

As if my weekend couldn't get any better, I wake up on Sunday to a text: *Mom is up and ready to chat with you about Sheila and Lyndon.*

I reply: *Give me 15 minutes and I will call.*

Coffee in hand, I dial the phone number, hoping that this will go well.

Mrs. Smith speaks warmly about her friends Lyndon and Sheila, whom she and her husband saw at club meetings and other social events. She points out that Sheila's accent was so distinctly Scottish, and she would have strange terms, such as referring to drinking tea as having a cuppa. Gloria recalls Sheila's tasty baking and chuckles over her quirky avoidance of cinnamon. Mostly, she fondly recounts her friend's fierce love of dogs and nature. Lyndon and Sheila's annual Nature Study

Club wiener roast at their farmhouse is a special memory for her.

"We brought our own camp chairs to sit around on the lawn. The Beals property was so beautiful, and it was a great location for a fun gathering. At other meetings, members asked the funeral home to deliver folding chairs if they needed extra seating for their houses; of course, this was before we had a clubhouse with plenty of room for everyone."

I gently steer the focus to memories of her friends in particular, so I inquire about Sheila's relationship to Lyndon and how she would describe it. From her tone of voice, I sense Mrs. Smith getting defensive.

"Why are you asking? It was nothing out of the ordinary. You know they met in London during World War II when she was a volunteer driver for American officers. I remember the story Lyndon told us about how they fell in love, and he brought her over as a war bride."

I don't mention that Sheila arrived in 1947 and didn't marry until 1952, so the term "war bride" seems a bit of a stretch to me. Still, here is another person telling me the story about Lyndon and Sheila's meeting in London during the war.

"I'm just trying to get a sense of Sheila's life here in Indiana. I'm renting her farmhouse until the park officially opens," I reply soothingly, and divert the conversation back to her stories of club meetings. Gloria talks about traditions like the Christmas gift exchange, which always had a nature theme. All the ladies wanted to receive one of Sheila's hand sewn aprons with embroidered flowers.

"Thank you so much for talking with me, Mrs. Smith. I appreciate hearing about Sheila and Lyndon, as well as the Nature Study Club. I might see you at an upcoming meeting."

When we end the call, I muse over what I know about the sensibilities of the Fifties and Sixties. Ladies didn't talk about their marriages or what went on behind closed doors. It wasn't proper to air your dirty laundry in public, so to speak. The prevailing attitude was that the man was the head of the house, and his little lady was there to stay home and cater to his needs. I'm sure that a few eyebrows rose when Sheila became a little more independent, with a driver's license and her own car. From today's viewpoint, I feel unsettled about such chauvinistic attitudes. Still, it was a thrill to chat with a woman who could give me personal recollections of my Sheila.

***

Still bubbling with excitement, I arrive at work the next day, ready to tell my coworkers about my wonderful walk in the woods scouting for wildflowers. Parking and entering through the employee entrance, I find room for my lunch in the little break room fridge and check my slot for any mail. I find a plain envelope with neatly printed words on the front: *For the new librarian* and a swirl underline with two slashes in the middle. I freeze. That distinctive curlicue flourish is something my ex-husband wrote on the envelope of every card he gave me. My hand is shaking and I look around. With all the calm I can muster, I try to keep my voice steady.

"Does anyone remember putting this in my mailbox?"

"Oh, some guy was asking Julie at the circulation counter about our newest librarian on Saturday. She explained you weren't on duty. After he left, Julie told me about the encounter, and that's when he came back in with this envelope. I said that we would make sure that you got it," George reflects, grinning. "You have a fan club already?"

He halts when he notices that I have gone pale.

"Can we step into Jan's office for a moment?" I insist.

With a quick knock on the director's door, we slip into her office and George guides me over to a chair. Jan watches with a concerned look on her face as I open the envelope with trembling hands. I read the cryptic message:

My accountant friend heard them calling you Meg.
Such a nice name, but I prefer Lucy.
I found you. As soon as I get out, we will be together again.
All my love,
Trent

The note falls from my hand. I take a deep breath and tell my trusted colleagues the full story of my escape from an abusive ex-husband, who I hope is still behind bars.

"It's terrible to have experienced everything that happened to you in Wisconsin. You have our full support. We can make an appointment with the police to discuss a strategy in case Trent shows up at the library. George and I are here for you," Jan assures.

I know I can count on my friend Charlotte; now my co-workers will also gather round and see me through any challenging situation that may transpire if Trent ever gets out on parole.

Chapter 16 - Sheila

"Those who contemplate the beauty of the earth find reserves of strength that will endure as long as life lasts. There is something infinitely healing in the repeated refrains of nature - the assurance that dawn comes after night, and spring after winter."

- Rachel Carson

Indianapolis, Indiana 1977

Sheila is sleeping in a hospital room and wakes with the image of another medical ward from years ago. She remembers when the groans of wounded British soldiers from the front had startled her from slumber. Her last memories were of working as a Land Girl in Shrewsbury, doing her part in the war effort. Yet when she opened her eyes, she was recuperating in a bed, her friend Millie by her side. A doctor arrived and was telling her how the surgeries - an appendectomy and a hysterectomy - had saved her life, but not that of her unborn child.

She shudders at the memory of antiseptic and hushed voices. Sheila glances over at the recumbent form of her husband, checking on the slight rise and fall of his chest under the covers. Lyndon is gravely ill, and she is keeping vigil.

Hospital staff pass by seemingly unconcerned, as she notes her husband drifting in and out of consciousness; he's addressing her as if she is his long-departed mother. She gathers from his delirious utterances that he both admired Mabel Beals and yet felt that, as hard as he tried, he could never live up to her expectations. From past conversations with her sister-in-law, Sheila learned that the late Mrs. Beals was an avid student of nature and history, with a keen intellect and a sharp tongue. Lyndon's brother, Thomas, had left home as soon as he was able. Was he driven away by her overbearing and demanding personality? His sibling moved to Baltimore, where he found a loving woman and settled down. Lyndon was more attached to their mother and had stayed in Indiana. Sheila recalls him talking about his time away from home during the war years; he had never gotten over the guilt of not being with his mother when she died in 1943.

The thought dawns upon Sheila that this domineering mother had passed some aspects of her personality on to Lyndon. He had tried to turn her into the submissive wife of his dreams. When they first met, Sheila probably looked like an impressionable spinster who would fit into that role. Little did he know she possessed a fierce resolve to be her own woman.

It was good fortune that they shared a passion for nature and music. They had enjoyed traveling to Scotland and South Africa to visit her sisters. There were, however, significant times when she had a differing opinion from his demands and had stood her ground: taking in stray dogs, refusing to move to Noblesville, and getting a job. Did Sheila show traits that would have gained Mabel's stamp of approval?

Sheila is here now to keep watch and to comfort her husband, who tried so hard to earn his mother's blessing. In all the community projects he had undertaken, and with all the organizations he joined, she understands now that his underlying need was to gain validation and admiration. His credentials were medals to be worn; his titles were accomplishments he hoped were worthy of praise. She looks back over the last twenty-five years and is sad that Lyndon had never come close to being an ordinary man, willing to sit at home and enjoy the quiet life with her and her dogs.

Lyndon stirs and murmurs, "Mother, did I do well?"

Sheila strokes his hand. "Yes, son. You can rest now."

He settles and breathes his last.

Westfield, Indiana 1977

Sheila calls to her current rescue dogs, a scruffy black and white border collie, MacDuff, and Sherlock the Basset Hound. They look up at their master and she gives them both a chin rub, grateful for their company. She wonders, as she sets off into the early morning mist, how she is going to make it through this day. Her dearest and oldest friend, Millie, and her husband, Bud, will be here later in the morning to escort her to the church. A tear trails down her cheek. These have been challenging times. She has maintained the public image of a supportive wife while privately remaining independent, deciding when to stand up to her husband and when to let things slide.

Trudging down the well-worn forest path, Sheila mentally reviews the planned funeral and reception. So many of her husband's family members, co-workers, and friends will want to express their condolences and reflect on what a prince of a man Lyndon had been. She gathers up her fortitude to face the American customs of grieving their dead. Tonight, she will arrive safely at the farmhouse with two people who knew firsthand how difficult the real Lyndon could be. Mille and Bud will join her in the Scottish way of bidding farewell to her husband with a bottle of Scotch.

***

In the days that follow, Sheila faces both loss and loneliness. The dogs keep her company, but unless one counted the month when Lyndon had stubbornly moved to Noblesville, she has never lived alone. The widow is feeling overwhelmed dealing with the lawyers concerning estate matters; in a vulnerable moment, she makes the awful decision to allow a developer to cut down a stand of her oak trees. It was a necessary action, for the proceeds from this lumber sale went to pay off death taxes. Now on her daily walk past the cleared section of forest, she often sits down on a stump and weeps.

However, she also experiences times of relief; to be the captain of her own ship again is an empowering feeling. Sheila has good friends to lean on, and the regularity of her job as assistant librarian is a warm blanket wrapped around her soul. She has places to go, a car to get there, and library patrons who depend on her for book recommendations. Life settles into a more comfortable routine.

August 1977

Dear Mona,

Greetings dear one. Thank you for your letter and your concern about me being alone here in the countryside. Never fear. I have friends who are ringing up and checking in on me. You know me; I am never truly alone with my exuberant gang of four-legged companions.

Is it naughty to say that because Lyndon isn't around to express his opinion about how many dogs are too many, I'm free to come to the aid of any canine in need of shelter? My most recent rescue shares a name with our famous wartime British Prime Minister. Here's how we met:

I was ending my shift at the reference desk when a library patron said the police were trying to apprehend a dog outside. The fugitive had evaded capture and was leading his pursuers on a merry chase through the park next to the library. I joined the throng of spectators. In our sleepy little town, we seek entertainment where we can get it! It was only hunger and my roast beef sandwich that won the day when the little English Mastiff puppy caught the scent of my lunch and came right over to me. I kept him occupied until the police officer got hold of him. Winston (yes, I named him on the spot!) maintained his air of dignity as they escorted him to the pound.

The next day, when I learned no one had laid claim to him, I marched in with purpose and proclaimed, "I've come for that wee dog with the face of Winston Churchill. We shall get along famously."

Then I addressed the stubborn waif of a pup, "We shall fight on the beaches; we shall never give up."

He sniffed my hand, no doubt hoping for more roast beef, but was happy enough to have found a sympathetic Clementine who would put up with his shenanigans.

Winston has been at my side ever since. Even in inclement weather, he is up for the trail, no matter how mucky it is in places. Even my faithful but moody Sherlock has been welcoming to the recent addition and MacDuff made friends right away, as is his wont. Well, must dash as Millie is at the door, come for a walk in the woods.

Hope you and Malcolm are keeping well. Also, sending hugs for your boxers.

With love,
Sheila

Millie is checking in on Sheila and agrees to a walk in the forest with her. They start off with MacDuff, Sherlock, and the recent addition of Winston, all scampering ahead along the trail.

"Lead on MacDuff," Millie calls out. "Do you know how long I've waited to quote Shakespeare to your dogs?"

"Sorry, my dear, but the actual quote from the Scottish play is 'Lay on, MacDuff.' The line you're quoting is actually from the 1885 novel, *King Solomon's Mines* by Rider Haggard," Sheila notes.

Millie sighs, "Of course, I stand corrected! How is it you know so much? You are the consummate librarian, and Westfield is so fortunate to have you in their employ."

Sheila beams at the compliment. She loves to research literary puzzles and to follow popular quotes to their sources. The Carnegie Library in Westfield is indeed her cherished place of wisdom and peace. It gives her time to immerse herself in armchair travels throughout the world, and all things historical, as well as all the plays of Shakespeare.

"To quote the Bard, I say, '*This above all: to thine own self be true*' - you to be the brilliant confidante that you are, and me to be the helpful librarian. Now let us carry on as the hikers we both are."

With that, the dogs do indeed lead the way, and the friends follow down the trail, arm in arm.

Westfield, Indiana 1979

Sheila is excited to host the Druthers today. She reflects on their Christmas party when they assigned dates and places for the upcoming calendar of meetings. The schedule doesn't change much from year to year. Betsy always hosts in May because her showcase garden is spectacular then. Jane puts on a spread for Christmas at her north Indianapolis home, as she loves to decorate for the season. They all know that Donna and Millie want the summer months, so the ladies can have a dip in their pools after lunch. Linda claims March; no one objects because she makes Irish coffees for St Patrick's Day, and they all agree to wear something green. One member even dresses up like a leprechaun. Such antics for a group of ladies in their fifties and sixties! September is Glenda's month, and everyone goes home with a basket filled with the bounty from the farm she and her husband own. And so it goes that April belongs to Sheila when she can lead a wildflower walk through her forest.

In anticipation of their arrivals, Sheila fusses over the table settings and arranges a teacup for every member. She has ironed the cloth napkins and made sure the tablecloth is just so. The little sandwiches are prepared, and her shortbread cookies are just coming out of the oven. Of course, she will serve sherry; no meeting is complete without sips of their traditional apéritif. She is grateful that today is sunny and dry, the perfect weather to conduct a guided tour of her property. They will meander past carpets of delicate blooms and everyone will have a pamphlet with illustrations she has painted of what plants to look for in the woods. For fun, she plans to divide them into groups and can't wait to announce that the first team to find each kind of wildflower will receive a homemade prize.

Sheila marvels at her diverse group of friends, each who have interesting stories about what they did for the war effort. The monthly gatherings are a time when they let down their guard, remember their roots and feel at home. Now, they are an even more important support group, as four of the twelve members are widows.

***

Sheila has retired from the library, and she celebrated the occasion with the little party her coworkers arranged on her last day. Now her time is totally her own. It's a hazy August day, and she is busy in the kitchen with the windows thrown open. Her baking project is in the oven, and she is ready to enjoy an afternoon cup of tea. Hearing a nicker, she steps out onto her porch in time to see her young neighbor astride a lovely palomino horse.

"Hello, Carol. Would you like to join me for a scone?" Sheila calls, waving her over.

"Hi, Mrs. Beals. Thanks again for letting me ride your trails. I'd love to stop, but begging your pardon, what's a scone?"

"Come on in and see," Sheila replies, pleased that this young neighbor feels comfortable dropping by.

"First, let's find a good place to tether your beautiful steed." Sheila strokes the horse's velvety nose and lets him graze in the backyard. She knows enough not to let the horse wander around to sample flowers from her front garden. The late afternoon is pleasantly warm, and she brings out a tray with a teapot, two teacups, and a plate of warm blueberry scones. Carol settles herself in a porch chair and accepts her cup of tea, with the milk and sugar that Sheila has already added. The teenager nibbles on her scone and nods her head in appreciation.

"It seems I will make a Scottish lass of you yet," Sheila remarks.

"Why, thank you. Will you be sewing a tartan kilt for me soon?" Carol teases back.

"A tartan is a very serious matter, as you learned from the talk I gave to the Hinkle-ettes a few weeks back."

Sheila had been the presenter to the Home Demonstration club members, and their daughters had all wanted to try on the kilt and sash that she had brought.

"Well, I'll have to earn the right to wear my clan's tartan. Should I start by learning how to make a proper cup of tea and these delicious scones?"

"That would be a good start. Oh, and one more thing before you go. I wanted to mention something about your dog. Evidently, Schwartz has this thing about my garbage container. Yesterday, I saw him dragging one of my pails across the fields, heading home. If you could return my bin sometime, that would be great, and I will find a better place to keep it safe. I wonder, does he like the smell of my leftovers?"

"Oh, that dog! Sorry about that. He's a rascal. I'll check when I get home and we'll bring your trash can back. I should go now so I can finish my ride before completing my chores. Thank you for the tea and scone. It's always so nice to stop for a visit." Carol rises and carefully places her teacup on the tray. She touches her linen napkin to her lips, folding and tucking it under her plate.

"Come again soon." Sheila watches her trot off and waves. Yes, she will have to write Mona and regale her sister with news of the sweet neighbor's visit and her aspiration of becoming a Scottish lass.

***

Snow dusts the forest as December comes around. Much to her delight, a Christmas package arrives in the mail from Mona. Sheila marvels at how the shortbread cookies survived their transatlantic journey and chuckles when she discovers a colorful paperback book as well. It's a new science fiction novel by Douglas Adams, which has not yet been published in the United States. Her sister informs her that this book is all the rage, so she hopes Sheila will enjoy it.

She reserves each evening to read a few chapters of *The Hitchhiker's Guide to the Galaxy*. It turns out to be a fun intergalactic adventure with space travel and aliens. Even though she is a retired librarian, Sheila still tries to read a variety of popular books, both fiction and nonfiction. At age seventy, her only desire to travel is alongside characters like Arthur Dent, the hitchhiker in space. She doesn't mind flying through the galaxy during the day, but is always content to return at night to her own home, this place of healing and solace. The forest will shelter her for some years and then will come another time of testing.

Chapter 17 - Meg (May)

It's been two weeks since I received the note from a man I have tried hard to leave in the past. Living in my forest haven has been a respite after a year of preparation and the stress of implementing my exit strategy from an emotionally abusive relationship. Trent is a controlling borderline psychopath; there are no other words to describe my ex-husband, who is in jail for accounting fraud. Now I learn prison officials might grant him parole for good behavior. He can be quite charming when he wants something or someone. The man obviously still has influence and connections, which he has used to discover my whereabouts, yet I am resolved to stand up to him. The more I have discovered about Sheila, the more I take courage from her example of resilience and fortitude.

Her story is one of grit and pluck. I admire her wisdom in gathering strength and encouragement from Millie and the Druthers group, as well as from her sister, Mona. Pouring coffee into my new red mug with the words *Stay Calm and Carry On* emblazoned on its side, I'm grateful to have found my support team composed of Charlotte, plus my boss and coworkers at the library. The police are aware of my situation and have my restraining order on file. I even signed up for an eight-week class that teaches women who have experienced domestic abuse about how to set boundaries for themselves. My classmates have become my morale boosters. Finally, Badger is at my side nudging my hand, the last, and in some ways, the most faithful member of my defense squad.

I glance down at his sweet face and imploring eyes.

"Yes, walk first, but then I have to head to work."

He wags his tail and shivers with excitement. If only I could solve my problems as easily with a brisk jaunt through the forest and an occasional head massage.

Charlotte has been encouraging me to consider prayer once again, and I have gotten back into the habit of praying while I walk among the towering trees. I have been expressing my frustrations and concerns to a God who was a part of my childhood until my faith waned with adult skepticism. When I am in nature, I feel closer to a sense of the divine, and maybe it will calm my nerves to articulate my worries to a higher power. That gets me wondering about Sheila, the daughter of a much-loved vicar. Was this forest a place where she worshiped the Creator of heaven and earth? Or had life handed her one too many sorrows for her to believe in God? I make a mental note to ask Sheila's goddaughters what they knew of her faith.

Walk complete, I check my computer and see an email from Anna with a photo attachment. She has continued to rummage through boxes in search of more of Sheila's artwork. I love this ink sketch of a Scottish bagpiper who is standing with what I call a Scottie dog. Sheila must have loved the traditional music of the Highlands. On the back of the sketch, she wrote - *Memorial Day weekend, Indy 500*. Another question for the goddaughters. I review the month of May on my phone's calendar. It helps calm my current anxiety to remind myself of fun upcoming activities. One item is my first official meeting with the Nature Study Club. Members take time at the beginning of the gathering every month to report what they have seen or experienced outdoors, whether it be a bird sighting or the discovery of a new plant. I am ready to share my nature observation of a group of turkey vultures roosting in a tree by the White River. On Memorial Day weekend, I will be with Charlotte and her family. They have invited me for my first ever visit to the Indianapolis Motor Speedway, where we will attend the famous Indy 500 race.

Tomorrow, I finally have the long-awaited lunch with Anna and Bea. I can't wait to get together with Millie's daughters in person. Until now, they have both been wintering in Florida, so we have only had a series of emails and phone calls. They've been so helpful in supplying personal information about their mother and Sheila, along with sending old photos. I imagine just sitting back and listening to their memories of the woman they called Aunt Sheila. The sisters will have answers to my many questions, and I hope some of their responses will lead me to new avenues of inquiry.

When we meet the next day at the Field Brewing Restaurant, we find a table and order salads. Anna hands over some snapshots from their family vacation in Hawaii when Sheila joined them. There is also a sweet print of Millie and Sheila together in a garden.

"It is thrilling that you are doing this research into our Aunt Sheila. We also appreciate all the background information about our own mother."

"Agreed. So, do you have questions? Is there anything in particular you want to hear about?" Bea chimes in.

"Tell me more about spending time with your aunt when you were growing up," I suggest.

Our food comes as they reminisce about summers when they got to hang out on the farm whiling away lazy days, running after dogs and coming in only when the sun had gone down.

"Sounds like sweet memories. Do you remember Sheila and Lyndon coming over to your house often? Your mother and Sheila were close friends, but did your father and Lyndon get along as well? Weren't they both in the army? I've read old newspaper accounts about how he was a friendly fellow, so did you call him Uncle Lyndon as well?" I ask, bubbling over with queries.

Then Bea puts her fork down. Anna had warned me that her older sister could be blunt in the way she expressed herself, not holding back in how she felt about Lyndon. She wasn't wrong.

"You know, I have waited to tell you this in person. Our time with Sheila was wonderful, but Lyndon was a jerk. As children, we picked up on vibes between the adults and listened to brief comments even after we had been sent to bed for the night. As I grew older, I got the impression that he tried to control Sheila and keep her on the farm as much as he could. That self-centered man would drive off to work in the morning, leaving her all alone. Lyndon expected that dinner would be on the table when he got home, and that she would accompany him to all those meetings and conferences with his various organizations. She was supposed to be dressed and ready at his beck and call."

Bea is just getting started.

"I think Lyndon tried to keep Sheila in a box: you know, the pretty little wife who should spend all her day keeping house and cooking for him. I always bristled at the limitations Sheila experienced for so many years. She didn't even have her own means of transportation."

Anna adds, "But she was resourceful and found activities to fill her time, such as the daily walks she took with her dogs, rain or shine. Sheila was also an amazing seamstress and liked to look nice. As an artist, she designed her own outfits. Mail-order catalogs were her friends, and she would order clothes and material plus other sewing supplies. Lyndon probably didn't mind spending money on that; the better his wife looked, the more it made him look good. Sheila always had to rely on others to give her rides, but it seemed she had lots of her friends who were happy to pick her up when she got involved in various clubs. She was very active with a Home Demonstration Club called The Hinkle-ettes, as well as the Woman's Club of Westfield and the Nature Study Club."

"However, she still had to depend on others if she wanted to go anywhere," Bea points out, continuing her story. "It got to a point that I just couldn't stand the way he left Aunt Sheila stranded on the farm. I said to myself, enough is enough, so my fiancé and I went over when Lyndon wasn't there and taught her to drive. Anna and I found her a used car with help from mom and dad, and from then on, Sheila was finally free to come and go as she pleased. It made us so happy to see her independent at last."

I can just picture Sheila driving around the countryside, the wind in her hair and a dog hanging out the passenger side window, ears flapping in the breeze. I'm drawn back from my mini reverie when I hear Anna say, "Yes, after she got her own car, Sheila even got a job as a part-time librarian in Westfield. Of course, she worked in the old Carnegie library building, which is near the corner of Union and West Main Street. This was before they built the new building where you work."

"Wait a minute! She worked at my library?" It will be a thrill to verify Sheila's employment at Westfield Public Library, but that means going through old staff meeting minutes where they recorded every hire and retirement over the years. A timeframe of when she worked there would be helpful.

"When was this?"

Anna holds a finger to her lips, "Late sixties, maybe?"

Bea suggests the early seventies and then they are off on a tangent about dates and where they were living when their aunt started work at the library. This is an amazing discovery for me: Sheila as a fellow librarian. I sit back to listen as the two sisters joke about how complicated family memories can be, yet they can agree on how much they loved their Aunt Sheila. I'd be proud to have these two strong and passionate women call me friend.

Back at work, I find Sheila's name up on the wall, where they commemorate all the people that have worked here since 1901. George kindly goes through all the minutes from the 1970s to confirm the dates they hired Sheila and when she retired. There may be books that I have handled that she filed on the shelves. I live in her farmhouse and now I work at the same library. No wonder I feel such a kinship with her as gardener, dog lover, and now fellow librarian.

***

The phone call comes as a complete surprise. Bea gives me the good news that the last of the Druthers is still alive. Winifred is in her nineties and lives in a retirement home in Indianapolis. What a marvelous contact this could be if this nonagenarian will agree to a meeting with me. I get the contact information for Ellen, who visits this old friend of Sheila's frequently.

Considering the older lady as her own auntie, Ellen checks in on her and they share a cup of tea regularly. Her mother, Betsy, and Win were best friends, similar to Sheila and Millie's relationship. Staying in touch with Aunt Win is natural because she cares for her like a member of her own family. I get the sense it is something all the Druthers passed along to their children: the ethos of friends looking out for one another like family.

I contact Ellen to make sure that Winifred is up to a visit, and make plans to meet the last living member of this courageous group of women. As I show my identification at the front desk, Ellen, who has offered to be our go-between, steps forward to greet her aunt in the lounge area of her care facility.

"Hello, Auntie Win. I have a friend with me who wants to meet you. Do you remember I told you about the librarian who is doing research into Sheila Beals and Millie Ostrom?"

The old woman, dressed elegantly in tailored slacks and a violet cardigan over a beige silk shirt, turns to me with an appraising glance. "Well, how do you do? I'm extremely curious about your fact-finding project and just what I can do for you." She speaks with a soft voice, looking me directly in the eye. "Will you join me for tea?"

I offer my gift of homemade shortbread, which I set on the table between us. Ellen pours tea for everyone and we all sit comfortably, taking sips from our fine china teacups. Winifred enjoys her cookie with a murmur of delight. She sets her cup back into its saucer.

"Such a wonderful memory of home. My mother made us shortbread biscuits for a treat."

I brush cookie crumbs from my lips. "I used my grandmother's recipe and they are a favorite of mine as well. Let me introduce myself. My name is Meg Livingstone, and I have been renting Sheila's old farmhouse for the last year. When I first discovered the story of how she donated her land to create a forest preserve, I wanted to learn more about her journey here to Indiana. Then, I met Sheila's goddaughters and learned about your group called the Druthers." I'm encouraged to see a smile play on Win's face.

"I can't tell you how exciting it is to talk to someone who knew Sheila Beals personally. With all my questions, do you mind if I take some notes just to remind myself of the details?" Win nods her assent to my request of recording her memories.

"Would you start by telling me when you first met Sheila, and what were your first impressions?"

"As you have learned from Anna and Bea, we were both members of the Druthers in 1948. Sheila was petite and always well dressed, but you learned not to let her size fool you. She would confidently speak her mind if you asked for her opinion, and she didn't suffer fools. Sheila listened politely to viewpoints that ran contrary to her own, but wasn't afraid to refute illogical arguments. She regularly wrote to the editor of the newspaper to express her thoughts on various topics." Win pauses, taking another sip of her tea.

"As the only Scot among us, Sheila was proud of her heritage. You couldn't mistake where she was from with that accent of hers. Most of us had a British lilt to our voices, but none with that musical way of talking. She and Millie were as thick as thieves, and it was so interesting when they got talking about their war experiences during the Blitz in London. They also reminisced about the farm near Shrewsbury where they were Land Girls together." Win seems caught up in a flashback, as if this was one of their meetings.

"What about the formation of the Druthers group?"

"Well, Ellen's mother, Betsy, was the first to suggest we break away from the Association of Daughters of the British Empire. Their meetings were so stuffy. She hosted our inaugural meeting, and it was as if we all let out a breath when Millie, Irene, and I settled into comfy chairs in her living room, sipping sherry. After that first gathering, the word spread to our friends and we stopped at twelve, so each member could pick a month to host. The schedule worked out naturally because each of us would pick a favorite holiday or a season that showed off someone's expertise or interest."

"That was my mom, the talented gardener, who loved hosting in May when our backyard was overflowing with color." Ellen continues, "Didn't someone else compose a club anthem that you would sing to the tune of *There'll Always Be An England?*"

"Why yes, we were always coming up with creative ways to express our happiness in being together."

"Can you tell me about your journey to Indiana? Did you all compare stories in the early days of your club meetings about how you came to America? Although, I had heard that there was one American among your numbers."

"Oh yes, that would be Linda, who lived next door to Jane. She married a war veteran, so that was close enough for us. Besides, she needed a supportive group of friends, as she was new to Indianapolis. Almost all of us met our husbands during the war, and Indiana was the place we now had in common. I was in the Auxiliary Service and drove officers around. That's how I met my husband, Albert. He's gone now, but he was in the American Medical Corps, stationed in England. He volunteered to help at the base hospital near to where I was living and would require a ride to other bases as the need arose. We agreed that none of us intentionally meant to fall in love with American soldiers, but it was different during the war when we all faced life-altering situations. Coming to the United States was both a glorious adventure and a frighteningly huge decision to move so far away from family." Win is looking out the window as if into a distant memory and tears come to her eyes.

"How are you feeling, Auntie Win? Are these questions making you feel sad?"

"Thank you for your concern, but no, these are fond recollections of how much we helped each other adjust to a new country. We became like family to each other." She reaches over to pat Ellen's hand affectionately.

Putting down my pen and notebook, I ask, "Are you getting tired? Do you have questions for me?" I want to give her a break and take the focus off her.

"I would like to know how you got started with this project, and just what you plan to do with all these stories that you have collected."

"Well, my first impression of Sheila was from information on a future park sign. It describes how Lyndon brought her to Indiana after they met during the war in London. It seemed like such a romantic story, and I wanted to find out more about her. Really, I think I'd like to write about her adventures, both before and after she arrived in the States. I want the written summary of her life to be more than the simple phrase from her obituary - *she was a homemaker.*"

I let out a sigh at the last statement, hoping they perceive that the heart of my mission is to right a wrong. Every woman deserves to have her story told.

"Well said. All the Druthers have led interesting lives," Win confirms. She stifles a yawn and motions for Ellen. "It's time for my nap. I will leave it up to you to arrange for another meeting with this budding author. Perhaps we can find some pictures to share for the next time."

"I will be grateful to hear anything more you want to tell me about the Druthers and, of course, Sheila in particular. Thank you for this visit." I stand and extend my hand and feel Win's firm grasp.

As we say our goodbyes in the parking lot, Ellen and I marvel over her aunt and how we want to be as mentally sharp as she is if we ever live to such an old age. She is eager to look through her mother's scrapbooks to see if she can find more photos of the Druthers and the words to their club song. I promise to call to schedule another teatime together with Auntie Win.

***

A month has passed now since I found Trent's missive waiting for me. My mind has been whirling between the exciting advances in my research and the lingering threat of my ex showing up at work.

An excursion to a famous racetrack is the perfect outing to divert my thoughts. Back in Wisconsin, I had neighbors who made the trip down to Indianapolis to attend the Indy 500 festivities every Memorial Day weekend. I often wondered what the draw was, but now that I am sitting in the stands and watching from a distance as cars whizz by, I am caught up in the crowd's excitement and the kaleidoscope of color and movement. It is so nice to tag along with Charlotte, Raffi, and their delightful daughters, Maya and Tara.

Positioning ourselves near the entrance, we hear the Gordon Pipers Band and Drum Corp play in the opening ceremonies. We stand up with everyone else as they pass, and I ponder how there is something ancient about the music. It stirs my soul. The two little girls dance and twirl and then giggle in delight as the adorable band mascots strut past: a West Highland White Terrier and a black Scottish Terrier, in honor of the iconic black-and-white checkered race flag. Does this experience call to the Scottish heritage in me, even though I've never heard a live performance with bagpipes before? Is this something that Sheila reveled in, something that transported her back to her homeland?

When I get home, I am exhausted and ready for a quick walk, a long soak in the bathtub, and bed. I thoroughly enjoyed the day of sunshine, movement, and companionship.

Just before I turn out the bedside light, I check my phone. There are emails from both Anna and Bea with photo attachments on each. There is a scan of a fun sketch that has a Westie dog looking up at a bagpiper. Another is of a grinning Sheila, so petite, beside a rather tall gentleman in full bagpiper regalia. They are posing together outside the Old Tavern pub in Carmel just after a Fourth of July parade. The last photo shows a group of the Druthers with their husbands, everyone dancing with joy and abandonment around a kilted piper. Anna mentions she took this picture at Sheila's birthday bash. I plan to print the images out at the drugstore and then slip them into Sheila's art portfolio.

Well, that answers one question about bagpipes. Sheila indeed loved the national musical instrument of Scotland; its music no doubt brought back memories of home. I fall asleep to the familiar strains of *Scotland the Brave* playing on my phone. Sheila and I dance together in my dreams.

Chapter 18 - Sheila

"I would rather walk with a friend in the dark, than alone in the light."

- Helen Keller

Westfield, Indiana 1979

As is their routine, Sheila and her dogs take the perimeter hike slowly, savoring the fall air and enjoying the sound of crunching leaves underfoot. When they make it back to the cozy farmhouse, the canines settle in for a nap and she tidies up from breakfast. It's been two years since Lyndon died and two months since she has stopped working at the library; she doesn't mind the solitude. The dogs keep her company, and she has plenty of social activities that keep her connected with the outside world. Sheila is looking forward to a visit from Millie this morning, but wonders if her friend will question the wisdom of her living alone in the forest now that she is in her seventies. She resolves to put Millie's mind at ease. Someday, circumstances may force her to move into the city, but that time is not now.

Sheila leaves MacDuff out on the porch to greet Millie when she arrives, and waits in her favorite blue plush wingback chair with her newest rescue in her lap. The ironically named Peanut is a golden retriever/poodle mix, who is a solid 75 pounds. Sheila can't wait to see the look of surprise on her friend's face.

Millie arrives and bends down to pet MacDuff, then calls into the house, "Sheila, I'm here. How is everyone today?"

She takes in the sight of Sheila's petite frame, engulfed by the furry dog.

"Really, Peanut?"

They both laugh and Sheila gives the erstwhile lap dog a gentle push, so she can give Millie a hug.

After lunch and many assurances to Millie that she is doing fine, Sheila waves goodbye and settles back into her armchair. The sun filters in through the window where Sheila can watch the squirrels in their frenetic search for acorns. The birds are flitting from branch to branch.

Sheila reaches for her current library book, *Smiley's People*, the most recent book by John le Carré. The Westfield Public Library staff put aside the newest novels from her favorite authors for her to borrow as a special favor, since she is a former librarian. She joins the cat-and-mouse spy game and imagines the posh British tones of George Smiley, alongside the Russian accent of Karla, his Soviet nemesis. Absorbed in the plot, it takes the dogs shuffling around for her to realize that it's mid-afternoon. She makes a phone call to confirm a ride to the Nature Study Club meeting tonight; she cannot drive safely at night anymore.

Sheila spends the rest of the afternoon working on her latest sewing project, a dress with delicate smocking, for her goddaughter's new baby. Classical music plays quietly in the background. Then, after a quick bite for supper, her friend, Gloria, picks her up for the meeting. It has been a full day, when she finally settles into her upstairs bedroom with the dogs and slips into Spymaster George's fictional world until sleep claims her. The crickets sing a lullaby into the dark night, and all is well.

Westfield, Indiana 1985

The Druthers have wrapped up their first meeting of the year. Millie is Sheila's designated winter driver and gets her settled in the passenger seat. They chat together on the drive home, laughing over the latest gossip from the club members. When they get up the icy driveway to her farmhouse and are inside, Millie sits down in a wingback chair across from her friend.

"Sheila, come with me to Hawaii for a holiday."

"And where, dear friend, did you get this extravagant idea?" Sheila teases indulgently.

"Indiana is cold, Hawaii is warm! Bud and I agree that this should be a long overdue celebration of your retirement, our treat. I know my birthday isn't until August, but I will also celebrate turning 65 this year." She reaches over to give Sheila's hand a squeeze. "Do say you will join us. Everyone in the family will take this trip and they want their Aunt Sheila to come as well."

"I wouldn't miss it for the world. The only arrangement I need to make is to find someone to take care of Maisie."

At the mention of her name, the Australian terrier perks up her fluffy ears and looks from Sheila to Millie, then back to her mistress. Sheila pets her beautiful tan and black fur.

"Don't worry, my sweet, I will return."

Maui, Hawaii 1985

Millie and Bud, their children and spouses, grandchildren, and Aunt Sheila have been on the island of Maui for a few days. The food is exotic and there are plenty of activities to keep everyone engaged. Yesterday, they all enjoyed their big adventure driving up to Haleakala National Park to see the sun set over the volcano in a spectacular blaze of oranges and reds. After breakfast today, Sheila is reading in the shade with the palm trees swaying in a breeze that is lulling her into a sense of security. Millie slips into a chair beside her and Sheila looks up from her paperback into her friend's face. She sees a strain that she hadn't noticed before.

"Let's take a walk along the beach while Bud is off golfing," Millie suggests, extending her hand.

"Alrighty then, but you know I won't go near the ocean. One narrow escape in the North Sea is enough for me to stay well clear of any body of water." Sheila lays her novel aside with a bookmark to mark her place.

With low tide, Ka'anapali Beach is wide enough so the women can admire the azure blue of the ocean but keep a respectful distance from the crashing waves. Millie knows her friend's fear of drowning better than most and understands that she will never get over her childhood near-death experience.

In a stroke of luck, a resourceful fisherman was there to save the young girl before a rogue wave swept her away. Sheila made it through her traumatic experience, but now she steers clear of water altogether, including swimming pools.

They settle in beach chairs and Millie casts off her sandals and digs her toes in the silky white sand. With a heavy sigh, she begins.

"You know how I haven't been feeling well since Christmas. Well, I finally got in to see my doctor. I really didn't want to ruin our time here in Hawaii, but honestly, I need my closest friend to know what is going on. Sadly, I have cancer and the prognosis is not good. This is a secret I'm not yet ready to share with the children. They will know soon enough. For now, you and Bud are my only confidants."

Sheila grasps her friend's hand and tears spring to her eyes.

"I can't believe it! Ach, no. You and I have been through so many things. The bombs in London didn't take us out; I always thought we would grow old together."

Millie laughs at that. "We are getting on in years, my dear."

"I mean doddery and in the old folks home together," Sheila retorts, "really infirm."

Millie bows her head, also picturing the two friends bundled up in blankets and shawls, sitting on the lawn of some grand old estate with their cups of tea. Then she makes balls with her fists.

"When we get home, I want to come to your forest and scream. Then have a good stiff drink."

"You come and we will rage together just like in the poem, *Do Not Go Gentle Into That Good Night* by Dylan Thomas."

Sheila hugs her best friend and strokes her blonde hair. They sit in silence, ignoring anyone passing by. What would her sister Mona say at this moment?

What will be, will be.

She holds on a little tighter and says quietly, "Tell me more."

Indianapolis, Indiana 1986

Sheila enters the den, tucking the blanket snugly around her friend Millie. The afternoon sunlight has lost its brilliance, bathing the room in a dusky amber glow. What did her brother-in-law say about this time of day? *This is the golden hour.*

Many months filled with agonizing chemotherapy and radiation have gone by. The battle was waged, and the troops rallied to surround Millie and Bud with support and love. Sheila quietly expresses her anger on her own while grappling with the thought of losing her best friend. She falls in line when she is with Millie, who has settled on the sentiment of "let it be."

Most of the time, Sheila sits in silence, listening to the birds chirping outside. Millie has always been an attentive gardener, tending to her bushes and flowers, coaxing them to grow and flourish. This sunroom is Millie's favorite place for sitting and enjoying her verdant garden, with full-length windows to let in the natural beauty. She waits for her friend, wondering how this can be happening. How will she cope when her rock and mainstay is gone? This is the friend who lured her to America and who gave Sheila refuge in her own small house. Millie's daughters are like family to her.

Whenever her friend becomes lucid, there is time for quiet conversations. With a little snuffle, Millie opens her eyes and looks over. With a half smile, she whispers, "Like old times? Me falling asleep and you keeping watch?"

"Always. I will be with you through thick and thin. How many bombing raids did we dodge in London during the Blitz? How many times did we make it down to the Tube station to shelter from the bombardment? We'd always look for the French men to sit next to; they smelled the best."

Millie's eyes crinkle at the hazy memory.

"You'd fall asleep on my shoulder, our heads together. We would wake stiff and sore when the all-clear sounded. I'd look over and see your face, so creased with worry. All I wanted was to keep you safe, my dear friend." Sheila leans over to stroke her fingers across Millie's forehead, smoothing over the wrinkles. "Did you have a good nap?"

"Let's talk about our farm days. Those were good times, eh?" Millie prompts, remembering the days as Land Girls in England.

"How about that time Bud came over to visit us on the farm? Were you engaged to him by then?" Sheila wonders.

"Somehow, you convinced him to milk a cow, seeing as he was from Indiana. As if everyone from the Midwest was a farmer. He was not, but gave it a go, working for a long time with no results. Not one drop of milk in his bucket. You finally took pity on him and told him it had slipped your mind that the cow was dry. Of course, they were getting ready to sell the poor beast off the next day. Bud took it well even as all the Land Girls in the barn laughed out loud and he realized the joke was on him. Oh, you loved to tease!"

Millie suppresses a smile. It hurts to laugh, and she coughs painfully.

"I couldn't help playing that joke on him. Americans could be so gullible."

Sheila retorts, "I imagine he was so in love that you could have convinced him to do almost anything!"

Millie replies with a wicked look on her face, "Why, what on earth do you mean? Like getting a quickie divorce from the wife he didn't love, just so he could marry me and bring me here to Indiana?"

She sighs at the thought of those passionate days when they could not bear being apart. The immediacy of desire. The longing to be together was so strong that she followed Bud and moved across the ocean.

"It was war all around us, and we didn't know if we would make it through alive." She stops and brings her frail hand to her mouth. "Forgive me, Sheila. I wasn't thinking. You lost loved ones in the war. I'm sorry. How could I have forgotten?"

Sheila shushes her friend and looks to one side in order to wipe tears from her eyes. The thought of her brother dying in that horrible Japanese prisoner of war camp surfaces. She tamps it down. The memory of Millie giving her the news of her beloved Gilbert's plane crash rises to overwhelm her once again. She turns back to lay an arm around Millie's shoulders.

Silence lingers as each dwells on their past pain and sorrow.

"Enough about the war. We made it and you saved me. You brought me here to Indiana and the beautiful farmhouse that is now my home. I will always be grateful that you and Bud took me in and that your children are so fiercely protective of us. I love your family as my own."

It is rare that she expresses her deepest thoughts and emotions.

"Now, how about a cuppa and a biscuit?" Sheila rises and hurries to the kitchen to retrieve the British solution for any awkward moment. Tea!

The two friends sip their Darjeeling and sit in the gloaming, happy to be together. In the coming days, Sheila will do what she can to keep Millie comfortable. Then, after the unthinkable, she supposes she will tackle each day and learn to carry on without her friend.

***

The summer day is oppressively hot as Sheila arrives at the Crown Hill Cemetery Mausoleum in Indianapolis. She squeezes into a pew in the Peace Chapel with the other Druthers, who are all teary-eyed. Millie is the first one of them to go. Sheila looks up at the beautiful stained-glass window that glows as the bright afternoon sun pours through it. She thinks how peaceful it will be to come back to visit Millie in her resting place, but for now, her sorrow is overwhelming. Rising when the bagpiper comes down the aisle playing *Amazing Grace*, her heart is close to bursting. On either side of her, a Druthers member places a hand under each of her elbows and holds her up. The funeral is beautiful as they honor their friend, but the pain of loss will stay with her for the rest of her life. Millie's favorite motto comes to mind - *"To thine own self be true"* - and she vows to follow her friend's advice.

"Carry on, Sheila," she whispers to herself as they exit the chapel.

Chapter 19 - Meg (June)

'Come, Watson, come!' he cries. 'The game is afoot.
Not a word! Into your clothes and come!'
- Sir Arthur Conan Doyle
The Return of Sherlock Holmes

My time at the farmhouse is flying by and I can hardly believe it is June already. With longer days and warmer temps, I consider this time of the gardening season to be the most enjoyable. Every morning, after my walk with Badger, I take my coffee on the front porch and look over the flowers that are blooming in Sheila's English Garden.

I admire the delicate pink blossoms of the wild rose bush that I have attempted to trim back and tame. The peony bush I discovered in the spring, choked with weeds, is now flourishing in its corner; its creamy white flowers take my breath away as childhood memories surface of my father with his green thumb. The hardy purple coneflowers are once again in full color alongside delphiniums and yarrow. I am happy to see the English lavender plant, which I purchased especially in honor of Millie, has fragrant leaves and delicate purple flowers on stalks.

I glance over to a little wrought iron side table where I have a framed picture of a woman sitting amidst flowers with a book on her lap. The quote from Marcus Tullius Cicero under the image reads: *If you have a garden and a library, you have everything you need.* So true Marcus, so true.

After today's shift at the library, I am looking forward to dinner with Charlotte. She texted me last night and said that she would bring Indian curry à la Raffi and meet me at the farmhouse. She has news. Who doesn't love a good mystery? My curiosity piqued, I readily agreed. I will never turn down good food and time with my best friend. Maybe I'll set out a chair in front of the flower bed and have her take a photo of me reading a book to save the image of this lovely summer day.

Badger barks as the little Honda pulls up the long driveway. Charlotte gets out smiling, holding up our food.

"Your order of Chana Masala, Spicy Chicken Curry, and rice has arrived. There is also homemade naan in this bag."

My mouth waters with the promise of tasty fare. "Ooh, that smells amazing. We can load up our plates in the kitchen and eat alfresco on the porch. I have chilled mango juice in the fridge."

We dig into our feast and laugh over the latest antics of Charlotte's girls, who are having an end of school celebration with their friends. Raffi is holding down the fort.

"Did I tell you how my favorite patron, Simon, has hinted about wanting to meet for coffee? He suggested we could spend more time chatting about the authors we both admire. Does that sound like we are both sci-fi nerds? I wonder if he has been to Gen Con? If we met after hours, we would not have to be interrupted by other library patrons coming to ask me questions. It's also a plus that he is an avid baseball fan, though he cheers for the Cardinals, and not the Blue Jays. Do you think it is too soon to think about dating? …"

I trail off when I get no reaction, as if she hasn't been listening.

"Charlotte?"

She gives her head a little shake. "Sorry, what were you saying?"

"I'll tell you later. Tell Raffi his curry was delicious and such a treat. Before we lose the light, can you take a picture of me reading in Sheila's Garden? Then I have some fresh raspberries and blueberries for dessert."

I show her the framed picture and Charlotte takes a photo as I pose with my book. We also take a selfie and I check the shots. She doesn't look as lighthearted as I feel. I gather up the dinner plates and bring out two bowls of fruit. We munch on the berries and look out at the darkening forest. The fireflies dance in the clearing in front of the farmhouse. Reluctantly, we move inside.

"Shall I make tea?"

My friend reaches out to take my hand.

"It might be a good idea to bring out a stronger option. I have information that is better delivered with stiff drinks."

"This sounds serious. I have some Scotch whisky that was Sheila's favorite brand. It's Friday night. Can you stay the night?"

"Yes, Raffi is prepared for me to sleep over."

We fill two glass tumblers and sit side by side on the sofa. "Okay, tell me what I assume to be bad news."

"As we agreed, my lawyer friends in Wisconsin have been quietly monitoring parole hearings at the Dodge Correctional Institution. They told me that Trent's hearing was yesterday, but I didn't want to alarm you until I heard how it went."

"Parole? Are you serious? How could they think of letting that horrible man out of prison?"

"You know how Trent can turn on the charm and seem remorseful. They convicted him of a white-collar crime, and in the parole board's opinion, they probably don't consider him a major threat to society. The ruling will come out in ten days, after which they could release him. However, he will have restrictions on his travel outside the state."

I take a gulp of whisky. "Do you think he will find me? Is there anything I can do? What if he shows up here?"

"We'll be ready for that possibility. We will tell the police about the latest news, and they can arrest him for violation of his parole if he sets one foot outside of Wisconsin. You will need to inform your boss at work if Trent gets paroled. A good offense is the best defense. Stand strong, my friend."

We spend the rest of the evening talking through strategies and worst-case scenarios. We don't want a paper trail, so in the future we agree to no texting or emails about our plans. I compile a list of phone calls to people who can be on standby to help. I feel like I have a similar support group to what Sheila had after Lyndon died. She was all alone on the farm, but her good friends looked in on her and were ready to help at the drop of a hat. I will try to be as brave as she was throughout her life.

***

Most of the week is a blur of meetings with the police and my library director. I host an informal gathering of my self-help group made up of ladies who have had experiences with abusive partners. My emotions are all over the map, ranging from utter despair to glowing confidence in my supportive friends and myself.

I set up a time to have coffee with Anna and Bea, as they have more stories of their Aunt Sheila to share. It's a welcome distraction on my day off as we settle into a corner table at Bica Café, a cozy little European coffee shop in downtown Noblesville. As the two sisters chat, I savor my flat white and key lime pie parfait, and they discuss how Sheila handled life with Lyndon, whom they considered an overbearing husband.

"I can't believe that Lyndon has inserted himself into the limelight again. I met with the people at the Westfield Washington Township Parks & Recreation Department to talk about the official opening for MacGregor Park. They let me see the signs that they plan to install all along the trails. I almost gagged when I saw the one titled *Sheila's Trail*. The information about how Sheila came to Indiana is wrong," Anna insists with the thump of her fist on the table.

My detective senses are tingling.

"You mean the story about how they met in England during the war when she was a volunteer driver for officers? Then, they fell in love, and he brought her over to Indiana? That was part of the reason I really delved into Sheila's life. It sounded like such a romantic story."

"Ha! That's rubbish. They didn't meet in England; I'm almost certain Lyndon was serving in the Pacific, but I don't have any paperwork to prove it. I told them some details were incorrect, but they said it would be too expensive to get the sign reprinted. Besides, they have their sources, and I would need verifiable evidence to the contrary to get it changed. I can't stand to think that Lyndon gets the last word and that it's wrong."

"Anna, this is a major issue. We need to sort this misinformation out. Detective Meg Livingstone is on the case. It really is too bad Sheila didn't leave behind a journal."

"I will send you a copy of Sheila's wedding photo with our mom and grandmother watching on in the background. That those two women are standing together is significant. Our mother hated how her mother-in-law tried to control our dad. Grandmother McWhirter was never around much, but she showed up at Sheila's wedding and I remember hearing her take credit for introducing them. Lyndon and Grandmother worked for the same newspaper and were both very active members of the State Historical Society."

"All good information. I can work on finding out where Lyndon served during the War to disprove the story of where and when he met Sheila. We will challenge Lyndon now, though perhaps Sheila chose her battles with him?"

Chuckling at a memory, Bea declares, "Oh, Aunt Sheila certainly picked a huge issue to defy Lyndon this one time. I specifically remember, she refused to move into Noblesville when Lyndon declared they were moving to the childhood home he inherited."

They are just getting warmed up, and Anna continues, "Yes. Aunt Sheila put her foot down. She loved living in the forest amongst the birds and the creatures, starting her walk every day by just stepping out onto her porch and whistling to her dogs. It wouldn't have been the same living in a city neighborhood. I wish I could have been there to see the expression on Lyndon's face when Sheila said no. I think he stayed in the house alone for a few weeks, but couldn't explain to the neighbors why his wife wasn't living there with him. He finally gave up and childishly insisted that if he wasn't going to live there, then no one would. Lyndon boarded up that lovely old home and left it to become the 'spooky building' on the street. Kids would come by and throw rocks at the windows and dare each other to break in."

"Wait a minute, that beautiful house on the historic street in Noblesville?" It hits me - the address for Lyndon as a young man in the census records matches where Sheila's goddaughter Anna and her family live now. How could I have missed that connection?

"After Lyndon died, his childhood home came to Aunt Sheila in the will. She asked if my husband and I were interested in buying the decrepit old place. We did and what a mess it was inside and out. All the glass from broken windows and garbage everywhere. Lyndon had abandoned the place for almost twenty years; the neighbors were so pleased that we wanted to restore it back to the grand home it had been. I will send you photos of the before and after."

"Did you find anything interesting amidst the detritus?"

"There were papers and junk galore in the basement. We even found a dusty old photo of a woman who looked like she was from the South Pacific. We couldn't bear to keep anything that had belonged to Lyndon, so it all went up in smoke in an enormous bonfire."

Inwardly, I groan about the destroyed documents, but I understand, considering Anna's distaste for the man. However, those old artifacts and letters would have been invaluable to me in my attempts to plumb the mind of this enigmatic man. Part tyrant, part lost soul?

Anna goes on, "I talked to an older neighbor who grew up down the street when Lyndon lived at home. This gentleman was a deacon at his church and traveled with Lyndon's father, Homer, who was a traveling shoe salesman. They would keep each other company, one peddling shoes, the other spreading the good news. The neighbor's wife told me *Lyndon had been kept too long in his knickers.* It's an old-fashioned expression, but she clearly believed that Lyndon was under his mother's influence much longer than was healthy."

So, an overbearing mother and a father who was away for long stretches? Mentally, I add finding an obituary for each of Lyndon's parents to my research task list. The goddaughters are providing primary source material for Sheila; however, where Lyndon is concerned, there may be a bias in their opinions. I inquire about letters that Sheila may have left behind. Sadly, the answer is no. As was so often the case with older people, they destroyed most of their personal correspondence and diaries. Who would want to read about regrets, sorrows, and thoughts of what might have been?

The last interesting thing I learn is that Anna accompanied Sheila on one last trip to Scotland to visit her sister Mona, and brother-in-law Malcolm.

"I was so happy to tag along on this trip with Aunt Sheila and to see the places that were close to her heart. Her sister Mona was living in a town near to where they grew up. We drove and walked around, seeing the houses they lived in and schools they attended. If they had the energy, we hiked the hills as they did as children. After teatime, Malcolm stoked the fire and brought out the whisky, and we settled in for an evening of reminiscing about their youth. When the grey heads started nodding and the conversation waned, I bundled up Aunt Sheila and took her back to our B & B. As soon as she was asleep, I jotted down as many of the details as I could remember. These were memories of a tough childhood as orphans, in the care of guardians who were less than loving. Still, what most impressed me was how the siblings clung together for support. They had all been through so much, but staying close got them through many of the hard times."

"You know, your Aunt Sheila had such a fascinating life. I've always wanted to write a book and her story would be an interesting tale. I want to prove that she was much more than just a homemaker! Perhaps I can even take a research trip to Scotland."

"I'd buy your book," Bea says, grinning.

Anna smiles as well and they both seem pleased with this prospect. With a promise that Anna would send me a copy of her notes from that trip to Scotland, we say goodbye. Trying not to forget anything, I write all my own impressions and thoughts once I am sitting in my car. Over the next couple of hours, I ponder all the information I've learned about Lyndon. In the opinion of Sheila's goddaughters, he was probably not the best of husbands and had made such a foolish decision to board up his beautiful childhood home. He was like a sulky little boy stomping his foot when he didn't get his way. However, I am only hearing their side of the story. Lyndon is not here to defend himself. What about the glowing memorial from his colleagues at the newspaper printed after his death?

I wish I could talk with Millie about why her friend married Lyndon. I believe she was Sheila's confidante and biggest supporter during challenging times in England and Indiana. Given the conventions of the 1950s and the 1960s, expectations were that a woman's place was in the home and that she would not be an independent thinker. Of course, the couple shared interests in nature and music, yet I realize from my research that privately Lyndon could have been controlling, and that put Sheila in an unpleasant position.

I imagine how she must have felt a burden lifted when Lyndon died, and she could live life on her own terms once again. I surmise that, like many of her generation, Sheila knew how to push down any emotion that threatened to overwhelm her. Would a psychiatrist say that she knew how to compartmentalize? Setting aside the negative while accentuating the positive?

After the war ended in Britain, Sheila had to work hard to make ends meet. When she married, she was more comfortably situated. She had many hours alone on the farm, yet she turned that time into creative pursuits. Her dogs kept her company, and once she branched out to join the different women's clubs in the area, she had her social needs met. She even had good friends who switched off to give her rides before she got her driver's license.

Encouraging Lyndon's community and civic involvement to boost his reputation while being true to herself was a balancing act. He needed affirmation; she played the part of a dutiful wife while also pursuing her own passions. It was a bargain with the devil that benefited her. I am sure that designing and sewing her own outfits and dressing up for social events was not a burden but a pleasure. She maintained her own self-worth and autonomy while doing what she must in order to support her husband.

I compare Sheila's situation to my disastrous marriage in Wisconsin. Did I trade off my independence to have the comfort of an upscale home? Was the price I paid, of quitting my librarian job I loved, to play the role of a devoted wife worth it? Somehow, after I realized I was married to a controlling and abusive husband, I lost confidence in myself. Sheila proved to be wiser about maintaining her self-esteem. She relished the time to pursue her own interests, all the while being the wife that Lyndon needed in the public eye. What went on behind closed doors is anyone's speculation.

The next day, I have a follow-up phone call with Bea. Once we greet each other, I start with, "If I write a book, I want to be careful with getting it right. You know, representing the real Sheila to the world."

"Oh, from our conversations, I'm pretty sure that you understand our Aunt Sheila." Bea is frank and upfront with her opinions.

"My sister is like Sheila, in that they both turned to art in their careers. I am like my aunt in the way she spoke her mind and wouldn't take guff from anyone."

"Can you give me a sense of her physical presence in a room?"

She laughs and replies, "There is an actress who played in one of those CSI series, a spin off maybe. This woman is petite, about the same height as Aunt Sheila, and the character she portrays is just the same sort of no-nonsense person as Sheila. You should look that up, then you'll have the perfect image in your head. Aunt Sheila was someone who didn't suffer fools and called a spade a spade. As children, we got up to shenanigans on the farm, but she called us on the carpet if we tried to put anything over on her."

I think I have seen this show which is set in L.A. and mentally put that on my list - check out CSI Los Angeles.

"You know, we are just so happy that you are interested in Aunt Sheila and want to tell her story. I told some friends of mine that you were thinking of writing a book about Sheila's life, and they all said they wanted to read it."

"I hope to write a novel. It's great to hear that your friends bring the total of potential readers up to ten."

"Don't sell yourself short. Look at all the research you've done in the past few months. You found us and that was something. We have had a lot of fun sharing our memories and photographs."

"I agree that my investigation has been very rewarding, and I'm thrilled to have found you both. I will keep you posted on my progress."

***

On my way home from work the next day, I drive to the Summit Lawn Cemetery, where they buried Lyndon with his mother's family. His gravestone is an unassuming granite marker, set close to the ground, in the shadow of his maternal grandparents' resting place. His parents' graves are close by. I sit down cross-legged, place some wildflowers next to his headstone, and lean in to have a quiet word with him about his aspirations in life. Despite all the negative things the sisters have told me, I reflect on all the positive newspaper reports and information that I have gleaned.

"Lyndon, you would be happy to know that people spoke highly of you when you died. There were two obituaries printed in the newspaper where you worked for your entire career. I believe many respected your passionate pursuit of history. Your musical endeavors and service to society no doubt brought peace and joy to others. Your mother would have been proud of all your accomplishments. You were a proud founding member of the Hamilton County Nature Study Club, which is still meeting and close to celebrating their one-hundred-year anniversary. I dare say that you would approve that your family's land will soon be open for people to walk in nature and appreciate the seasons."

I brush away some mown grass from his grave. "Your public persona has been well documented; your private life and relationships will remain shrouded in mystery. Sheila was an amazing woman and from what I've learned, I just think that you could have been a kinder husband."

Tracing his name in the rough stone, I whisper, "Please forgive me for whatever I get wrong if I ever write a book."

It seems fitting that when I get home and sort through the last few copies of sketches that Anna has given me, I notice that one is a lovely rendering of Lyndon's house in Noblesville, which her family refurbished. It is once again a dwelling that is filled with love.

There is a small dog, who I imagine is Whisky, on the front porch. On the reverse, it reads *"Noblesville 1979 - a home again."* Seeing the restoration after all those years, she must have felt at peace. Maybe Sheila contemplated how her life had returned to a level of calm and equilibrium now that she was an independent widow.

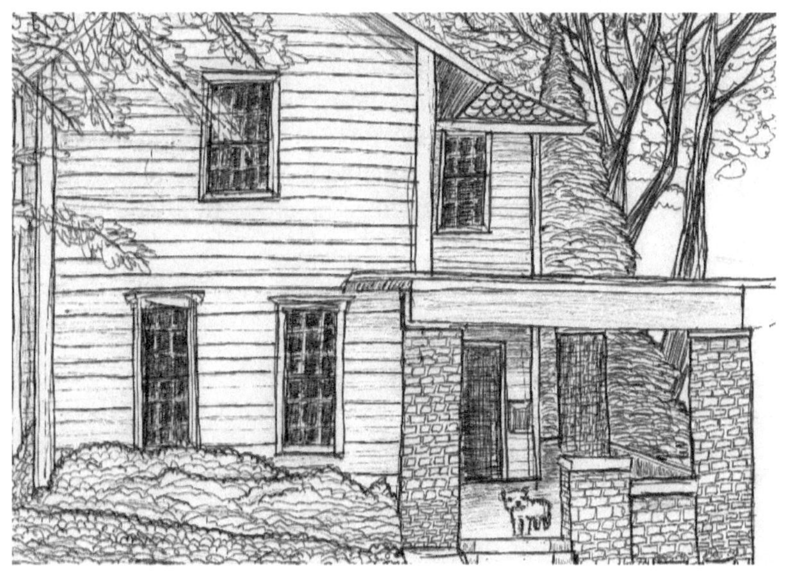

Chapter 20 - Sheila

"Let us be grateful to people who make us happy;
they are the charming gardeners who make our souls
blossom."

- Marcel Proust

Westfield, Indiana 1988

Sheila looks out the front window and sees that the photographer, who is a new member of the Hamilton County Nature Study Center, has arrived. His project is to take pictures of some of the long-standing members at their homes, highlighting their own gardens. She moves out to the front porch where her faithful and fierce-looking German shepherd is at his station in front of her; he growls menacingly when the stranger with the camera approaches. She quickly steps in between them, hushing her guard dog with a rub under his chin.

"Hello Michael, I am so glad that you found my nature hideaway. Don't worry about Dougan. He is just doing his job."

"And a fine job taking care of you so far off in the forest as you are. Are you ready for a few shots in front of your house? Then perhaps you can show off your beautiful trail."

"Of course, but the dog will be in every picture. He never ventures far from me," she admits.

"That's fine. Now both of you - smile!"

Dougan manages a doggie grin as best he can, sensing that his mistress is pleased and relaxed to have the camera pointed at them. She plays with his large ears, but they always revert to their alert and pointed state.

Sheila gestures to the path that meanders along the perimeter of her land, and they set off at her pace, which these days is a tad slower.

"I don't go anywhere now without my cromack," she says, holding out her old Scottish walking stick. Sheila poses for several more shots along the way.

"I bought it when I was back home for my niece's wedding. That was the last time I saw my sister, Biddy, in person. We were there in time to see the fields of heather blooming in the Scottish Highlands. Such a beautiful sight."

The day is fine, with a slight breeze that stirs the fallen leaves. The air has turned cooler, but the weather does not deter Sheila from her walks and her appreciation of the woods and meadows that surround her home.

"And you say that you walk this trail every day, no matter the temperature or precipitation?" the young man asks.

"Habits formed over years are hard to break. Besides, every time I set foot in these glorious surroundings, I observe something different; whether it be a new bird, the bud of the first flower of spring, or the beauty of the light reflected off freshly fallen snow. The colors are beautiful every day, from the blue hues of a cloudy afternoon to the welcome pinks of a sunrise. If I didn't complete my daily tour, I'd miss some breathtaking nature observation to share at the club meeting."

He stops to glance around at the view as Sheila extends her arm. "Pay attention or you will miss the glory." Michael nods in agreement.

They admire the sloping hillside behind them, where the magnificent trees reach for the sky. The waning afternoon light gives the meadow ahead a golden tint, lending a warm glow to each variety of grass that gently waves. They are in the middle of an enchanted place.

"Thank you, Mrs. Beals, for the tour. That is excellent advice about being more intentional in observing the natural world around me." He almost whispers the words so as not to break the spell.

Dougan barks and they both start.

"Please call me Sheila, and it looks like our guide is encouraging us to complete the circuit before we lose the light. He doesn't think that we should walk after dark."

They carry on, the young naturalist and his aging guide. She thinks he might have gained a new appreciation for the older members of the Club. They round back to the farmhouse, and Sheila listens intently as he talks about his aspirations to be a park ranger. She shares her wish that this property would become a nature preserve some day. Packing up his equipment, he thanks her again for allowing him to take photos. He will present his slide show at an upcoming meeting and promises to let her know the date.

Sheila heads inside to have her usual tea, toast with marmalade, and an apple cut neatly into quarters, feeding Dougan his kibble at the same time. She put some classical music on the record player. The young people in her life have offered to buy a better sound system, but she prefers to slip a record from its sleeve and gently place the tonearm onto the spinning vinyl. Tonight, it is *The Four Seasons* by Vivaldi. The two settle in for a quiet evening of reading and snoozing, Sheila in her favorite wingback chair, Dougan at her feet. Night falls, and the music enfolds them like a fluffy blanket as they rest content in their woodland retreat.

Village of Elgin, Scotland 1991

Taking this trip is her goddaughter's idea, but Sheila remembers having tea with Anna one day and wistfully talking about seeing her sister Mona one last time. Admitting her hopes for a visit was probably the seed planted that grew into this adventure. The last time she had been "across the pond" was for her niece's wedding in 1974; now it is 1991 and the pull of seeing Mona and Malcolm is strong. As soon as they get off the plane, she feels robust and confident. Going home is going to be bittersweet, but she is looking forward to showing Anna all the places she has told her about in those long-ago bedtime stories.

Her sister, Mona, is not well enough to meet them at the airport, but friends from the village of Elgin have offered to pick them up. That is the thing about living in a small village; everyone knows your business, yet there is always someone willing to lend you a hand. Mona and her husband Malcolm have certainly come alongside many of their neighbors. During the war, they looked out for refugees, feeding those in need, and housing couples and their young children. They had taken in Biddy and her daughter Susan for a time when their brother-in-law was overseas with the Royal Medical Corps. It seems everyone in town knows there will be visitors from America staying at the local B & B.

Seeing her sister for the first time in almost twenty years is emotional. She finds Mona sitting in the garden with her boxer dog named Bruno, standing sentinel. She smiles to see Mona feeding him treats under the table. Anna brings two cups of tea and gives them some privacy.

"Ach, here we are, two old ladies at leisure," Sheila says with a satisfied sigh.

"Don't you know how long I have been waiting for you? You should have come sooner!" Mona chides.

"I am getting too old to go gallivanting about. Why didn't you and Malcolm come to see me?" Sheila retorts.

"Malcolm takes pride in the fact that he hasn't been south of Edinburgh since 1938 and besides, we couldn't abide that man you married! He thought too much of himself."

"Mona, really, Lyndon died fifteen years ago!" Sheila laughs. "You'll have to come up with a better excuse than that."

"I appreciated every letter you sent asking us to come visit, but you know us. We don't travel far from home."

"You'd miss your dog too much?" Sheila raises an eyebrow.

Mona chuckles and takes a sip of her tea. "How different it would have been if we both had children. Imagine that out of all the siblings, only Biddy, the baby of the family, had daughters of her own."

"Here's my thought. There are plenty of children in this world who need our love without us being their parents. During the war, look how you took your neighbor's children under your wing; their parents were at their jobs, working night shifts, just trying to put enough food on the table."

"It's true that there have been children in the village that Malcolm and I have cared for as our own. And don't forget the time that Biddy and her wild child came to live with us when her husband was in the Medical Corps overseas. I prefer to take care of my wee doggies than to have children to worry about all the time. And here you are with your goddaughter, Anna, who is just like a child of yours, the way she fusses. Millie would be happy to see the two of you together."

Mona reaches over to scratch her dog behind his ear while he looks at his master with love. Was it their niece, Susan, who commented that Aunt Mona cared more for her dogs than children?

"I feel blessed to have Millie's children in my life. They call me 'Aunt Sheila' and take care of me as if I am family."

The women nod at each other in understanding. They think of the goddaughter who helped Sheila arrange the trip and whose laughter bubbles up when she hears a new story.

"Would you like to go down to the bottom of the garden to see where Malcolm buried my lovelies? Oh, how Biddy fussed when I wrapped each one of my dogs in a cashmere shawl from Johnson's Mill. She said that expensive cloth would have served her better than being buried in the ground! Stuff and nonsense that my beautiful boxers weren't worth the money. They have been my joy and comfort all these years."

Sheila reaches over and squeezes Mona's hand.

"I know."

Malcolm comes out to the terrace and coughs a little to signal his presence.

"Here they are. Are you ready for a drive to see where it all happened? Fordyce awaits." His bushy eyebrows rise. "Or we could go fishing!"

The sisters groan. Malcolm is president of the salmon fishing club.

Later that day, Anna and Sheila are standing next to the memorial for the Rev. John MacGregor.

"Aunt Sheila, I am so happy to be seeing all these places that you've told me about, like the village where you grew up. I'm so sorry that they turned the manse into a restaurant."

"Well, I was just a wee one when we lived there, and once our da was gone …" Sheila trails off.

"I'm glad that we could see where he is buried. Such a beautiful headstone."

"Aye, all the people that he helped wanted to honor his memory. They buried our mother with her family. We must drive by and see my grandparents' house. Then you will appreciate it when we tell the story about Mona and me playing a trick on poor Iain by dangling him out the second-story window by his heels."

"No!"

"We were young and left to our own devices, so we didn't realize what might have happened if we dropped him. It's a good thing the servant came running as he hollered and squirmed to get free. We got a thrashing that we remembered for days, but it was so worth it for the fun we had."

Coming home for steak and kidney pie, and a lovely orange drizzle cake for tea, they all gather in the back room while Malcolm stokes the fire. They sit comfortably and sip their whisky as the stories percolate like sparks from a summer bonfire. Mona relates the horrible ordeal of her accident and how the doctor who treated her burns only made them worse. She recounts the memories of her year being bedridden and how far back it had put her back in school. The only relief came when Sheila would creep in at night and tell her stories of the day and the mischief she had been up to. After Mona's recovery, Sheila remembers the trip to the TB sanitorium to visit their mother. A physician there had looked at her scars and commented in no polite terms on how the first doctor had botched her treatment. Mona chuckles and says how marvelous it was to hear the physician swear. They had sung for the other patients and Sheila had done a poetic recitation to great applause.

"Oh, do give us a repeat performance, Aunt Sheila," Anna encourages.

"Yes, give us some Robbie Burns, lass," Malcolm chimes in.

Sheila stands and starts in on the poem, *A Red, Red Rose*. Her lilting voice is like a song as she delivers all the lines, just as the Scottish poet would have composed them at his desk.

Applause erupts when she finishes. As Sheila and Anna prepare to leave, they all stand and sing softly,

For auld lang syne, my jo
For auld lang syne
We'll tak a cup o' kindness yet
For auld lang syne

Westfield, Indiana 1992

Home again and finished with travel for the foreseeable future, Sheila reflects on the memories of the trip. She is grateful that Anna has recorded the stories in a journal. She has just finished reading a letter from Mona, who says how happy the visit made her. It seems just like yesterday that she was in Scotland, though it has been over a year. She knows that her mind is not as sharp these days. There was the unfortunate incident when she took a shortcut across the frozen field. The driveway had looked icy, and she didn't think the farmer would mind. Bea was adamant that Sheila's driving days were now over.

The goddaughters keep hinting that she should not be living alone here in the country. Until now, she has stubbornly refused to contemplate a move from the farm. However, Sheila knows she will soon need a more secure place to live. The conversation she had with the young photographer, Michael, comes back to her. Can she afford to move to the city to live close to Bea and still donate this forest to create a nature preserve? Perhaps they can rent out the farmhouse? That would be a little income to pad her nest egg. Already she has turned away developers who are eager to build luxury homes on her land. She wants this property to be enjoyed by many, rather than a few elite people, making it their private domain. She writes a note to her lawyer and one to Anna.

The time has come. The forest will be open to everyone.

Chapter 21 - Meg (July)

"You've got to jump off the cliff all the time and build your wings on the way down."

-Ray Bradbury

Badger and I are out on the trail and, as we pass Bruce and his work crew, I wave and shout, "Happy Canada Day!"

"Well, we haven't seen you in a while. Happy what?"

"July First is the day we celebrate the great country of Canada. It's just like the Fourth here in America."

"Oh, I didn't know that. Eh?" He adds for effect.

Yes, that's how most people think Canadians end all our sentences, but I chuckle.

"Can you believe it's July already? How are the finishing touches coming along on the trail? I see that you're installing the information signs. What's the date for the official opening? I want to make sure I have it on my calendar."

"September 15th is the day, and we still have a lot to do. There are benches to install and a gazebo to build. We will get it done, mark my words." Bruce pauses. "I guess that means that you will move out soon."

"Sadly, yes. I'm going to miss this place terribly."

He grins, "Well, the good news is that you can come back anytime to walk. MacGregor Park will be open to everyone."

I smile in agreement. This is the realization of Sheila's dream - her forest accessible for all people to enjoy and appreciate as much as she did. Even though she probably dreaded leaving her home of almost forty years, Sheila knew she had to make way so the nature preserve could become a reality. Still, it must have been a difficult transition. It will soon be my turn to get on with my life in a new home. It's time to look for a new place to live.

Badger is circling around me, which means we need to carry on. We continue, and I'm curious to read the new panel titled "Sheila's Trail," which is close to the parking lot area. Disappointingly, the information about Lyndon and Sheila's wartime meeting in England is still in place. Anna claimed that the Park officials opted for the initial version they received from individuals they believed were knowledgeable about the story. Without definitive proof of facts to the contrary, they understandably don't want to incur the expense of creating a new sign.

I need to really focus on finding information about Lyndon's war service, but I don't have high expectations based on my initial research. Back in 1973, there was a fire at the National Personnel Records Center, the warehouse that housed military records, and many of the Army files were destroyed. Acting as a genealogist, I plan to send a request through for Lyndon's file and see if his military records still exist. My other effort will be to comb through old newspaper articles.

Putting aside the thoughts of more research for now, I go inside, get Badger settled with a treat, and gather my purse. My reference desk shift at work starts in an hour.

As I enter the library building through the back staff entrance, Brianna, one of the high school students who works at the circulation desk, waves me over.

"I didn't want to forget to tell you. There was this man asking for you yesterday." Sighing, she goes on, "He was so good looking for an old guy, tall, dark hair, blue eyes. You could never forget someone who looks like he could be a famous actor on TV. That smile."

Half listening, I'm rummaging in the mail slot for my name badge but stop when I hear this news. I sit down at my desk and spin my chair around.

"When I say old, I mean someone your age." Brianna giggles at her faux pas, but then looks over at me. "Are you okay? You look as pale as a ghost."

"Did he mention me by name?" I ask.

"Well, no. And now that I think about it, he just said he was looking for the new librarian who started last year."

"And what did you say?" I ask hesitantly, fearing the worst.

"Hmm. Only that you must have the day off, but you'll be here today," she admits. "I thought he might be a friend of yours from Minnesota."

I smile weakly. "Perhaps he had the wrong library. It doesn't sound like anyone I knew back home."

I had hoped that the situation with my ex-husband wouldn't be an issue so soon. A pang in my heart comes back as I remember the note that was delivered to me in April. Has he known that I work at this library since the man from Wisconsin came in with his mother? Had that accountant who recognized me mentioned it to coworkers and somehow the news reached Trent in jail?

Was I naïve enough to think that my escape from Trent could be as simple as a magician's disappearing act? Now you see her, then poof, she's gone without a trace. I left Wisconsin in the middle of the night, without giving a forwarding address, leaving my friends completely unaware of my destination. Just a puzzling disappearance with hurt feelings for some acquaintances. I secured a name change and a fresh start in a new community. Charlotte and I had been so careful about not putting anything on social media about my arrival in Indiana. All I wanted was to live under the radar for my first year and figure out if I needed to move again. Now I realize that I have become too comfortable here.

The only people who know everything at the library are Jan, George, and the police. Others on staff might have to be informed if this man is spotted. I make a quick call to Charlotte.

"I'll check with my Wisconsin friend who has been monitoring parole hearings. Stay calm and tell your boss, and I will get back to you as soon as I can," she cautions.

Shaking off the shiver that runs down my spine, I head toward Jan's office and knock before entering. She looks up and sees my anxious expression.

"I think Trent is in town."

"I will call the police so they can start doing a regular patrol. Do you want to go home?"

"No, I think I feel safer here."

The library has that hushed atmosphere as I take my turn at the information desk, tucked away in the non-fiction section. It is separate from the hubbub of the main entrance and children's story time, and that suits me just fine.

I hear Jan, who has positioned herself at the checkout counter, call out cheerfully, "Welcome to the library. Can I help you find anything today?"

It must be a stranger who has caught her attention. A tall gentleman with a confident stride has gone by without acknowledging the friendly greeting to the Westfield Library. I look up from the reference desk and see the stormy appearance of the man I thought I loved so long ago. He is scowling and has a determined look on his face.

"Hello Trent," I murmur in my calmest voice.

"Hello?" he bellows in rage and disbelief, and heads turn to watch the scene unfold. "Is that the only thing you have to say after disappearing into thin air?"

He charges toward me, reaching over the counter to take hold of my arm. I cringe and recoil with absolute dread. Words elude me as I watch Trent turn to those staring at us, sweet ladies who resemble startled deer in the headlights. "This cheating woman left me." Then he clutches me tighter, and his face clouds with bitterness and disgust. "I gave you so much and you do this? Abandon me without a word while I sit alone in a jail cell?"

My library director, bless her soul, shepherds the adult patrons out of harm's way. She watches me with concern: this is an impossible situation to predict, but that is why our plan is in place. George is also helping to keep people away and I'm sure that the police have been called. Still, I'm grateful when she returns to serve as a witness until they arrive.

My agitated ex-husband spits words in my face, "I have spent this past year trying to track you down, sick with worry, calling in all my favors, and here you are, Meg Livingstone. You disowned me and changed your name?"

As if possessed, Trent tightens his grip, causing me to cry out. "You're coming with me, you worthless piece of garbage." He laughs maniacally and adds, "Yeah, they'll thank me for taking out the trash."

Coming around the reference desk, he pulls me into an embrace, my back against his wide chest. I can feel his heart beating like a wild animal as he presses an icy blade against my throat. The smell of alcohol on his breath makes it hard for me not to gag as he hisses, "You are mine, dear wife."

What would Sheila do? I ask myself

Be strong and say no to this bully, I hear her say, *just like I stood up to Lyndon.*

I am sure the police would not approve of this action, but I agree with Sheila. Summoning the strength, I resolve to stop us from moving forward by digging in my heels.

Despite the wavering in my voice, I protest, "No! I don't belong to you." More firmly, I demand, "Let me go. Our divorce is final, and you are not supposed to be near me."

I am refusing to move, which momentarily shocks and surprises Trent. Then we both hear, "Sir, please let go of our librarian." Jan is now standing in front of us with hands up in a supplicant's pose. "We can work this out."

Distracted and losing patience, Trent snorts. This was supposed to be a snatch and grab affair. He didn't expect resistance.

"I'm not here to talk. I'm taking what's mine." Yanking me along, Trent knocks my director aside, but around the corner we run into a wall of blue. We halt as a burly male police officer blocks our way.

"Police. Down on the ground," he yells.

Trent is momentarily stunned by the sudden appearance of authority, but recovers and lunges toward him with his knife. I take this opportunity to squirm frantically away from my attacker. My boss pulls me to the side and puts herself in front of me. We back away, as the officer disarms Trent and forces my ex-husband's arm behind his back. More police have arrived, and the space reverberates with shouts and protests from my would-be kidnapper. Jan turns and her arms envelop me while the police arrest him; I collapse to the floor, trembling and crying tears of relief. An ambulance arrives and my EMT friend, Simon, helps me up and stays with me while I recover.

***

Charlotte is making tea in the kitchen and Badger is standing guard as I sit in my favorite chair in the den, a shawl around my shoulders to ward off the cool evening air. They took Trent away and Jan had called her after the only words I could say were: *I need Charlotte.* My friend brought me home from the hospital after they checked me over and documented my injuries. Wordlessly, she places a mug into my still shaking hands, and sits down beside me. I didn't recognize the weight of tension I have been carrying these past few months until today.

"Thank you for being here. What happens now?"

"Well, you're going to drink that red bush tea, and we are just going to rest here."

"Come to think of it, I feel as if Sheila saved my life today. She was my example and helped me stand up for myself. I shudder to think how badly events could have turned out." Shaking my head, I ponder, "How could Trent have made such a poor choice to confront me in the library?"

"Three cheers for Sheila for giving you the courage to say no. Trent's an idiot. That scumbag wanted to humiliate you in a public place, but you're alive and there is no need to go through the list of what ifs. He's in custody, and the police will escort him back to Wisconsin."

"I need to focus on my next steps. Move to another state and start again?"

"Trent should not determine where you live, but that is a discussion we can have later. Right now you just need to stay calm and take a deep breath. No decisions have to be made today. You need to take some time to recover from the attack.

Maybe someone can stay with you at the farmhouse for a few weeks?"

"You're right. No decisions right away, but I have found a home here, and friends. Carry on, as Sheila would say. I'm sure that I can find someone to sleep over until I feel more settled."

"That's the spirit. You belong here in Indiana. This is your home."

I stare at the trees outside the window. "My time at the farmhouse is going to be over in a few months, so I must make the most of soaking in the atmosphere of this woodland retreat that meant so much to Sheila. Then there's my writing project; I want to stay close to the people who can tell me their memories of her in person. Also, my goal is to resolve the discrepancies in the stories of how Sheila and Lyndon met. My work is not done."

Just as a distraction, I ask Charlotte to get Sheila's portfolio from my office. Anna was kind enough to sort through boxes of Sheila's art supplies and discovered a folder with some of her last sketches. She scanned most of them and gave me a thumb drive the last time we had lunch. We look through the ones that I printed out and then find a lovely drawing of a trio of women, sitting on what looks like a stone fence and facing off into the distance. It's only their backs that we can see, but I imagine these are the two people in Sheila's life who supported her the most. Sheila is in the middle and the others are probably her sister Mona and best friend Millie. The only face we can see is of a sweet little Westie snuggling up next to Sheila.

We both laugh. "Of course, there's a dog."

This may be my favorite sketch; Sheila has featured those women who helped most to inspire courage and steadfastness in her. I think of Charlotte, who assisted in the plan for my escape from Wisconsin and let me stay at her place when I first arrived in Indiana, just like Millie did for Sheila. I admire the bravery of Jan, who stood up to a deranged man and defended me today. There were so many people in Sheila's life who encouraged her just as my friends helped me to stand on my own and face my fears.

"When you feel up to it, we are going to drive into Noblesville and look at a few rental places. As you said, you'll be moving out just before the park opens."

I squeeze her hand and nod in agreement. I will stay in Indiana.

Chapter 22 - Sheila

"My little dog—a heartbeat at my feet."

- Edith Wharton

Noblesville, Indiana 1991

Sheila has taken a seat on her new front porch to watch as Anna and Bea and their teenagers carry furniture into the condo. She reaches down to ruffle the fur of her West Highland Terrier named Whisky. They are both a little at sea with the move, but happy to be together. Dougan found a different home with a neighbor, ending his days still romping in the countryside; Sheila and Whisky will shuffle along in the suburbs of Indianapolis.

In the last forty years as wife and widow, Sheila has lived in the same farmhouse and walked her forest trail daily. Making her half of this duplex feel like home will require a major adjustment on her part. Thankfully, there is a paved path leading into Forest Park, which is close by, so her morning outing will be where both she and her little dog can stretch their legs and create an alternate routine.

This accommodation is not her first choice, but she is grateful for the care of her nearby goddaughters, and she must come to terms with the ever-increasing unreliability of her aging body. Her sister Mona complains about her own move with Malcolm to a care home in Scotland, where they don't allow pets. At least here, Sheila can enjoy the companionship of her dog. Whisky looks up at her for confirmation that this will be where they sleep tonight. Wherever his mistress is, he is content.

"How about a walk, Whisky? Shall we find some squirrels?" she asks, picking up his leash.

A little bark and wag of the tail is his response. They see Bea and Anna on the way out, organizing the kids they have wrangled into helping her move.

"We're going for a wee amble," she says to them. "Thank you for moving in my things."

Sheila turns to the young men who are carrying her boxes of books that she insists must be within reach in her new reading nook and cautions, "Those are heavy, so watch your backs!"

Bea looks at her, "Please don't get lost."

"Always worrying about me? Whisky will know the way back, won't you, my friend?" Sheila winks at her dog.

They set off to explore the neighborhood where they will spend the next chapter of their lives, Whisky adjusting his stride to her slower pace. There will be time enough to sniff out and mark his favorite trees. For now, Sheila leads the way into this next adventure.

***

Over the next few years, her sisters pass away, like petals falling from a beautiful bouquet. She grieves for Mona and Biddy, the siblings who made it into old age with her. Sheila mourns the loss of comforting letters that bridged the distance between them.

She gets one last letter from an aging Malcolm, who is also missing Mona. He explains that the people at the care home informed him of the need to deal with his papers. While sorting through things, her brother-in-law came across the graduation certificates from Gray's School of Art in Aberdeen, the school where she and Mona both studied years ago. He enclosed her copy and Sheila fingers the old parchment, thinking of her dream of being a fashion designer.

She has taken up sketching again, and the familiarity of charcoal in hand brings to mind the classes she took at the Herron School of Art in Indianapolis. Sheila wonders what happened to the art portfolio that was her pride and joy when she first was acclimatizing to life in America. She had done ink sketches to chronicle her life and wishes now that she could look back through them.

The Druthers are still going strong, but daytime meetings are now quarterly and hosted in the homes of some of the members' daughters. The Christmas gathering is a highlight; since someone else is providing rides, no one has to worry about driving when they pass around glasses of sherry and toast the members no longer with them. It's at moments like these that Sheila feels the absence of Millie the most, wanting to just sit with her old friend and reminisce about old times.

To keep her mind active, she arranges for Anna to take her to the Hamilton East Public Library each week to check out new books that keep her company when she is alone. Every time she walks into the building, she remembers many happy hours as a librarian in Westfield. Sheila is grateful for the company of her goddaughters and their families, which now include married children and grandchildren. There are holidays to celebrate and parties to attend, but she also appreciates quiet evenings at home with her books and her dog.

She is keen to hear stories about the people who rent her farmhouse, from Anna's daughter and her son-in-law to a lively group of art students who create woodland creatures out of timber found in the backyard. It warms her heart to know that they have not abandoned the house and that there are those who still wander the paths she trod.

The seasons pass and, while life sometimes feels overwhelming and unpredictable, the rhythm of nature is reliable. She no longer has a garden of her own to tend, but she admires the flower beds in the neighborhood. Sheila can still spot wildlife in Forest Park and has a little bird feeder outside her window. Evenings are challenging, as she feels exhausted by the end of the day, so her attendance at the Nature Study Club meetings tapers off. Her daily walks with Whisky are a time to feel the wind on her face and the sun on her skin. As long as she can go outside, she feels anchored by the earth under her feet.

Indianapolis, Indiana 1998

While her mind is clear, Sheila has come to terms with the frailty of her slight frame. She knows that the time will come when she joins her family and friends who have gone on ahead. These are not morbid thoughts, just reality. While she has had many passions - art, literature, dogs - she wants her love for the natural world to be her lasting legacy.

Her inquiries about the negotiations for her forest becoming a nature preserve are regular, but responses from the township and Anna and Bea are vague. Sheila knows the girls are conscious of her desires and recognizes that patience is necessary. However, she will feel more at ease when the deed is done, and they protect her land from the encroachment of suburban development. She resolves not to die until then.

***

Sheila shifts in the leather seat, just one of the luxurious seating options in the plush lawyer's office. Her goddaughters and their husbands are close by; Sheila reaches for the comforting feel of her dog's fur. Her hand comes away empty. No dogs allowed in this building; they told her. She wonders why these Americans have no regard for how important it is to have a loyal friend at your side, no matter the occasion. Smoothing her stylish dress, she sits up straighter. Official looking paperwork is on the polished table in front of her, and the lawyer is explaining the pending transaction.

"Mrs. Beals …" he begins.

"Please, just Sheila," she interrupts.

"Of course, Sheila. The document before you states your intention to donate 42 acres of your Westfield property to the Westfield Washington Township Parks & Recreation Department for the creation of a nature park which will be minimally developed and used only for passive nature activities. Does that reflect your wishes accurately?"

"Yes, indeed. As my forest has brought me joy, it is only proper to dedicate it to the quiet surrender and enjoyment of nature. I wish to have the forest remain as undisturbed as possible."

"Then all being in order, it is time for you to sign."

Sheila takes up the pen and adds her signature to the sheet of paper that will make her dream come true. Her forest and the meadows and the burbling creeks will be safe, and soon others will discover the joy of walking the trails.

Indianapolis, Indiana 1999

Sheila must adapt to another new rhythm in the retirement home. Living on her own turned out to be too challenging, and this new facility is a place where staff provide her meals and administer her medications. She has her own room that she shares with Whisky, and they make do with short walks about the property.

She wakes one morning to see the leaves spiraling from tree branches outside her window, and she has a sudden urge to walk over to her best friend's house. With her bathrobe carefully cinched at her waist, Sheila sets off determinedly. She has a vague idea about the direction of Millie's home but gets turned around and calls out with agitation as she scans for street signs.

"Millie! Millie!"

If only her friend could hear her, she would come and take her home. It's hard to concentrate with the noise of the traffic and blaring horns.

A woman's voice says, "Ma'am. Are you lost? Here, let's get you off the road."

She feels a hand grasp her elbow and steps up to the sidewalk. Sheila clasps this unfamiliar woman's arm.

"Do you know where Millie lives? She's my best friend, and I haven't seen her in such a long time."

"Let's sit on this bench together. First, tell me where you live. Maybe we can find someone there who knows the way to Millie's place."

"I think I live at an old folks' home that has a name about trees, but there are more buildings than greenery. I much preferred living in my farmhouse."

"Do you mean Forest Crossings? I noticed it a few blocks back from here. Shall I call them? What is your name?"

Sheila looks at this concerned stranger and knows she is not Millie; thoughts of the past and the present are all mixed up in her mind.

"I am Sheila MacGregor, newly arrived from London, England. My friend Millie was kind enough to invite me to Indiana. I am living at her house while I get settled and look for employment. I seem to have lost my way, but I know her house is on 53rd Street, here in Indianapolis."

Sheila marvels as this lady sitting beside her who taps on a glass device then holds it to her ear. She hears her talk to someone about an old woman whom she found wandering in the middle of the busy road.

Why hadn't she brought Whisky along? He would have guided her in the right direction.

Indianapolis, Indiana 2001

Sheila sits in the common room, dressed and propped up with pillows. Her eyes are closed, and her hand rests on her beloved white dog. She senses visitors and overhears their hushed conversation.

"I'm sad to see her looking so frail. I hope they don't let her walk outside like the last time. Imagine finding her wandering down 86th Street in her bathrobe, calling out for my mom? I'm also worried about how attached she is to that stuffed animal," Anna says with a catch in her voice.

"At least she's comfortable and feels she has a canine companion to keep her company," her husband suggests. "The move to memory care was the right decision. Just consider how fortunate we were to get all the legal documents in place before her decline. Now we can carry out her wishes and this park will be her legacy to show how much she loved nature."

Sheila opens her eyes, and a smile plays on her wrinkled face as she notices this middle-aged couple.

"Millie and Bud, how very nice of you to come and see me."

"No Aunt Sheila, Millie was my mom. I'm her daughter Anna, and we have come to visit you. How are you feeling this morning?"

Sheila turns to look at them both and tries to rise out of her chair.

"How about a nice cup of tea for you both? I'll just pop into the kitchen and put the kettle on."

"No need. We've both had breakfast and we're fine right now. You stay put." Anna says with a reassuring hand on her shoulder.

Sheila nods and repositions the dog on her lap.

"I want to show you the design of the entrance sign for your park that will open soon." Anna gets out her portfolio and Sheila starts in surprise.

"Oh, MacGregor Park! That's my family's name. Where is this park?"

"Auntie, remember your farmhouse and the beautiful forest? This sign will go at the entry to the nature preserve that you envisioned for your property in Westfield. People from the Park Department are going to come tomorrow and present you with an award for your generous donation. We hope you are happy that your park will open soon."

A light goes on in Sheila's eyes, and it's as if the idea of a nature preserve has turned a switch on. "My trees, oh yes, now I remember. Ach, no fuss and bother for me about getting an award. I am only relieved that the developers won't be building houses in my forest!" She sighs, remembering the feel of the autumnal breeze on her face and the sound of crunching leaves underfoot.

Her memories swirl and fade and she glances up at Anna.

"Oh, good. Are you here to help me? I was wondering when Whisky and I could take our walk along the trail. You know we go out every morning no matter what the weather is like. Brave wee boy; he doesn't mind the cold or rain." She gives her dog a scratch behind his ears and an affectionate hug.

"Well, we will have to see about the walk, but we'll be back for the ceremony. We love you Aunt Sheila," Anna says, and with warm embraces, they leave.

Sheila bends over and whispers to her stuffed toy, who is a realistic facsimile of her beloved pet Whisky.

"I can't imagine for the life of me what exactly those people wanted, can you? Did I not ask nicely if they could help me up so we could take our daily constitutional? We cannot miss walking our trail together." She drifts back into pleasant memories until she wakes up in bed.

"Good morning Mrs. Beals." The distilled sunlight filters through the curtains as she opens her eyes. She wonders why they insist on using her married name.

"Please, call me Sheila."

"Okay Miss Sheila, time to rise and shine," is the pert reply from a woman dressed in what looks like a nurse's uniform.

Thoughts skitter through her head: *How can I manage another day? Where is my best friend, Millie? Today is the perfect day for an outing. Where are my dogs?*

"Today is a special day at Forest Crossings, Miss Sheila," another attendant prattles on. "We must get you up and ready for your special visitors."

As they help her dress, she resumes her thoughts: *So why is this place called Forest Crossings when no one is going anywhere? And where are the majestic trees? When was the last time I had visitors? I am a pilgrim in a strange land. All those I love have gone on ahead. Who is coming to see me?*

Slowly, the name Millie comes to her mind: *A kindred spirit. Millie had a baby girl. Let's call her Anna, she whispered to me. I clasped the tiny hand and vowed to be a caring godmother. Anna and I got into such mischief. Could Mille and her charming husband Bud be coming to take me away? Back to my woodland retreat?*

"Really, Mrs. Beals. Time is of the essence. You must dress and have your breakfast."

She sighs and raises her arms like an obedient child, shivering in the chill morning. *Whatever is the fuss all about?* She pats her dog Whisky and smiles. *Ready for a walk, old thing?*

Officials from the Westfield Washington Township Parks & Recreation Board are making speeches about her generosity and handing her an award. Anna and Bea are there with their husbands, looking so happy. She takes the plaque and reminds them that the forest is to remain untouched. A gentleman assures her that will be the case. That is all Sheila needs to hear, and as the talk flows around her, she enjoys her cup of tea.

Chapter 23 - Meg (August)

"I may not have gone where I intended to go, but I think I have ended up where I intended to be."

- Douglas Adams

It's no wonder that I love reading mystery novels. The female detective catches and neutralizes the criminals by the end of the book. In addition, after resolving all her personal issues, she starts a new life, happy and content. Everything tied up with an enormous bow. I sigh. Too bad that's not my current situation.

Yes, they arrested Trent, and he will face charges of aggravated assault, attempted kidnapping, and violation of my restraining order. He is currently in jail here in Indiana; is it too much to dream about the police sending him back to Wisconsin to face charges of violating his parole? I don't even want to think about his upcoming trial and the aftermath of his actions. There are days when I feel like throwing my possessions in my car and just driving off with Badger with no plan but escape.

Then I stop and remember all that has happened over the last year and say a prayer of gratitude for my friends here in Indiana who have supported and sheltered me. Charlotte has been by my side through thick and thin. The members of the Boundaries support group keep checking in with me and sending texts of encouragement; many of them have faced similar situations with abusive partners. Jan and George have been amazing at work, covering my shifts at the library so I can have a couple of days to recover. That gives me time to take a trip to Indianapolis so I can deliver a letter to a woman who has inspired me by her example of resilience and fortitude. I don't think I could have found the courage to stand up to Trent without her.

There is a hush in the air, and I may be the only one in this austere and historic building. I've been wandering around Crown Hill Cemetery's mausoleum for almost an hour, looking for Sheila and her friend Millie. I'm almost ready to quit. In the main building, the Peace Chapel is lovely, and I stop to admire the beautiful stained-glass window. I imagine sitting in the pew during the funerals for these two beautiful women alongside the Druthers members. As I realize there is another building, my search continues. Anna sent me photos of Millie and Sheila's resting places, and I finally spot the adage *To Thine Own Self Be True* etched above Millie's name. I place my hand on the cool marble and consider this is the closest I will be to Sheila's best friend. Bea told me that her mother wanted a view of water, and I look out onto the quiet pond outside the window at the end of this hallway. The birds' chirping outside filters in to suffuse the peaceful stillness with the sounds of nature. Sheila is in a columbarium niche, just around the corner. I smile to see that the person who engraved her name put *MacGregor* in the large font and *Beals* in a smaller font. I sit on a bench and quiet my thoughts. This is a solemn moment to honor a woman I've spent the last year pursuing. With a deep breath in, I read my letter to her out loud.

Dear Sheila,

Let me introduce myself. My name is Meg Livingstone, and I have been renting your farmhouse for the last year. I also have your senior art portfolio and will give it to your goddaughters soon. The sketches have given me glimpses into your past, and I appreciate your bravery and spunk. I am grateful for your example of facing difficulties with a "carry on" attitude.

Anna and Bea have encouraged me to write a book based on what I have learned while researching your life. I really hope to do my best in depicting you, Millie, and the other Druthers - such a lovely group of women. It's

Folding my note to Sheila in half, I slip it into a crack. Wiping a tear away, I stand and check that the hallway is empty. All is quiet, so on a whim, I open my phone and press play on a bagpipe recording of *Scotland the Brave*. With the distinctive reedy notes trailing behind me, I leave with a smile on my face, knowing that Sheila would have been pleased.

Returning home, I organize my research files to prepare for setting up my new home office. As soon as I move, in the middle of the month, I want to get back to writing about Sheila. Bruce and his crew have finished installing all the interpretive signs. I am even more determined to find irrefutable proof that the story of Lyndon and Sheila meeting in London during the war is erroneous. One half of the puzzle is to confirm that Lyndon did most of his service with the Army stateside or in the Pacific arena, not in Europe. The other half needed is evidence that Sheila came to America because of Millie's invitation, not Lyndon's.

Despite the hubbub of packing, I couldn't sleep one night and while searching the online newspapers, happened upon an article in the Noblesville Ledger about Sheila winning a Women's Club fashion competition in 1962. At work, I print out the news clipping, which includes a photo of Sheila wearing an outfit that she designed and sewed herself. The photo is black and white, but the reporter describes her brown and gold-colored patterned wool crepe dress and coat. A gold-braid hat, long black cloth gloves, and black kid shoes and bag complete her ensemble. A well-known sewing instructor as chairperson of the judging committee is quoted as saying they chose the winning outfit based on appropriateness for club occasions, becomingness to the wearer, overall fashion effect, and workmanship. Sheila evidently scored 96 out of a possible 100 points.

I find Sheila's achievement impressive, and the information proves that she was a skilled seamstress and designer. However, the additional personal comments drew my attention.

The newspaper reporter asks when Mrs. Beals first began sewing. *"Oh, it was many years ago,"* Sheila replies, *"when I was a young girl attending boarding school in my native country of Scotland. Each evening, one of our instructors read to us for an hour and during that time we did hand-sewing. Perhaps that's when I started to enjoy it."*

Sheila adds that the reason for her visit to America 15 years ago was initially to visit a girlfriend in Indianapolis, but she ended up staying. She lived with Millie and attended art school at night with the goal of pursuing her dream of fashion design. Three years later, she met Lyndon and was married soon after.

"Music and flowers are hobbies we both enjoy at our home, just north of Westfield."

Excitedly, I share the newspaper article with Anna and Bea. The account authenticates that Sheila's reason for coming to Indiana was Millie's invitation, not to follow her fiancé after WWII. We are one step closer to disproving the sign, with a quote in Sheila's own words.

The sentence about their mutual hobbies strikes a note with me. Music and flowers. Sheila found common ground with Lyndon, creating sources of joy amidst what Bea insists was a troubled marriage. Doesn't every relationship start with attraction and passion? My own reflections about Trent start with memories of delight in his devotion to me. He showered me with gifts and treated me to nights out on the town to win my affection. Caught up in the whirlwind of romance and the promise of a lifetime of security, I didn't see the signs of manipulation and deceit. Too late did I discover the real Trent. By then I was married and, like Sheila, striving to make the best of a challenging situation.

Lyndon died, and that event released Sheila. Trent is back in jail, and I am determined to live my life with optimism despite the continued threat of his return. I am planting my flag in Indiana, investing in new pursuits and relationships. I even have a date with Simon to go see the newest Star Wars movie.

For now, I tuck the photocopy of the old article in a file folder labeled *Change the sign* and continue with my packing.

***

My day to move has come and I'm sad to be leaving this snug little home in the woods. Charlotte is waiting out on the front porch, giving me time to say goodbye to the farmhouse. The original furniture will stay, and I go to each room for one last look. Upstairs, I touch the dresser in Sheila's bedroom, remembering the art school locker receipt for her portfolio that fluttered down and launched my research into her interesting life. From the window, I can see her cherished forest and a glimpse of the golden meadow from above.

Coming down the stairs, I take a step into the den at the back of the house, picturing the scene of my friend pouring wine and vowing to stay the night to map out my options after hearing about Trent's parole. Here is Sheila's comfy wingback chair, where I often got lost in a good book. I walk through to the cheery kitchen and run my hand over the smooth wooden tabletop, where I shared cups of tea with people who cared about me. Sheila did the same with her friends. The last area to visit is her old office, set off to the side of the front entrance. This space is where I sat at her desk with my laptop. I spent many hours here with Badger at my feet, working late into the night, caught up in my detective pursuits. According to Anna, this was where Sheila had her sewing machine, material, and art supplies.

I smile, remembering the last copy of Sheila's sketches that Anna printed out for me - it was of Whisky, her West Highland Terrier. Both of us found solace and an outlet for our creativity here, and I'm grateful for the opportunity to follow her trail over the last year.

A little bungalow in Noblesville will be my next rental, and I will have the footpaths at Forest Park to explore with Badger. The official opening of MacGregor Park is next month, and I plan to attend and walk in Sheila's footsteps again. Unfortunately, I will have to pass by the sign with the inaccurate story of Sheila and Lyndon's meeting in England. I don't blame the park officials for wanting definitive evidence disproving the original account before making changes. After all, I heard that same London story from two different people when I first started my research. The person in charge of the signage no doubt felt reliable sources had provided a truthful version of that first encounter. Sheila's goddaughters and I will all rest easier when they correct the information.

Charlotte and I load my belongings in both our cars. I have been buying some used furniture for my new home, but just the basics. Raffi and some of his friends will meet us in Noblesville to unload the bigger pieces. I want to take my time to find a special desk for my new writing room. My dream is to write a historical novel that is partly based on Sheila's life, using my notes and research. That project will keep me busy for the next year at least.

I gather up one last box containing my purse, Sheila's art portfolio, plus all the other sketch printouts, and the notebooks and files that have been a source of fulfillment and inspiration. Stepping slowly outside, I take the steps down from the front porch and Charlotte opens my car door for me. Badger has one last sniff and scrambles into the car.

Turning to Charlotte, I nod and say, "I think Sheila would agree. It's time for me to move on."

***

I miss living at the farmhouse and having the pleasure of nature just outside my front door. Our new little rental off the downtown square in Noblesville suits Badger and me just fine. We are close to the White River, which meanders through the center of town; it's an easy jog across the pedestrian bridge over the waterway to the lovely old Forest Park. I have learned that the founder of the Hamilton County Nature Study Club, Dr. Brooks, and other members mapped out these forest trails nearly one hundred years ago. For me, it is like walking in the past.

Speaking of this area's history, I have been combing digitally through old newspapers. I'm in search of the last piece of the puzzle about how Sheila met Lyndon. My goal is to disprove that they first became acquainted in London, England. Thankfully, I uncovered that article where Sheila says her friend, Millie, invited her to Indiana.

Now, the key is tracking down Lyndon's army service record. I print out the form requesting his army records as a genealogist, since his time in the military is over sixty years ago. It's discouraging to get a form letter back from the National Archives and Records Administration stating they could not locate any information concerning Lyndon Beals.

Finally, I'm overjoyed to happen upon a lengthy newspaper account from the Noblesville Daily Ledger dated February 13, 1946, titled "Lyndon K. Beals Returns Home." I suspect Lyndon composed the article himself; it starts with a meticulous outline of his Army training and service stateside. He then gives details of being assigned to the Headquarters South Pacific Base Command in New Caledonia in 1944. Ironically, it seems Lyndon himself has disproved the theory that he brought Sheila to Indiana.

So, during the war, Lyndon was in the South Pacific and Sheila was a Land Girl in England. Curious to think about how Lyndon and Sheila would no doubt have shared their wartime experiences with each other. Was it too painful to talk about how her brother served in the Pacific arena and was captured and held in a Japanese prisoner of war camp? Iain MacGregor died in captivity and was buried on an Indonesian island. Lyndon survived and returned to his home.

I can't wait to share the official documentation with Charlotte, Anna, and Bea. This proof is exactly what we need to correct the historical record. Anna will be in touch with the parks department, and we will wait to hear their response. My file folders sit beside my new desk in a sunny alcove. I have made copies of some of Sheila's sketches and framed some of them to hang in my writing nook. Whisky, who was Sheila's last dog, looks down on me from the wall, with a hopeful look on his face.

Chapter 24 - Sheila

"Everybody needs beauty as well as bread, places to play in and pray in, where nature may heal and give strength to body and soul alike."

- John Muir

Indianapolis, Indiana 2002

The Peace Chapel is aglow with the light that filters in through an amazing floor-to-ceiling stained glass window that was donated by the Eli Lilly family. Sheila would have met Mr. & Mrs. Lilly through the Hamilton County Nature Study Club meetings. Bea and Anna are in the front row; they've been here twice before for the funerals of their parents, Millie and Bud. There is a piano on the platform at the front, but a bagpiper provides the music that Sheila loved so much as he comes up the aisle playing *Amazing Grace*. Everyone stands, and there is not a dry eye in the place.

Millie's children gather at Anna's home, together with the few remaining members of the Druthers club, to celebrate the life of Sheila MacGregor. Exchanging stories of summers on the farm, they pass around a few photos. They have other aunts and uncles, but this woman was special. She weathered many storms, yet life had not beaten her down. Sheila carried on with a stiff upper lip and a sense of humor. She had lived her life with joy, especially in the company of her dogs. Most of all, she felt at home in nature, always taking a hike in all kinds of weather until her body had failed her. Even then, she would ask for details of the park that would be her legacy. No, she didn't need her name on the sign at the entrance - why would they do such a thing? She only wanted to protect her trees from being cut down and preserve a place for the wildflowers and the birds - and trails for the dogs.

Sheila's goddaughters invite everyone in attendance to meet up again at the official park opening, which is still a few years off. They all raise a glass of sherry or whisky. Sheila MacGregor will be warmly remembered by Millie's family and by all who will walk her trail.

Epilogue - Meg

"The best remedy for those who are frightened, lonely, or unhappy is to go outside, somewhere they can be alone, alone with the sky, nature and God. For then and only then can you feel that everything is as it should be and that God wants people to be happy amid nature's beauty and simplicity."

- Anne Frank

MacGregor Park

Anna was happy to present officials at the park with evidence that contradicts the original story of Lyndon and Sheila meeting in England during the war. They received the information, and with little fanfare, installed a corrected sign. No matter how that first version came about, we plan to have a little party to celebrate the new plaque titled "History of Sheila MacGregor Beals."

A small group of women gather around to admire the verified account of how a remarkable woman came to Indiana. If Sheila were present, I imagine she would ask, *whatever is all the fuss about?* I picture her half smile as she bends to pat the head of her faithful Whisky, then the two of them head off to complete their daily trail walk. Thinking back to the obituary I found, was the injustice huge, to have Sheila misrepresented as just a homemaker? I think so. The woman donated her land as a way of preserving this mighty forest land from the encroachment of developers. She also had such an interesting life and faced so much loss with grace.

Other women in her life came alongside and kept her going; this park is as much a tribute to the friendship and power of ordinary women carrying on in the face of adversity as it is a remembrance of Sheila. Scotland would always be her true home, but this forest was Sheila's dwelling place where she ultimately found shelter and peace.

She left a glorious place of nature to mark her extraordinary life.

Sheila is still here in spirit.

***

Sitting down on a bench in the middle of MacGregor Park, I feel that I have finally come to the end of my research. I am now ready to finish writing about this amazing woman. Just as I had invited Sheila back into her farmhouse, I now ask for permission to chronicle her life's journey as a historical novel.

Before Sheila can object to the project, I say, "It's not just for you, but for all the women out there who dare to forge into places unknown and who deserve to be noticed. They have the potential to be an encouragement to those around them. Do you realize that you have inspired me to be brave and dream about making my mark in the world?"

With her Scottish brogue, I hear Sheila's soft but strong voice in my head, "*Well, what are you waiting for?*"

Pen in hand, I start to edit my first draft.

~ The End ~

Author's Notes

Not Just a Homemaker: The Extraordinary Life of Sheila MacGregor is a work of fiction inspired by true events. When my husband and I moved to Indiana in 2019, we discovered the trails of MacGregor Park. Captivated by the lovely park photo of Sheila who wanted her beautiful forest protected, I began my four-year research project to uncover the story of this woman of nature.

At the beginning, I read the story posted on an informational sign which stated: *Sheila MacGregor Beals was brought here from Scotland by her husband, Lyndon Beals, after WWII. They met in England during the war while she served as driver for officers.* It sounded like a romantic tale, and I wanted to know more. A pivotal moment was finding Sheila's scant obituary, compared to both of Lyndon's two detailed memorials. The summary of her life seemed to be that she was Lyndon's widow and a homemaker. I knew it was an injustice for any woman to be known only as just a housewife, and that thought spurred me on to digging deeper into her life and times.

It puzzled me to find a five-year gap between Sheila's arrival in 1947 and her subsequent marriage in 1952, which didn't seem to mesh with the passion of a wartime love affair. Everything changed when I discovered Sheila's friend Millie, with her name and address listed on Sheila's immigration form as her destination. When I tracked down two of Millie's daughters, who as goddaughters considered Sheila as part of their family, they confirmed my suspicions. Their mother, not Lyndon, invited Sheila over to Indiana and gave her a place to live until her wedding. After meeting them, my mission was two-fold: find the documentation that would correct the park sign story and prove that Sheila was so much more than just a homemaker.

Most of the narrator Meg's discoveries were like my journey of putting together genealogical timelines and identifying the people in Sheila's life who knew her best. The challenge in writing historical fiction is fabricating scenes and conversations that remain true to what I have learned about the main characters. I remain indebted to Millie's daughters, who spent time with me, sharing memories and photos of their Aunt Sheila. They both watched over Sheila after Millie's death in 1986.

As a librarian, I am familiar with the genealogy website Ancestry.com and found a lot of personal information about Sheila, Lyndon, and Millie. Thanks to the local library databases, including Newspapers.com and archives of the local Noblesville Ledger newspaper, I found vital answers to the many questions about family relationships and timelines. Newspaper reporting back in the day resembles our present-day social media platforms, naming names and giving details to everyday life occasions. I could track the various club meetings that Sheila attended, along with wedding notices, obituaries, and the like. In print, they recorded the social lives of citizens, making this resource a treasure trove of information.

Sheila was born in Fordyce, Scotland, and her father was the Presbyterian vicar. Orphaned at a young age, her family moved in with her maternal grandparents. Sadly, she had lost her parents and grandparents by the time she was 10 years old. I found the teenaged Sheila's name on a ship's manifest bound for South Africa and verified that she had an uncle and aunt who lived in the Transvaal. In the early 1930s, she traveled to Nyasaland (today's Malawi) to serve as a children's nurse for a British doctor, his wife, and young daughter. They all stayed for three years. While her presence in Africa is accurate, the characters and scenes are the product of my imagination. I have seen old photos of a woman named Nurse Muir who worked at the Blantyre Hospital around the same time, who had a reputation of giving medical support throughout the region. She was a fun character to recreate.

When the goddaughters hinted that their aunt might have had a romantic attachment during the war, I conjured up Gilbert to be that man. Sheila sailed back to England alone, and I found her at an address in a Kensington neighborhood in London upon her return.

Much to my delight, I found a memoir written by Sheila MacGregor's actual niece, Sue MacGregor, who had a successful career in the British Broadcasting Corporation with her own show called *The Woman's Hour*. In her memoir, *Woman of Today: An Autobiography*, [Headline Publishing Group, 2003] she mentioned that Biddy, her mother who was Sheila's younger sister, was working in London around the same time that Sheila lived there. Ms. MacGregor also recounts how, during WWII, when her father was posted overseas, she and her mother took a trip to Holcroft Farm to visit her Aunt Sheila, where she was working as a Land Girl. She also mentions an encounter with Aunt Topsy. That account, along with family stories from Millie's daughters, served as verification that Sheila and Millie volunteered together in the Shrewsbury countryside during the war.

The Internet Archive is an American nonprofit digital library founded in 1996 by Brewster Kahle. It provides free access to collections of digitized materials, which meant I could access old Indianapolis City Directories in search of where Sheila first lived when she arrived in Indiana. She was renting with Bud and Millie until she got married. With the help of Ancestry.com and resources such as the Internet Library and online newspapers, I found Sheila's immigration forms listing her friend Millie as her intended destination and her occupation as designer. On her wedding announcement, she listed her education as having graduated from Gray's School of Art in Aberdeen, Scotland. Sheila was a talented artist and an accomplished seamstress. When she won a Westfield Women's Club Fashion Contest, a local reporter wrote about how Sheila revealed she moved to Indiana at the invitation of her friend Millie.

The city of Noblesville has a charming downtown, Lyndon's childhood home has been restored, and the parks in Hamilton County are as lovely as described in my book. However, because the Blatchley Nature Study Club is private, I moved its location up the White River a few miles north and referred to it by its original 1922 club name of the Hamilton County Nature Study Club. Every year in mid-April, when the spring wildflowers bloom, members hold a Wildflower Walk that is open to the public. I highly recommend the activity if you are in the Noblesville area! You can find them on Instagram: https://www.instagram.com/blatchleynaturestudyclub/

An article posted in the Noblesville Ledger in 1945, titled <u>Lyndon K. Beals Returns: Discharged After Four Years Service in Army</u>, listed every detail of his military career. Contrary to the information on the original park sign that claimed he met Sheila in wartime England, he did not serve in the European Theater. After several years at Camp Breckenridge in Kentucky, they assigned Lyndon to the South Pacific Base Command of Admiral William F. Halsey on New Caledonia, just off the coast of Australia.

Curiously, I talked to two people who knew Lyndon personally and heard them repeat the description of how Lyndon met Sheila in England during the war and that he brought her to America. How that flawed account came about is a mystery, but I made up a scenario to explain how others may have heard the story from Lyndon and believed his faulty version of events. I am happy to report the actual story of how Sheila ended up coming to Indiana is now corrected on the MacGregor Park sign.

Meg's joy at working at the library is in line with the fond memories I have from my former job at the Elm Grove Public Library in Wisconsin. It was a delight to learn that Sheila was a part-time librarian herself at the Washington-Westfield Public Library in the 1970s.

The Druthers was indeed a group of women who, all except one, immigrated to Indiana from the British Isles after WWII. They found comfort and friendship with each other being so far from home. Meeting the last living member of the club and hearing about her memories was a highlight of my research journey. This delightful centenarian was alert and keen to share her own wartime experiences and impressions of Sheila and Millie.

My goal was to introduce readers to an extraordinary woman of nature who loved her dogs and the forest that now is MacGregor Park. She traveled the world and was so much more than just a homemaker.

Acknowledgements

Dear reader,

You have no idea how wonderful it is that you have finished my first book. A huge THANK YOU to everyone out there for your interest in my debut novel. Now, let me tell you about all the support I have received in the writing of this book. Here are the people who deserve my gratitude. My sincere apologies for anyone I have inadvertently left off my list.

I am grateful to Sheila MacGregor's real goddaughters, Sheila and Beets, for believing in this project and spending hours telling me stories about the woman they know as Aunt Sheila and their mother, Millie. Their photos and memories were a great addition to my research journey. A special thanks to the actual last living member of the Druthers, Ruth, for talking to me about their group and her memories of Sheila, and to her goddaughter Lisa, who helped set up the meeting.

My friend and author, Sylvia May, deserves so much credit for the many hours she has put in, reading multiple drafts of my manuscript and offering her expertise, advice, and encouragement along the way. She has been my writing coach, editor, and a consummate cheerleader. This book has been a long time coming. Thanks for the push!

Thank you to my friends who are part of my Indiana writing community: Hella, Nichole, Karen, Joanne, Allison, Kerry, Myra, and Tasha. I'm grateful for the self-publishing tips from Carol, Chris, and Katherine! Thanks also to the other supportive members of the Central Indiana Writers Association and those who attend the Hamilton East Public Library monthly zoom, called *The Write Stuff*, hosted by librarian Jan.

Thank you to my stylist, Katie McGuire, at Blown Away Hair Salon in Noblesville. After my appointment, I went straight home to get my author photo taken and was so happy with the results.

NaNoWriMo was a great help in providing the structure to begin on my first draft in November 2020 and to keep going. Thanks especially to the Indianapolis regional MLs for their positive feedback.

I am now a member of the Blatchley Nature Study Club. Thank you for hosting the annual Wildflower Walk in April 2020, where a kind gentleman helped me get in touch with a long-time member who knew Sheila personally.

Many thanks to the Washington-Westfield Park Department staff who allowed me to peruse the binders with information about the founding of MacGregor Park. Special appreciation to Jeannine, Susie, Danielle, and now Markine.

Members of my book club in Wisconsin got behind this book project from the start and especially Linda, who has kindly provided a writing haven many times over the last three years. I appreciate you all and can't wait to discuss the novel with our group soon! I'm grateful for the friendship and encouragement expressed by Betsy, Janet, and Margaret, three gems I call The Rubies, because we met at the Ruby Isle Panera regularly. We are still there for one another through thick and thin. Also, thanks are in order for the anticipation of members of my Indiana book club.

Much love to Jane for her listening ear and prayers. My good friends Deb, Joan, and Pat have also been a source of morale building over many cups of coffee.

Special thanks to the librarians, staff, and members of the FOEGL at Elm Grove Public Library in Wisconsin. Also, I am grateful to the wonderful staff at the Indiana Room (now the Crossroads Discovery Center) at the Noblesville branch of the Hamilton East Public Library system for help with my genealogy and local history research.

Sheila was indeed a librarian at the Washington-Westfield Public Library - kudos to the current director, Sheryl, for verifying her employment in the 1970s and for allowing me to browse the history cabinet at the library.

I appreciate the honest feedback and helpful advice from my exceptional Beta readers: Andrew, Emily, Liz, Mary, Noah and Ann Marie.

Thanks and love to my whole family, including the grandkids, who have been amazing in supporting me with positive vibes. Warm affection for the Canadian branch who listened to my research adventures and asked for more. Many thanks to David, my Texas son-in-law and brilliant artist, for all the original ink sketches. Thank you to Elissa and Andy for their interest and encouragement. My husband, Phil, has been behind me all the way and is now promoted to webmaster and business manager. You're the best.

Finally, thank you God for all your goodness. You are the Great Author and Finisher of my faith.

Epigraph Attributions

Prologue
"You shall walk where only the wind has walked before and enter the living shelter of the forest … too few of us aware that to any beauty we must come as lovers, not destroyers, come humbly, softly, to look, listen, to cherish and to shield."
-Nancy Newhall

This is The American Earth (Sierra Club, San Francisco, 1960)

Chapter 1
"When I was growing up, I dreamed about becoming a cowgirl, a detective, a spy, a great actress, or a ballerina. Not a dentist, like my father, or a homemaker, like my mother - and certainly not a writer, although I always loved to read."
-Judy Blume

Quote permission given by author
https://judyblume.com/about-judy-blume/author/

Chapter 2
"Life can only be understood backwards, but it must be lived forwards."
-Søren Kierkegaard

This quote comes from volume IV of the philosopher's journals and notebooks written around 1843

https://www.oxfordreference.com/display/10.1093/acref/9780191826719.001.0001/q-oro-ed4-00012432

Chapter 3
"An early morning walk is a blessing for the whole day."
-Henry David Thoreau

From Journal I - April 20,1840

https://www.walden.org/collection/journals/

Chapter 4
"… I shall try to hold myself in readiness to go anywhere, provided it be forward."
-David Livingstone

Livingstone, D.; Schapera, I. (1961).
Livingstone's Missionary Correspondence, 1841-1856
(University of California Press. p. 48)

https://www.google.com/books/edition/Livingstone_s_Missionary_Correspondence/M9X7vglJLgAC?hl=en&gbpv=1&pg=PA48&printsec=frontcover

Chapter 5
"I awoke this morning with devout thanksgiving for my friends, the old and the new."
-Ralph Waldo Emerson

From his essay "Friendship"

https://emersoncentral.com/texts/essays-first-series/friendship/

Chapter 6
"Carry on! Carry on!
Fight the good fight and true;
Believe in your mission, greet life with a cheer;
There's big work to do, and that's why you are here."
-Robert W. Service

From Rhymes of a Red Cross Man, published by Barse &
Hopkins, New York, U.S., © 1916, pp. 97-99

https://allpoetry.com/Carry-On

Chapter 7
"Begin doing what you want to do now. We are not living in
eternity. We have only this moment, sparkling like a star in our
hand and melting like a snowflake."
-Marie Beynon Ray

From the article, Stay Young with a Hobby, published
February 8, 1953 in The San Francisco Examiner, Section:
The American Weekly. Start Page 20, Quote Page 23,
Column 2, San Francisco, California. (Newspapers.com)

Chapter 8
"The land army fights in the fields. It is in the fields of Britain
that the most critical battle of the present war may well be
fought and won."
-Lady Denman, Honorable Director of the Women's Land
Army

From the foreword to the Land Army Manual, 1941

https://www.womenslandarmy.co.uk/world-war-two/

Chapter 9

"It is said that truth is far too often eclipsed, but never totally extinguished."
-Titus Livius (Livy)

The History of Rome, Book 22 Chapter 39 [Rev. Canon Roberts, Ed.]

Chapter 10

"In war as in life, it is often necessary when some cherished scheme has failed, to take up the best alternative open, and if so, it is folly not to work for it with all your might."
-Sir Winston Churchill

Sir Winston Churchill: a self-portrait (1954).

Chapter 11

"Yet nothing delights the mind so much as faithful and pleasant friendship: what a blessing it is when there is one whose breast is ready to receive all your secrets with safety, whose knowledge of your actions you fear less than your own conscience, whose conversation removes your anxieties, whose advice assists your plans, whose cheerfulness dispels your gloom, whose very sight delights you!"
-Lucius Annaeus Seneca

Of Peace of Mind, Section VII -From: L. Annaeus Seneca, Minor Dialogs Together with the Dialog "On Clemency"; Translated by Aubrey Stewart, pp. 250-287. Bohn's Classical Library Edition; London, George Bell and Sons, 1900

https://en.wikisource.org/wiki/Of_Peace_of_Mind#VII.

Chapter 12

"If you don't have a dog, at least one, there is not necessarily anything wrong with you, but there may be something wrong with your life."
-Roger A. Caras

A Celebration of Dogs (Time Books, 1982)

Chapter 13

"When you take a flower in your hand and really look at it, it's your world for the moment."
-Georgia O'Keefe

http://www.arthistoryarchive.com/arthistory/modern/Georgia-OKeeffe.html

Chapter 14

In this very attitude did I sit when I called to him, rapidly stating what it was I wanted him to do … Imagine my surprise, nay, my consternation, when without moving from his privacy, Bartleby in a singularly mild, firm voice, replies, "I would prefer not to."
-Herman Melville

Bartleby, the Scrivener: A Story of Wall-Street was published anonymously in 1853 in Putnam's Monthly Magazine. It was collected in his 1856 volume, The Piazza Tales.

Chapter 15

"If you look the right way, you can see that the whole world is a garden."
-Frances Hodgson Burnett

The Secret Garden, first published in book form in 1911, after serialization in The American Magazine
(November 1910 – August 1911)

Chapter 16
"Those who contemplate the beauty of the earth find reserves of strength that will endure as long as life lasts. There is something infinitely healing in the repeated refrains of nature - the assurance that dawn comes after night, and spring after winter."
-Rachel Carson

Silent Spring. Published on September 27, 1962 (Houghton Mifflin)

Chapter 17
"The world breaks everyone, but afterward some are strong in the broken places."
-Ernest Hemingway

A Farewell to Arms. The work was first published serially in the United States in Scribner's Magazine between May and October 1929. Book published September 1929 (Scribner)

Chapter 18
"I would rather walk with a friend in the dark, than alone in the light."
-Helen Keller

This line was spoken by Helen Keller in a question-and-answer session in the early 1920s, recorded by biographer Joseph P. Lash for later use in Helen and Teacher: The Story of Helen Keller and Anne Sullivan Macy (Delacorte Press,1980)

Poem reference, *Do Not Go Gentle Into That Good Night*
-Dylan Thomas

The Collected Poems of Dylan Thomas (New Directions Publishing Corporation, 1957)

Chapter 19
'Come, Watson, come!' he cries. 'The game is afoot. Not a word! Into your clothes and come!'
-Sir Arthur Conan Doyle

Line appears at the beginning of the short story titled, "The Adventure of Abbey Grange." It is part of The Return of Sherlock Holmes, a collection of 13 Sherlock Holmes tales, published in The Strand Magazine (1904).

https://sherlockholmes.stanford.edu/2007/notes7_1.html

Chapter 20
Let us be grateful to people who make us happy; they are the charming gardeners who make our souls blossom.
-Marcel Proust

From Les Plaisirs et les Jours - Chapitre 55 [Pleasures and Days Chapter 55] (short story collection)
https://www.atramenta.net/lire/oeuvre2682-chapitre-55.html#:

Poem reference, A *Red, Red Rose* by Robert Burns

https://www.poetryfoundation.org/poems/43812/a-red-red-rose

Poem reference, *Auld Lang Syne* text by Robert Burns

https://en.wikipedia.org/wiki/Auld_Lang_Syne

Chapter 21
"You've got to jump off the cliff all the time and build your wings on the way down."
-Ray Bradbury

From the article, Learning is Solitary Pursuit for Bradbury by Luaine Lee, 1990 October 14, Herald-Journal, [N.Y. Times News Service], Page C1, Spartanburg, South Carolina. (Google News Archive)

Verified by Quote Investigator®
https://quoteinvestigator.com/2012/06/17/cliff-wings/

Chapter 22
"My little dog—a heartbeat at my feet."
-Edith Wharton

The Yale Review Volume IX (new series Edited by Wilbur L Cross) p. 348. Part of Lyrical Epigrams (Yale Publishing Association 1920)

Chapter 23
"I may not have gone where I intended to go, but I think I have ended up where I intended to be."
-Douglas Adams

The Long Dark Tea-Time of the Soul (William Heinemann, 1988)

https://www.panmacmillan.com/blogs/general/hitchhiker-s-series-top-phrases#:

Chapter 24

"Everybody needs beauty as well as bread, places to play in and pray in, where nature may heal and give strength to body and soul alike."
-John Muir

The Yosemite, page 256. (The Century Company, 1912)

https://vault.sierraclub.org/john_muir_exhibit/writings/the_yosemite/chapter_16.aspx

Epilogue

"The best remedy for those who are frightened, lonely, or unhappy is to go outside, somewhere they can be alone, alone with the sky, nature and God. For then and only then can you feel that everything is as it should be and that God wants people to be happy amid nature's beauty and simplicity."
-Anne Frank

The Diary of a Young Girl
Entry dated Wednesday 23rd Feb 1944

https://archive.org/stream/AnneFrankTheDiaryOfAYoungGirl_201606/Anne-Frank-The-Diary-Of-A-Young-Girl_djvu.txt

About the Author

A retired librarian and debut novelist, Paulette Brooks holds a bachelor's degree in Honors English Literature from University of Waterloo (Ontario, Canada) and a master's degree in Library and Information Science from University of Wisconsin-Milwaukee.

Her short story, *Dream Piper,* won first place in the Hamilton East Public Library Adult Writing Challenge 2023: Classics Reimagined.

Paulette was born in Toronto and lived in Canada for the first half of her life. According to her Scottish grandfather, they had a distant family connection to the explorer David Livingstone.

She lives with her husband outside of Indianapolis where, when not writing, she loves to read, bake pies, garden, and work on jigsaw puzzles, all the while trying to keep up with the activities of her six grandchildren.

Learn more about Paulette at

www.PBrooksAuthor.com

 /PauletteBrooksAuthor

 PauletteBrooksAuthor